TIME SHELTER

TIME SHELTER

A NOVEL

GEORGI GOSPODINOV

TRANSLATED FROM THE BULGARIAN BY ANGELA RODEL

LIVERIGHT PUBLISHING CORPORATION

A Division of W. W. Norton & Company

INDEPENDENT PUBLISHERS SINCE 1923

TO MY MOTHER AND FATHER,

WHO ARE STILL WEEDING THE ETERNAL

STRAWBERRY FIELDS OF CHILDHOOD.

Copyright © 2022 by Georgi Gospodinov
Translation copyright © 2022 by Angela Rodel

Originally published in Bulgarian as *Времеубежище*

"September 1, 1939," copyright 1940 and © renewed 1968 by W. H. Auden; from *Collected Poems* by W. H. Auden, edited by Edward Mendelson. Used by permission of Random House, an imprint and division of Penguin Random House LLC. All rights reserved.

For information about permission to reproduce selections from this book, write to Permissions, Liveright Publishing Corporation, a division of W. W. Norton & Company, Inc., 500 Fifth Avenue, New York, NY 10110

For information about special discounts for bulk purchases, please contact W. W. Norton Special Sales at specialsales@wwnorton.com or 800-233-4830

Manufacturing by Lakeside Book Company
Book design by Chris Welch
Production manager: Lauren Abbate

ISBN 978-1-324-09095-3

Liveright Publishing Corporation, 500 Fifth Avenue, New York, N.Y. 10110
www.wwnorton.com

W. W. Norton & Company Ltd., 15 Carlisle Street, London W1D 3BS

2 3 4 5 6 7 8 9 0

TIME SHELTER

All real persons in this novel are fictional,

only the fictional are real.

No one has yet invented a gas mask and a bomb shelter against time.
—*Gaustine, "Time Shelter," 1939*

But which is our organ of time—tell me that if you can.
—*Thomas Mann,* The Magic Mountain, *translated by H. T. Lowe-Porter*

Man is the only working time machine we have now.
—*Gaustine, "Against Utopias," 2001*

Where can we live but days?
—*Philip Larkin, "Days"*

Oh, yesterday came suddenly . . .
—*Lennon/McCartney*

. . . If the street were time and he at the end of the street . . .
—*T. S. Eliot, "The Boston Evening Transcript"*

Yesterday, and yesterday, and yesterday . . .
—*Gaustine/Shakespeare*

The novel comes as an emergency, with
lights blazing and siren blaring.
—*Gaustine, "Emergency Novel. Brief Theory and Practice"*

. . . and God will call the past to account.
—*Ecclesiastes 3:15*

The past differs from the present in one essential
way—it never flows in one direction.
—*Gaustine,* A Physics of the Past, *1905*

Once, when she was little, she drew an animal, absolutely
unrecognizable.
What is it? I asked.
Sometimes it's a shark, sometimes a lion, and sometimes a cloud,
she replied.
Aha, so what is it now?
Now it's a hiding place.
—*G.G.,* Beginnings and Endings

I

CLINIC OF
THE PAST

And so, the theme is memory. The tempo: andante to andante moderato, sostenuto (with restraint). Perhaps the saraband, with its controlled solemnity, with the lengthened second beat, would be good for a beginning. More Handel than Bach. Strict repetition, yet at the same time moving forward. Restrained and solemn, as befits a beginning. Afterward everything can—and should— fall apart.

1.

At one point they tried to calculate when time began, when exactly the earth had been created. In the mid–seventeenth century, the Irish bishop Ussher calculated not only the exact year, but also a starting date: October 22, 4,004 years before Christ. It was a Saturday (of course). Some even say Ussher gave a precise time of day as well— around six in the afternoon. Saturday afternoon, that sounds completely believable to me. When else would a bored creator set about building a world and finding himself some company? Ussher devoted years of his life to this, his work itself numbered two thousand pages in Latin; I doubt many have ever made the effort to read the whole thing. Nevertheless, his book became exceptionally popular, well, maybe not the book itself, but the actual discovery. They started to print the Bibles on the island with a date and chronology according to Ussher. This theory of the young earth (and of young time, if you ask me) captivated the Christian world. It should be noted that even scientists like Kepler and Sir Isaac Newton estimated specific years for the divine act of creation that more or less coincided with that of Ussher. But still, the most mind-boggling thing for me is not the year and its relative recency, but the specific day.

October 22, four thousand and four years before Christ, at six in the afternoon.

On or around December 1910, human character changed. So wrote Virginia Woolf. And one can imagine that December 1910, ostensibly like all the others, gray, cold, smelling of fresh snow. But something had been unleashed, which only a few could sense.

On September 1, 1939, early in the morning, came the end of human time.

2.

Years later, when many of his memories had already scattered like frightened pigeons, he could still go back to that morning when he was wandering aimlessly through the streets of Vienna, and a vagrant with a mustache like García Márquez's was selling newspapers on the sidewalk in the early March sun. A wind blew up and several of the newspapers swirled into the air. He tried to help, chasing down two or three and returning them. You can keep one, said Márquez.

Gaustine, that's what we'll call him, even though he himself used the name like an invisibility cloak, took the newspaper and handed the man a banknote, a rather large one for the occasion. The vagrant turned it over in his hand and muttered: But . . . I won't be able to make change. That sounded so absurd in the Vienna dawn that both of them burst out laughing.

For the homeless, Gaustine felt love and dread, those were the precise words, and always in that combination. He loved them and feared them in the way you love and fear something you have already been or expect to become. He knew that sooner or later he would join their ranks, to use a cliché. He imagined for a moment long lines of homeless people marching down Kärntner and Graben. Yes, by blood he was one of them, albeit a slightly more peculiar case. A vagrant in time, if you will. Simply through a concurrence of circumstances he had ended up with some money, enough to prevent his metaphysical adversity from turning into physical suffering.

At that moment he was practicing one of his professions—that of geriatric psychiatrist. I suspect that he was secretly swiping his patients' stories so he could take shelter in them, to rest for a bit in someone's place and past. Otherwise, his head was such a jumble of times, voices, and places that he needed to either place himself immediately in the hands of his fellow psychiatrists or he would do something that would force them to put him away themselves.

Gaustine took the newspaper, walked a little way, and sat down on a bench. He was wearing a Borsalino, a dark trench coat, beneath which the high collar of his turtleneck was visible, old leather boots, and he carried a leather bag in a nobly fading red. He looked like a man who had just arrived by train from some other decade; he could have passed for a discreet anarchist, an aging hippie, or a preacher from an obscure denomination. And so, he sat down on the bench and read the name of the newspaper—*Augustin*, published by the homeless. Some of the paper was written by them, some by professional journalists. And there, on the second-to-last page down in the left-hand corner, the most inconspicuous place in a newspaper as all editors well know, was the article. His gaze fell upon it. A thin smile that held more bitterness than joy flitted across his face. He would have to disappear again.

3.

Some time ago, when Dr. Alzheimer was still mentioned mainly in jokes—*So what's your diagnosis? It was some guy's name, but I forgot it*—a short article appeared in a small newspaper, one of those news items that was read by five people, four of whom instantly forgot it.

Here is the article, retold in brief:

A certain medical professional, Dr. G. (mentioned only by initial), from a Vienna geriatric clinic in Wienerwald, a fan of the Beatles, decked out his office in the style of the '60s. He found a Bakelite gramophone, put up posters of the band, including the famous *Sgt. Pepper* album cover . . . From the flea market he bought an old cabinet and lined it with all sorts of tchotchkes from the '60s—soap, cigarette boxes, a set of miniature Volkswagen Beetles, Mustangs and pink Cadillacs, playbills from movies, photos of actors. The article noted that his office was piled full of old magazines, and he himself was always dressed in a turtleneck under his white coat. There was no photo, of course, the whole piece was all of thirty lines long, stuffed into the lower left-hand corner. The news here was that the doctor had noticed that patients with memory issues were staying longer and longer in his office; they became more talkative, in other words, they felt at home. And that had radically reduced the number of attempts to run away from that otherwise prestigious clinic. The article had no author.

That was my idea, I've had it in my head for years, but clearly somebody beat me to it. (I must admit that in my case the idea was for a novel, but still.)

Whenever possible, I always supplied myself with that homeless newspaper, on the one hand due to my particular attachment to those who wrote it (a long story from another novel), but also because of the clear feeling (a personal superstition) that precisely in this way, through a scrap of newspaper, what must be said comes fluttering down gently or hits you upside the head. And this has never led me astray.

The paper said that the clinic was in the Vienna Woods and nothing more. I checked the geriatric centers nearby, and at least three of them were located in those woods. The one I needed turned out to be the last one I checked, of course. I introduced myself as a journalist, which actually wasn't such a big fib; I had an ID card from a newspaper so I could get into museums for free, and sometimes I actually wrote for it. Otherwise I used the related, but far more innocent and elusive profession of writer, for which there is no way to legitimize yourself.

Anyway, I managed to reach—with quite a bit of difficulty, I might add—the director of the clinic. When she realized what I was interested in, she suddenly became curt: The individual you are looking for is no longer here as of yesterday. Why? He resigned by mutual consent, she replied, stepping onto the slippery slope of bureaucratic-speak. Was he fired? I asked, sincerely astonished. I told you, mutual consent. Why are you so interested? I read an interesting article in the newspaper a week ago . . . Even as the phrase left my lips, I realized I had made a mistake. That article about attempts to run away from the clinic? We have submitted a claim for a retraction.

I realized I had no cause to stay any longer; I also understood the reason for the resignation by mutual consent. What was the doctor's name? I asked, turning back just before leaving, but she was already talking on the phone.

I didn't leave the clinic immediately. I found the wing with the doctors' offices and saw a worker taking the sign down from the third door on the right. Of course that was the name. I had suspected this from the very start.

4.

To catch a trace of Gaustine, who jumped from decade to decade just as we change planes at an airport, is a chance that comes along only once a century. Gaustine, whom I first invented, and then met in flesh and blood. Or perhaps it was the opposite, I don't remember. My invisible friend, more real and visible than my very self. The Gaustine of my youth, the Gaustine of my dreams of being someone else, somewhere else, of inhabiting other times and other rooms. We shared a common obsession with the past. The difference between us was slight, but fundamental. I remained an outsider everywhere, while he felt equally at home in all times. I knocked on the doors of various years, but he was already inside, ushering me in and then disappearing.

When I called forth Gaustine for the first time, it was to have him sign his name beneath three lines that came to me just like that, out of nowhere, as if from another time. I struggled for months, but still couldn't add anything to them.

> From woman is the troubadour created
> I can say it yet again
> she has created the Creator

One evening I dreamed of a name written on a leather book cover: *Gaustine of Arles, 13th Century*. I remember that even while still asleep I said to myself: That's it. Then Gaustine himself appeared, or I should say, someone who looked like him and whom I mentally took to calling that.

This was at the very end of the '80s. I must have kept that story somewhere.

5.

Gaustine. An Introduction.

This is how I'd like to present him to you. I saw him for the first time at one of those traditional early September literary seminars at the seaside. In the late afternoon we had sat down in one of the little pubs along the shore, every last one of us writing, unmarried, and unpublished, at that pleasant age between twenty and twenty-five. The waiter could barely keep up, scribbling down our orders of brandy and salads. When we fell silent, the young man at the end of the long table piped up for the first time. Clearly, he hadn't managed to order anything yet.

One creamer, please!

He uttered this with the confidence of a person who was ordering at the very least duck à l'orange or Blue Curaçao. In the long silence that followed, the only sound was the evening breeze coming from the sea, pushing along an empty plastic bottle.

Pardon? the waiter managed to say.

One creamer, if you would be so kind, he repeated with the same reserved dignity.

We were puzzled as well, but the conversations at the table quickly regained their previous boisterousness. Soon plates and glasses covered the tablecloth. The last thing the waiter brought was a small porcelain dish with a thin band of gold edging. In the middle of the dish, the creamer stood exquisitely (or so it seemed to me). Gaustine drank it so slowly, in such tiny sips, that it lasted him all evening.

That was our first meeting.

The very next day I went out of my way to get to know him, and in the remaining days we completely turned our backs on the seminar. Neither of us were extremely talkative types, so we spent a marvelous time walking and swimming in a mutually shared silence. Nevertheless, I managed to learn that he lived alone, his father had passed away long ago, while his mother had emigrated illegally for the third time a month ago—he very much hoped this time she would succeed—to America.

I also found out that sometimes he wrote stories from the end of the last century, that's exactly how he put it, and I barely contained my curiosity, trying to act as if this were something perfectly natural. He was especially preoccupied with the past. He would go around to old empty houses, digging through the ruins, clearing out attics, trunks, and gathering up all sorts of old junk. From time to time he managed to sell something, either to an antique dealer or to an acquaintance, and that's how he made ends meet. I reflected that the humbleness of his order the other night did not inspire confidence in that line of work. For that reason, when he mentioned in passing that at the moment he had three packs of Tomasian cigarettes from 1937 on hand, dusted off, double-extra quality, I, being a die-hard smoker, immediately offered to buy all three of them. Really? he asked. I've always dreamed of trying such an aged Tomasian, I replied, and he darted back to his bungalow. He watched me with true satisfaction as I casually lit up with an authentic German match from 1928 (a bonus he threw in with the cigarettes) and asked me how the spirit of '37 was. Harsh, I replied. The cigarettes really were jarring, they had no filters and smoked like crazy. It must be because of the bombing of Guernica that same year, Gaustine said quietly. Or perhaps it's because of the *Hindenburg*, the biggest zeppelin in the world exploded then, I think, on May sixth, about a hundred meters above the ground, right before landing, with ninety-seven people on board. All the radio announcers cried on the air. These things surely clung to the tobacco leaves . . .

I almost choked. I stubbed out the cigarette, but didn't say anything. He was speaking like an eyewitness who had managed to overcome the incident with enormous effort.

I decided to change the subject abruptly, and that day, for the first time, I asked him about his name. Call me Gaustine, he said, and smiled. Nice to meet you, I'm Ishmael, I replied, so as to keep up the joke. But he didn't seem to hear, he said he liked that poem with the epigraph from Gaustine of Arles, and I must admit I was flattered. And besides, he continued in utter seriousness, it brings together my two names: Augustine-Garibaldi. My parents never could agree on what to name me. My father insisted on naming me after Garibaldi, he was a passionate admirer of his. My mother, Gaustine said, a quiet and intelligent woman, clearly a follower of Saint Augustine—she did have three semesters of university philosophy under her belt, after all—insisted that they also add the saint's name. She continues to call me Augustine, while my father, when he was alive, used Garibaldi. And so early theology and late revolutionism were brought together.

That more or less exhausted the concrete information we exchanged during those five, six days as the seminar wound down. I remember, of course, several particularly important silences, but I have no way of retelling those.

Oh yes, there was one other short conversation on the last day. I only then learned that Gaustine lived in an abandoned house in a small town in the foothills of the Balkan Mountains. I don't have a telephone, he said, but letters do arrive. He seemed endlessly lonely and . . . unbelonging. That was the word that came to me then. Unbelonging to anything in the world, or more precisely to the modern world. We watched the generous sunset and kept silent. A whole cloud of mayflies rose from the bushes behind us. Gaustine followed them with his gaze and said that while for us this was simply one sunset, for today's mayflies this sunset was the sunset of their lives. Or something like that. I foolishly said that that was only a worn-out metaphor. He looked at me in surprise, but said nothing. A full few minutes later, he said: For them, there are no metaphors.

. . . In October and November 1989, a slew of things happened that have already been written and described ad nauseum. I hung out on the squares and never did get around to writing Gaustine. I had other problems, too, as I was getting my first book ready for publication. And I had gotten married. All lame excuses, of course. But during that time I thought of him often. He didn't write to me then, either.

I got the first postcard on January 2, 1990—an open Christmas card with a black-and-white Snow Maiden that Gaustine had additionally colored in, making her look like Judy Garland. She was holding some kind of magic wand that pointed to the year 1929 written in a large font. On the back there was the address and a short message, written in fountain pen and using all the quaint spelling conventions of that era. It ended with: "Yours (if I may be so bold), Gaustine." I sat down and immediately wrote him a letter thanking him for the pleasant surprise and saying that I truly appreciated his exquisite mystification.

I received an answer that same week. I opened it carefully; inside there were two pale green sheets of paper with a watermark, covered on one side only in the same elegant hand and strictly following the reformed Bulgarian spelling of the '20s. He wrote that he didn't go out anywhere, but that he felt wonderful. He had subscribed to the daily *Zora*, written "quite objectively by Mr. Krapchev," and the journal *Zlatorog*, so as to still keep tabs on where literature was heading these days. He asked me what I thought of the suspension of the constitution and the dissolution of Parliament by the Yugoslav king Alexander on the sixth day of the year, which *Zora* had reported on the very next day. He ended his letter with a postscript in which he apologized for not having understood what I meant by "exquisite mystification."

I reread the letter several times, turning it over and over in my hands, sniffing it in hopes of discovering some whiff of irony. In vain. If this was a game, Gaustine was inviting me to play without any clarification of the rules. Well, fine, then, I decided to play. Since I didn't have any knowledge of that ill-fated 1929, I had to spend the next three days at the library, digging through old issues of *Zora*. I carefully read about Prince Alexander. Just in case, I glanced at impending events: "Trotsky Exiled from the USSR," "Kellogg-Briand Pact for Germany Comes into Force," "Mussolini Signs a Treaty with the Pope," "France Refuses Political Asylum to Trotsky," and a month later, "Germany Denies Political Asylum to Trotsky." I got all the way to "Wall Street Collapses" on October 24. While still at the library, I wrote Gaustine a short and, in my opinion, cold reply, in which I quickly shared my opinion (which suspiciously coincided quite precisely with that of Mr. Krapchev) on the situation in Yugoslavia and asked him to send me whatever he was working on, as I hoped to be able to glean from that what exactly was going on.

His next letter did not come until a full month and a half later. He apologized, saying he had been attacked by some terrible influenza and hadn't been in a state to do anything. He also asked, by the by, whether I thought France would accept Trotsky. For a long time I wondered whether I shouldn't just put an end to this whole business and write him a pointed letter to sober things up, but I decided to keep up the charade a bit longer. I gave him some advice about influenza, which, incidentally, he himself had already read in *Zora*. I advised him not to go out very often and to soak his feet in hot water saturated with a salt infusion every evening. I highly doubted that France would offer political asylum to Trotsky— and neither would Germany, for that matter. When his next letter arrived, France had indeed refused to accept Trotsky, and Gaustine, enraptured, wrote that I had "a colossal sense of politics, in any case." This letter was longer than the previous ones due to two more sources of rapture. One was the recently released fourth edition of *Zlatorog* and the new cycle of poems by Elizaveta Bagryana published there, while the other was a wireless radio set, a real Telefunken, which he was now trying to get into working order. To that end he asked me to please send him a Valvo vacuum tube from Dzhabarov's warehouse at 5 Aksakov Street. He also described at great length some demonstration in Berlin of Dr. Reiser's twelve-tube device, which received short waves with automatic modulation of the frequency: *With this, they'll be able to listen to concerts all the way from America, can you believe it?*

After that letter, I decided not to respond. He, too, did not write to me again. Not the next New Year, nor the next. Gradually the whole story faded away, and if it hadn't been for the few letters that I have saved to this day, I surely would not have believed it ever happened myself. But fate had other plans for me. Several years later, I once again got a letter from Gaustine. I had a bad feeling about it, so I didn't hurry to open it. I wondered whether he had come to his senses after all this time, or whether things had gotten worse. I finally opened the envelope in the evening. Inside, there were only a few lines. I will quote them here in their entirety:

Forgive me for disturbing you again after so much time. But you yourself see what is happening all around us. You read the newspapers and with that political sense of yours, you certainly long ago could presage the slaughter that is now upon our doorstep. The Germans are amassing troops on the Polish border. Until now, I have never mentioned that my mother is Jewish (recall what happened last year in Austria, and "Kristallnacht" in Germany). This man will stop at nothing. I have made up my mind and made the necessary arrangements to leave tomorrow morning by train for Madrid, then Lisbon, and from there to New York . . .

Farewell for now.

Yours truly, Gaustine

August 14, 1939

Today is September 1.

6.

On September 1, 1939, Wystan Hugh Auden woke up in New York and wrote in his diary:

> I woke up with a headache after a night of bad dreams, in which Ch. cheated on me. The newspapers say that Germany has attacked Poland . . .

Now, there's everything you need for a true beginning—bad dreams, war, and a headache.

I was at the New York Public Library when I came across Auden's diary, which is otherwise kept in London, but by some happy accident his archive happened to be on loan there.

Only a diary could bring together the personal and the historical like that. The world is no longer the same—Germany is attacking Poland, the war is starting, my head is aching, and that idiot Ch. has the cheek to cheat on me in my dreams. Today in dreams, tomorrow while awake. (Was that what Auden was thinking?) Let us recall that after discovering such infidelity, Shahryar begins his slaughter of women in *One Thousand and One Nights*. Did Auden even realize how many things those two lines register, how precise, how personally and cynically precise they are? Two lines about the most important day of the century. Later that same day, when his headache eased a bit, he would start jotting down some lines of poetry:

I sit in one of the dives
On Fifty-second Street
Uncertain and afraid

And now the dive on Fifty-Second Street, the headache, the cheating and the bad dream, the invasion of Poland on that Friday, September 1—all of it has become history. And that's exactly what the poem will be called: *September 1, 1939*.

When does the everyday become history?

Wait a second. That so-oft-quoted *We must love one another or die* toward the end of the poem, which Auden later did not like at all and was constantly getting rid of, isn't it connected to exactly that dreamed-up infidelity? Who would want to remember such nightmares?

I would like to know everything about that day, one day in the late summer of 1939, to sit in the kitchens of the world with each person, to peek into the newspapers they have opened while drinking their coffee, to hungrily read everything—from the gathered troops on the German-Polish border to the final days of the summer sales and the new bar Cinzano, which had opened in Lower Manhattan. Fall is already on the doorstep, the ads in the newspapers, paid for in advance, now sit side by side with brief communiqués from the last hours in Europe.

7.

On another September 1, I'm sitting on the grass in Bryant Park, the dive on Fifty-Second has long since disappeared, I've just come from Europe, and, tired (the soul, too, has its jet lag), I look at people's faces. I've taken my little volume of Auden, we owe ourselves the ritual, don't we? After a day spent in the library, I sit "uncertain and afraid." I had slept badly, I didn't dream about infidelity, or perhaps I did but I've forgotten ... The world is at the same level of anxiety, the local sheriff and the sheriff of a far-off country have been trading threats. They're doing it on Twitter, all within the character limit. There's none of the old rhetoric, there's no eloquence. A briefcase, a button, and . . . the end of the world's workday. A bureaucrat's apocalypse.

Yes, they are gone now, the old dives and the old masters, the war, which was then impending, it is already over, other wars have come and gone as well, only the anxiety remains.

I tell you, I tell you,
I tell you we must die.

Somewhere nearby that Doors song was playing, and suddenly it seemed to me that there was a secret conversation going on, that

Morrison was actually talking to Auden. Exactly in that refrain, that line, as if resolving the hesitation in Auden's least favorite line, *We must love one another or die.* In Morrison's case there is no longer any hesitation, the answer is categorical: *I tell you we must die.*

After some searching I discover that in fact the song had been written way back in 1925 by Bertolt Brecht with music by Kurt Weill. Weill himself performed it during the 1930s in the most deranged, almost horrifying way . . . And this only made things more entangled. Auden had grabbed and twisted around a line from that song by Brecht and is in fact speaking to him. Both Brecht from 1925 and Morrison from 1966 have set off on death's trail. *I tell you we must die.* Against their backdrop, Auden sounds like he's still giving us a chance—*we must love one another or die.* Only before wars, even on the very eve of them, is a person inclined to hope. On September 1 most likely the world still could have been saved.

I had come here on urgent business, as one usually comes to New York, running away from something, seeking something else. I'd run away from the Continent of the past toward a place that claimed it had no past, even though it had accumulated some in the meantime. I was carrying a yellow notebook. I was looking for a certain person. I wanted to tell the story before my memory slipped away from me.

8.

Several years before that I would be standing in a city where there had been no 1939. A city that is good for living and even better for dying. A city quiet as a grave. Aren't you bored? they'd ask me over the phone. Boredom is the emblem of this city. Here Canetti, Joyce, Dürrenmatt, Frisch, and even Thomas Mann have been bored. It's somehow a bit presumptuous to measure your boredom against theirs. I'm not bored, I'd say. Who am I to be bored? Even though secretly I longed to taste the decadence of boredom.

Time had passed since I had lost Gaustine's trail in Vienna.

As I was waiting for him to give a sign from somewhere, I looked through the pages of the most obscure newspapers, but clearly he had become more cautious. One day I received a postcard, with no name or return address.

Greetings from Zurich, I've got an idea, if it works out, I'll write.

It could only be him. He didn't write anything in the following months, but I hurried to accept an invitation for a short residency at the Literaturhaus there.

And so—I had almost a month there—I wandered through the empty streets on Sunday, I enjoyed the sun, which lingered longer on the hill, and at sunset you could see, way back at the far end of the landscape, the peaks of the Alps changing color into a cold violet. I understood why everyone came here in the end. Zurich is a good city for growing old. And for dying as well. If there is some sort of European geography of age, then it must be distributed as follows. Paris, Berlin, and Amsterdam are for youth, with all its informality, its whiff of joints, beer-drinking in Mauerpark and rolling around in the grass, Sunday flea markets, the frivolity of sex . . . Then comes the maturity of Vienna or Brussels. A slowing of tempo, comfort, streetcars, proper health insurance, schools for the kids, a bit of a career, Euro-pencil-pushing. Okay, for those who still do not wish to grow old—Rome, Barcelona, Madrid . . . Good food and warm afternoons will make up for the traffic, noise, and slight chaos. To late youth I would also add New York, yes, I count it as a European city that ended up across the ocean due to a certain chain of events.

Zurich is a city for growing old. The world has slowed down, the river of life has settled into a lake, lazy and calm on the surface, the luxury of boredom and sun on the hill for old bones. Time in all of its relativity. It is no coincidence whatsoever that two major discoveries of the twentieth century tied precisely to time were made here, of all places, in Switzerland—Einstein's Theory of Relativity and Thomas Mann's *Magic Mountain*.

I hadn't come to die in Zurich, not yet. I was walking around the streets, I needed this pause. I was trying to finish a novel that lay bleeding, abandoned halfway through, and I was hoping to run into Gaustine, just like that on the train to Zürichberg or sitting on the hill in the Fluntern Cemetery near the statue of Joyce. I spent several afternoons there. By the smoking Joyce, one leg crossed over the other, with a small open book in his right hand. His gaze is lifted from the book, so as to allow time for the sentences to mix with the smoke from the cigarette, his eyes are slightly squinted behind the glasses, as if at any moment he will lift his head to you and make some comment. I find this one of the most alive tombstones I have ever seen. I've strolled through cemeteries around the world, like everyone who is deathly afraid of death and dying (actually, which are we more afraid of—death or dying?), who wants to see his fear's lair, to confirm that this place is calm, quiet, that it has been made for people after all, for a rest . . . A place for getting used to it, as it were. Even though there's no getting used to it. Isn't it strange, Gaustine once said to me, it's always other people who are dying, but we ourselves never do.

9.

And so, I didn't run into Gaustine either in the cemetery or on the Seilbahn to Zürichberg. My stay was coming to an end, I was sitting in a café on Römerhofplatz with a Bulgarian woman and we were chatting away breezily, enjoying the advantage of a small language, the calm assurance that no one will understand as you gossip about everything. We critiqued boldly—from the patrons at the café and certain Swiss eccentricities to the eternal sorrow and misfortune of being Bulgarian, a topic ripe for filling any awkward lull in the conversation. For a Bulgarian, complaining is like talking about the weather in England, you can never go wrong.

So at that moment a dignified, handsomely aged gentleman next to us who had been sipping his coffee turned and with the most blithe Bulgarian voice (blithe and Bulgarian usually don't go together) said: Pardon my eavesdropping, but when I hear such beautiful Bulgarian, I can't possibly turn off my ears.

There are voices that immediately tell a story, and this was an emigrant voice, from the old wave of emigrants, it was astonishing how they preserve their Bulgarian without an accent, just here and there some vowels have been left behind in the '50s and '60s of the language, giving it a slight patina. Our discomfiture at having been caught in the act quickly dissipated; after all, we hadn't said anything about this gentleman.

And so began that conversation between compatriots who have accidentally met up, and my role here was more that of an ear. An hour went by, but what's an hour to years of absence; the lady excused herself and left, we moved to share a table, *Do you have a bit more patience, just let me finish this story and we'll go*; I had, of course. When the conversation began, the sun had been drowsing on the windows of the café and on the clock, which showed three in the afternoon, then the shadows of our cups grew longer, as did our shadows, the coolness of dusk approached, but without hurrying, and it mercifully gave us time to finish a story that was more than fifty years long.

He was a man with an absolutely sharp mind, yet in places he stopped to find a more fitting word. *No, now I'm translating from German, wait a moment, it'll come, there, now, that's the word* . . . and he would continue on. The son of a forgotten Bulgarian writer and diplomat, with a childhood spent on the eve of war in the embassies of Europe. I knew of his father, which made him happy, even if he didn't show it. Then came the classic Bulgarian post-1944 story— the father was fired, tried, sent to a labor camp, beaten, threatened, broken; their apartment confiscated and given to a "proper" writer, while their family was sent somewhere on the outskirts of the city.

My father never said a word about what had happened to him in the camp, never, my new acquaintance, let's call him Mr. S., said. *Only, once, my mother had boiled potatoes and apologized that they were slightly undercooked, and he said: Don't worry, I've eaten them raw, too, I've rooted around in the dirt like a pig. And then he fell silent again like a man who had said more than he should.*

Then Mr. S. himself, as was to be expected, was thrown in jail for fifteen months, primarily for being his father's son, but also *just in case* after the Hungarian events of '56. Afterward life more or less fell into place. He told himself that he wouldn't think about prison or about the secret agents who continued to follow him, but one night, while he was waiting for the last streetcar, he saw a completely empty shop window and stared at it. Inside only a single light bulb hung down on a wire, casting its dim light.

A light bulb, a wire, and an empty shop window.

He couldn't take his eyes off it. As if in a dream he heard the streetcar come to a screeching halt, wait for a bit, then close its doors and rumble off. He stood and stared at the glowing filament of that simple electric bulb, dangling there as if hanged. *And then the light bulb in my own head went off,* he said, *that which I had always hidden, even from myself—I had to get out of here. The light bulb in my head went off,* he said, and laughed. *It was February seventeenth, 1966, I was thirty-three.*

From then on everything was subordinated to that thought: He had a plan. He would change jobs to find one that sought workers for East Germany. He would say goodbye to everyone, without them realizing it. First to his best friend, then to the woman he was with. He didn't let it slip to anyone, not even at home. When he left, his father just said, *Be careful,* and hugged him for longer than usual. And his mother had taken a bowl of water and splashed it on the stairs, an old Bulgarian custom for good luck, which she had never done before. He never saw them again.

On the train to the GDR, he got off at the station in Belgrade for a cigarette and disappeared into the crowd. He left his suitcase on the train. His father had once been ambassador in Belgrade, Mr. S. had spent the first years of his childhood there. And he still remembered how the war had started—with a telegram via diplomatic mail on September 1, 1939. *As a child I thought that's how wars started, with a telegram. Ever since then I've never liked telegrams,* Mr. S. said.

When he arrived months later in Switzerland, after many transfers and tribulations, a friend of his father's met him on this very date and Mr. S drank his first coffee in Zurich with him precisely in this spot. The sun was the same. Since then he had come here every year on that date.

Any regrets, nostalgia, at least in the beginning?

No, he said quickly, as if he'd had the answer ready. *No, never, never. I was curious about this world, I had lived in it as a child, I spoke its language, and in the end I ran away from a place where I had spent fifteen months in prison, I ran away from prison.*

From the haste with which he said this, I suspected that he had never stopped thinking about it.

He told me about a lunch with his friend Georgi Markov in London three days before Markov was killed. Clearly that story still gave him chills.

I had come by car and Gerry, that's what we called Georgi, wanted to leave with me, he had some business to attend to in Germany, but he could only leave in three days, while I had to get home. We went to see his boss in the BBC editorial office to see whether they'd let him go a bit earlier. They told him he had to find a replacement, he waved his hand and gave up on the idea. I left by myself, stopped for a few days in Germany, then came to Zurich, I bought a newspaper at the station, opened it up, and in front of me—a picture of Gerry, the same man I had hugged just a week ago, dead.

The conversation turned to other topics, it had gotten completely dark by then, my interlocutor was startled, he should have called his wife. And then, as we parted at the door, he suddenly said, *You know what, there's another fellow countryman of ours here, whom I've struck up a friendship with. He, like you, has an ear for the past. I help him out, he's started something up, a little clinic of the past, that's what he called it . . .*

Gaustine? I practically shouted.

Do you know him? Mr. S. replied, truly surprised.

Nobody knows him, I said.

That's how Gaustine chose to appear to me that time, through an accidental encounter with Mr. S., an emigrant from Bulgaria, at the Römerhof café, Zurich, one late afternoon.

I've saved my notes from that meeting with Mr. S., I had quickly jotted down in my notebook some of the stories I had heard that afternoon. Later I thought back on how he had so quickly denied having any nostalgia for his Bulgarian past. I wrote that, clearly, in order to survive there, in a new place, you had to cut off the past and to throw it to the dogs. (I could never do that.)

To be merciless toward the past. Because the past itself is merciless.

That obsolete organ, like some appendix, which otherwise would become inflamed, it would throb and ache. If you can survive without it, better to cut it out and get rid of it; if not, well, then you'd better suck it up. I wonder whether that was going through his head as he stood in that Sofia night before the empty shop window with the bare hanging bulb. Enlightenment comes in different ways. At the end of my illegible notes I sketched this . . .

Old Mr. S. lived a long time and would later spend his final days in the sanatorium of the past, in Gaustine's clinic, which he himself had helped with. He passed away happy, it seems to me, in one of his favorite memories, which he had told me during our very first meeting. Gaustine and I were standing there next to him. He asked for a piece of toast. He had been on IVs for a month and couldn't eat, but the smell alone was enough.

He is a child, his father has come home, he has received an honorarium for some translation, he has bought jam and butter from the shop with the money. After days of nothing but potatoes, his father toasts him a big slice of white bread, spreads it thickly with butter and jam, they are laughing, and his father, who is otherwise a stern man who doesn't believe in spoiling children, picks him up and puts him on his shoulders. They walk around the room like that, stop in the middle, and little S. looks point-blank at the glowing filament of the bulb, which is now at eye-level.

10.

The next day I was at Heliosstrasse first thing in the morning, Mr. S. had given me the address. I found the apricot-colored building on the western shore of the lake, separated from the other houses on the hill. It was massive yet light at the same time, four stories with a fifth attic floor, a large shared terrace on the second level, and smaller balconies on the other floors. All the windows looked to the southwest, which made the afternoons endless, and the day's final bluish glimmers nested in them until the very last moment, while the light blue wooden shutters contrasted softly with the pale apricot of the facade.

The whole meadow out front was dotted with forget-me-nots, here and there peonies and some big red poppies erupted. But the petite forget-me-nots shone blue amid the Swiss green of the grass—I am sure that Swiss green exists, I can't believe someone hasn't patented it yet. Was it some sort of joke, planting forget-me-nots in front of a geriatric psychiatric center? I went up to the top floor where Gaustine's clinic was, with several years' rent paid for in advance by Mr. S. I rang the doorbell and Gaustine himself in a turtleneck and big round glasses opened the door.

Weren't you heading to New York in 1939 last time I saw you? I said as casually as I could. When did you get back?

After the war, he replied, unruffled.

So what are we going to do now?

Rooms from different times. As a start.

Rooms of the past? It sounds like a title.

Yes, rooms of the past. Or a clinic of the past. Or a city... Are you in?

I had just gotten divorced, and I had the vague idea that I could make a living thinking up stories. I had a soft spot for the '60s. I tumbled easily into any past, but, of course, I did have my favorite years. I had no good reason not to stay for a short while, a month or two at most. (I thought of Hans Castorp and his intention to stay only three weeks at the Magic Mountain.)

Gaustine occupied one of the three apartments on the top floor. The smallest space near the front door, "the servants' quarters," as he called it—and it's highly probable that this was exactly what it had been used for—was now his office. The other three rooms of the apartment, including the hallway, were in another time. You opened the door and fell directly into the middle of the '60s. The entryway with the classic coatrack-and-bench ensemble, dark green, made of fake leather with brass studs. We had one like it at home. I should say that although I was born at the tail end of the '60s, I remember them clearly, from beginning to end, and they are part of my Bulgarian childhood, not because of any mystical reasons (although I continue to believe that memories are passed down directly from parent to child—your parents' memories become your own). The reason I have them in my head is actually quite trivial: the 1960s, just like everything in Bulgaria, were simply delayed and arrived ten or so years later. Most likely during the 1970s.

A light green coat with two rows of wooden buttons was hanging from the coatrack. I remember that when I stepped in for the first time that morning, I froze when I saw it. That was my mother's coat. It was as if any second she would open the living room door, the typical beveled glass would glint, and she would be standing there: young, twenty-something, much younger than I am now. Although when your mother appears at twenty, you automatically turn into a child and at that moment of awkwardness and joy you wonder whether to hug her or simply to casually call out: Hey, Mom, I'm home, I'm going to my room. All this lasted only a second . . . or a minute.

Welcome to the '60s. Gaustine smiled, observing my shock in the entryway to the decade with a furtive smirk. I didn't want to leave this transfiguration just yet and immediately turned toward the kids' room. Two twin beds along the walls, each covered by a yellow shag comforter made of some fake fiber (we called it *ledeka* back then, it must've been an abbreviation) with a brown chest between them, the two beds meeting perpendicularly at the chest. I glanced at Gaustine, he understood and nodded, and I threw myself down on the bed, just as I was, in my jacket, shoes, and fifty-year-old body, and landed in my eight-year-old body amid the tickling fringe of the comforter . . .

The wallpaper, how could I forget, the wallpaper was a true revelation. The pattern here—with a castle and green vines—was very similar to what had hung in my room, pale green diamonds with entwining vegetation, except instead of a castle there had been a cabin tucked deep in the woods, with a little lake in front of it. Hundreds of copies of green cabins with green lakes. Every night as I fell asleep, I would settle into the cabin from the wallpaper, until the unpleasant ringing of the alarm clock would suddenly kick me out into a concrete panel-block apartment. I glanced at the desk, yes, the alarm clock was there, not exactly the same, but more . . . how can I put it, more colorful and Western, with Mickey Mouse on the face.

And here's where the differences started. This other, Western boy had had a whole collection of those little Matchbox cars painted in what we called "*metalisé*" back then, just like real cars. With doors that opened and real rubber tires. From a Ford Mustang to a Porsche to a Bugatti, Opels, and Mercedes, there was even a little metal Rolls-Royce . . . I knew all those models by heart, I knew their top speeds, which was the most important thing for us, I knew how many seconds it took for them to go from zero to to a hundred miles per hour. I had the same collection, only on bubble gum wrappers. I got up off the bed and picked up one of the cars, I opened and closed the doors with my index finger, I rolled it across the desk. One of my classmates had had a car like this, brought back by his truck-driver father. (Oh, how crucial it was back then to have a father or uncle who drove a semi, who went to that obscure country known as "Abroad" and brought back real Levi's jeans, those hard ribbed Toblerone chocolate bars, which I never liked, Venetian gondolas that sang and lit up and which were used as night-lights, Acropolis ashtrays, and so on.) Plus an old copy of that *Neckermann* magazine, actually it was a German catalog of goods that you could never own in any case, so it lost its commercial character and transformed into pure aesthetics. And erotica, I might add, by the erstwhile standards of my ten-year-old self, especially the section with ladies' undergarments. I'll never forget how that magazine lay on the round marble coffee table in a classmate of mine's living room, right next to the phone—at one time a telephone was considered furniture as well. But it was the *Neckermann* that was the true treasure. You knew you would never have all the shiny things from that catalog, but they existed somewhere, and the world they existed in also existed.

The posters on the walls of the boys' room were slightly different. The Levski football team from the 1976–77 season, cut from a newspaper to adorn my room way back when, was here replaced by the Ajax team of 1967–68, and it was an enormous glossy poster with, wowie!, an autograph from Johan Cruyff himself, my father's idol, which meant he was also mine . . . I was Cruyff and my brother was Beckenbauer.

I had the Beatles on my wall, my most precious Western possession, obtained via barter with that classmate of mine, the trucker's son, which cost me fifteen teardrop marbles plus another three "Syrian" marbles. The boy in the looking glass of the Western world had a wall full of chaotically ordered posters, which, examined carefully, told the whole bildungsroman of his puberty. From Batman to Superman, those missing heroes from my Eastern childhood (replaced by the more available King Marko and Winnetou), through *Sgt. Pepper*, a Lolita-esque black-and-white photo of a young Brigitte Bardot strolling along the beach in a bikini, her hair flowing freely, in one of Roger Vadim's films, three more hot babes, anonymous, probably Playmates from the '60s, to Bob Dylan with a guitar and a leather jacket. I had Vysotsky.

The room is only for boys, I noted.

We've got a girls' room, too, if you want to check out Barbie and Ken.

Let's keep going.

The living room was bright and spacious; the philodendron in the corner by the window and the rushes in the tall ceramic vase in front of the photo mural once again sent me back to that decade. I remembered how we used to wipe the philodendron (what a name!) with a wet rag soaked in beer. That's what was recommended back then, so all living rooms back reeked of alcohol.

But the photo mural on the wall was a true epiphany, as well as the epitome of kitsch. Thanks to yet another international truck driver, a friend of my father's, even we had gotten our hands on a wall mural. Autumn woods with the sun shining through the trees. A schoolmate of mine had a wall with a Hawaiian beach, complete with a few bathing beauties in the foreground. The one here was more reminiscent of his: an endless beach and a sunset over the ocean. What else to put on a wall mural in Switzerland? Certainly not the Matterhorn and the Alps.

And there's the small square trunk of the television, standing uneasily on four long wooden legs, the exact same one we had.

Is it an Opera? I glanced at Gaustine in surprise.

No, it's a Philips, he replied. But guess who was stealing designs from whom.

Indeed, the shape and everything else was one hundred percent identical, the People's Republic of Bulgaria's industrial espionage department was not sleeping on the job. But what about those tulip chairs? Why didn't our guys didn't steal that design, too? They were familiar to me only from movies and the *Neckermann* catalog. Elongated, cosmically aerodynamic, deep red, with a single leg, or rather stem. Of course, I immediately wanted to sit down, just as I wanted to help myself to the box of chocolate candies wrapped in tinfoil on the coffee table. I reached, then stopped.

Wait, when are these chocolates from?

They're fresh, from the '60s. Gaustine smiled.

Does the past have an expiration date . . . ?

The living room was enormous, with a sliding door that separated the east end into something like a study. Standing on the tall desk was a small red Olivetti typewriter with a piece of paper in its roller. Immediately I wanted—my fingers wanted—to pound something out, to feel the resistance of the keys, to hear the bell ding at the end of a line, and to manually pull the small metal lever for the next line. A desire from a time when writing was physical exertion.

The study was my idea, Gaustine admitted, I've always wanted to have my own room, a small den with books and that kind of a typewriter. It's not completely in the style of the '60s, back then they stored their books everywhere, even on the floor, wherever they could . . . But I can tell you that the typewriter has been a big hit. Everyone's eyes light up when they see it, they put in paper and pound their fingers on the keys.

What do they write?

Most often their names, people like to see their names in print. Of course, we're talking about the ones in the earlier stages of their illness. The others simply hit the keys.

I recalled that this was exactly what I would do as a child with my mother's typewriter, which would result in strange missives.

Жгмцццрт №№№№кктррпх ггфпрı111111ı. . . .
внтгвтгвнтгггг777ррр . . .

A possible code, which we will never crack.

11.

Why here exactly, why Switzerland? I asked Gaustine, as we sat down in the living room of the '60s.

Let's just say it's due to a fondness for *The Magic Mountain*. I tried other places as well, but here I could find people to buy my idea and invest money. There are enough people here ready to pay to die happy.

It's astonishing how cynical Gaustine can be at times.

Let's just stick with the fondness for *The Magic Mountain*, I said. (The truth is, Switzerland is the ideal country due to its "time degree zero." A country without time can most easily be inhabited by all possible eras. It has managed to slip through—even during the twentieth century—without the identifying marks that keep you in a certain era.)

There's a lot of work yet to be done, Gaustine said, wiping the lenses of his round glasses. Here you see a middle-class '60s, the past is pricey and not everyone can afford it. But you do realize that not every past and not every youth was like this. We need to have a 1960s for workers, student dorms . . . as well as the '60s for those who lived in Eastern Europe, our 1960s. One day, when this business really takes off, Gaustine continued, we'll create these clinics or sanatoriums in various countries. The past is also a local thing. There'll be houses from various years everywhere, little neighborhoods, one day we'll even have small cities, maybe even a whole country. For patients with failing memories, Alzheimer's, dementia, whatever you want to call it. For all of those who already are living solely in the present of their past. And for us, he said finally after a short pause, letting out a long stream of smoke. This sudden groundswell of people who have lost their memories today is no coincidence . . . They are here to tell us something. And believe me, one day, very soon, the majority of people will start returning to the past of their own accord, they'll start "losing" their memories willingly. The time is coming when more and more people will want to hide in the cave of the past, to turn back. And not for happy reasons, by the way. We need to be ready with the bomb shelter of the past. Call it the time shelter, if you will.

Back then I didn't understand what he meant. Just as I was never sure whether he was joking or whether he joked around at all.

According to Gaustine, for us the past is the past, and even when we step into it, we know that the exit to the present is open, we can come back with ease. For those who have lost their memories, this door has slammed shut once and for all. For them, the present is a foreign country, while the past is their homeland. The only thing we can do is create a space that is in sync with their internal time. If it's 1965 in your head, Gaustine said, the year when you were twenty and you lived in a rented attic in Paris, Kraków, or behind Sofia University, then let the outside world, at least in the confines of a single room, be 1965, too. I don't know how therapeutic that is, who knows whether it will help regenerate neural synapses. But it gives these people the right to happiness, to a memory of happiness, to be more precise. We assume that the memory of happiness is a happy memory, but who knows? You'll see, Gaustine went on, how they'll start telling stories, remembering things, even though some of them haven't said a word in months. "Oh, I remember that lamp perfectly, it was in the parlor at home, then my brother broke it with a ball, then ... How did you get our sofa ... shouldn't it be right here, a bit closer to the wall?"

I asked for a cigarette. I had quit five years ago, but now we were in a different time, damn it, before I had quit. And before I had ever started smoking, to be precise, but never mind. We sat in silence for a while, watching the cigarette smoke of the '60s wafting beneath the round lamp. The January editions of *Time* and *Newsweek* from 1968 had been casually tossed on the coffee table. The whole back of one was an ad for these very same *Pall Mall Golds*, with an extended filter and the slogan *Because it's extra long at both ends.*

I remembered that when I met Gaustine for the first time many years ago, we smoked Tomasian cigarettes from 1937, which he had offered me. Well, at least we had moved thirty or so years ahead in time since then. I was about to remind him of that, but something stopped me. I figured he would give me a strange look as if nothing like that had ever happened.

Look—he lit up a new cigarette, pausing ever so slightly before his next sentence (I recalled that trick from the films of the '60s and '70s: you take a deep drag, holding the smoke in your lungs, then exhale slowly with squinted eyes)—I need you.

I'll make you an offer you can't refuse, as the classic movie scene puts it. But for the moment I played hard-to-get and pretended to be angry.

Well, in that case, you could've given me a sign. It was a complete accident that I found you.

There was no way you wouldn't have found me. After all, you thought me up, right? He muttered, barely bothering to hide his spite. Now and then I read one of your books, I come across an interview here and there. Besides, you're my godfather, you christened me, otherwise I would still be called Augustine-Garibaldi, or have you forgotten?

You really never can tell when Gaustine is joking.

What the hell did they drink during the '60s, anyway? I cut in.

Everything. Gaustine took the hint, grabbed a bottle of Four Roses bourbon out of the minibar, and filled two heavy crystal glasses. Look here, with these couches, tables, and the bourbon (cheers!), with these lamps and light fixtures, with the music and all the pop art of the '60s—all this we can handle fine on our own. But as you yourself well know, the past is more than a set. We're going to need stories, lots of stories. He stubbed out his cigarette and immediately reached for another one. (I had forgotten how much people smoked in the '60s.) We'll need everyday life, tons of everyday life, smells, sounds, silences, people's faces; in short, all the things that crack the memory open, *mixing memory and desire*, as our man would say. You have experience with time capsules that they used to bury, right? Well, that's the sort of thing I mean. Travel around, gather up scents and stories, we need stories from different years, with that 'premonition of a miracle,' as you made me say in one of your stories in some literary rag, he added with a laugh. All kinds of stories, big, small, lighter, let them be lighter this time. After all, for some of the folks here they will be the last stories they ever enter into.

It had grown dark outside. The clouds had gathered quickly above the lake and the rain poured down in long streams. Gaustine got up and closed the window.

Well, what do you know, in '68 today's date was also a Thursday, he said, glancing at the Pan Am Airlines wall calendar featuring models from different continents. And it also rained that afternoon, if you recall.

I got up to go. Before I started down the stairs, he said, almost off the cuff: The saying that you can never step into the same story twice is not true. You can. That's what we're going to do.

12.

And so, Gaustine and I created our first clinic for the past. Actually, he created it, I was only his assistant, a collector of the past. It wasn't easy. You can't just tell somebody: Okay, here's your past from 1965. You have to know its stories, or if you have no way of getting them anymore, then you have to make them up. To know everything about that year. Which hairstyles were fashionable, how pointy the shoes were, how the soap smelled, a complete catalog of scents. Whether the spring was rainy, what the temperatures were in August. What the number one hit song was. The most important stories of the year, not just the news, but the rumors, the urban legends. Things got more complicated depending on which past you wanted delivered to you. Did you want your Eastern past, if you were from the eastern side of the wall? Or on the contrary, did you want to live out precisely that past which had been denied to you? To gorge yourself on the past as if on the bananas you had dreamed about your whole life?

The past is not just that which happened to you. Sometimes it is that which you just imagined.

13.

Such was the case with Mircea from Turnu Măgurele. He only remembered what *hadn't* happened to him. He remembered nothing of socialism or his job at the factory, the endless party meetings, banquets, parades, and chilly warehouses—he had already erased all that while his mind was still working. When the empty-ing of his memory began, only the things he had yearned for (that's the right word, no two ways about it) as a young man remained. Even back then he had known everything about America, it was in his heart and soul. He said he had always felt like an American. He had a friend who back in the day had managed to escape to New York and they wrote to each other from time to time. The other guy, the friend, was always complaining, Here they do this, here they do that . . . Finally Mircea couldn't contain himself and wrote to him: Hey, jackass, so why do you keep sitting there wasting this chance? . . . Come back and let's switch places. Fate granted one share of good luck to the whole of Turnu Măgurele and it fell to you of all people, you friggin' whiner.

His son had brought him to the clinic one afternoon. And our Mircea felt right at home here amid those records, sofas, tables, and posters of that past which hadn't actually been his. He remem-bered all these things in detail, at the expense of the real past that fate had allotted to him in Turnu Măgurele under socialism. That which had not happened to him, which he had imagined, remained in his memory longer than what had happened. He continued to walk down streets that he knew only from books and films, to hang around all night in the clubs of Greenwich Village, to recount in great detail that open-air concert by Simon & Garfunkel in 1981 in Central Park, where he had never set foot, and to remember women he had never been with.

He was a strange bird both here at the clinic and back in his little Romanian hometown.

Happened stories are all alike, every unhappened story is unhap-pened in its own way.

14.

It was the perfect job for me. When it comes down to it, that's what I've always done—I've roamed like a flaneur through the arcades of the past. (Out of Gaustine's earshot, I could say that I invented him so that he could invent this job for me.) It allowed me to travel, to wander around ostensibly aimlessly, to write down even the most trivial of things—what more could I want? To gather up the bullet casings from 1942 or to see what is left of that dilapidated yet still important 1968. Past eras are volatile, they evaporate with ease like an open bottle of perfume, but if you have the nose for it, you can always catch a whiff of their fragrance. You have a nose for other times, that's what Gaustine said once, a nose for other times, that'll come in handy for me. And so I officially became something of a trapper of the past.

Over the years, I've realized that it tends to hide above all in two places—in afternoons (in the way the light falls) and in scents. That's where I laid my traps.

What I've come up with isn't a show, Gaustine would always say, in any case it isn't *The Truman Show*, nor is it *Good Bye Lenin!*, nor *Back to the Future*. (Somewhere his critics had tried to slap these labels on him.) It's not recorded on video, it isn't broadcast, in fact there's no show at all. I'm not interested in maintaining somebody's illusion that socialism continues to exist, nor is there any time machine. There is no time machine except the human being.

ONCE (NOT SO LONG AGO), as I was wandering around Brooklyn, I sensed for the first time with such clarity that the light was coming from another time. I could define it quite precisely, the light of the '80s, sometime from the beginning of the decade, I think it was from 1982, late summer. Light as if from a Polaroid picture, lacking brightness, soft, making everything look slightly faded.

The past settles into afternoons, that's where time visibly slows down, it dozes off in the corners, blinking like a cat looking through thin blinds. It's always afternoon when you remember something, at least that's how it is for me. Everything is in the light. I know from photographers that afternoon light is the most suitable of exposures. Morning light is too young, too sharp. Afternoon light is old light, tired and slow. The real life of the world and humanity can be written in several afternoons, in the light of several afternoons, which are the afternoons of the world.

I also realized that I wouldn't have recognized that light from 1982 if not for its synchronous appearance with a particular smell, which came from the same decade from my childhood. I think our whole memory for scents comes from childhood, it is stored there, in that portion of the brain responsible for our earliest memories. It was the sharp scent of asphalt, of tar melted by the sun, the greasy, yes, greasy smell of petroleum. Brooklyn offered me this scent, perhaps because of the heat, perhaps they were fixing the road somewhere nearby, perhaps because of the big trucks that crisscrossed the neighborhood. Or perhaps because of all of that taken together. (I will add here as well the scent of oil-soaked brown wrapping paper around the Balkanche bike that my parents brought home one evening for me. The scent of impatience, of newness, of warehouses and stores, a joyful scent.)

With light, you can make some pathetic attempt to preserve it, to take a picture of it. Or like Monet you can paint a cathedral in various hours of the day. He knew what he was doing—the cathedral was only a ruse, a trap for capturing the rays of light. But with smells, no such tricks are available to us, there is no film or recording device, no such instrument has been invented over the long millennia, how could humanity have overlooked this?

Isn't it truly astonishing that there is no recording device for scents? Actually, there is one, a single solitary one that predates technology, analog, the oldest of them all. Language, of course. For now, there is nothing else, thus I am forced to capture scents with words and to add them to yet another notebook. We remember only those scents that we have described or compared. The remarkable thing is that we don't even have names for smells. God or Adam didn't quite finish the job. It's not like colors, for example, where you've got names like red, blue, yellow, violet. . . . We are not meant to name scents directly. Rather, it's always through comparison, always descriptive. It smells like violets, like toast, like seaweed, like rain, like a dead cat . . . But violets, toast, seaweed, rain, and a dead cat are not the names of scents. How unfair. Or perhaps beneath this impossibility lurks some other omen, which we do not understand . . .

And so I traveled around, gathering up scents and afternoons, cataloging them. We needed a precise and exhaustive description of which scent brings which memories back, what age it affects most strongly, which decade we could call forth with it. I described them in detail and sent my findings to Gaustine. In the clinic, scents could always be re-created when needed. Although some attempted to preserve the very molecules of a given scent, for Gaustine this was a waste of effort. It was much simpler and more authentic to toast a piece of bread or melt a bit of asphalt.

15.

When I discovered Gaustine and the clinic, I was just starting to write a novel about the discreet monster of the past, its deceptive innocence, and so on, and what would happen if we began bringing back the past with a therapeutic aim. My work for the clinic and the simultaneous writing of that book were like interconnected vessels. Sometimes I lost my sense of what was real and what was not. One flowed into the other.

In any case, the basic question for both was how the past is made.

Will someone arrive like He the Messiah? Someone who will take mercy on the past's stiff dis-member-ed parts, its pale face and its stopped heart, and say, "Lazarus, come forth!" and it will gradually get its breath back, blood will start to flow beneath the waxy skin, its members will start to move, its plugged ears will clear up, and its eyes will open.

Or, while we're waiting, various false prophets, tempters, and mad scientists will perform experiments upon its corpse and every time will end up with Frankenstein's monster. Can the past be resurrected or re-member-ed again? Should it be?

And how much past can a person bear?

16.

Mr. N.

A person, whom I shall call Mr. N., at the end of his days is sitting by a window and trying to resurrect that which is over and done with. His memory is leaving him, just as his friends left him when he was blacklisted. He has no friends, no living relatives. No one to call. If we are not in someone else's memory, do we even exist at all?

Sometimes random people tell him stories in which he appears, but he doesn't remember any of them, they seem made up to him, as if they had happened to someone else. He comes across written works under his name. Most likely he had been relatively famous, then afterward they had erased him. Doctors advised him to go look at his dossier from socialist times. That, too, turns out to have been erased, almost nothing is left of it. But he manages to figure out (they whisper it to him) which agent had primarily kept tabs on him.

So he is forced to call that very same agent from back then. At first the agent recoils and refuses to meet him at all. Mr. N. has no intention of taking revenge on him, he even apologizes for disturbing him, but he would like to see him for a completely different reason. He has lost his memory and must gather up the pieces of himself before he passes away. And the only person left who was close to his past is the agent.

You know every detail of my past better than anyone, including myself, sir, please, let's meet.

And so their meetings begin. They have long, slow conversations every afternoon. Both of them are now outside the world, or at least outside of the system within which they had been young and enemies, the closest of enemies.

Some of the stories mean nothing to Mr. N., as if they are not about him at all. Others open long-forgotten doors in his memory, such as: A woman used to come visit you often. A very beautiful woman. Every Thursday at three in the afternoon. Then you would be alone in the apartment, your wife wasn't home, the agent recalls indelicately.

Mr. N. tries to remember and fails. Yes, there were such afternoons. He could reconstruct to some extent a vague feeling of guilt and excitement from back then. But who was this woman, and why had she later disappeared? She was clearly quite brave, since she had decided to have an affair with him. She must have known that he was kept under surveillance. For a person with his past, that was inevitable. What did the woman look like? The agent describes her in detail. How she walked down the sidewalk, how all the old men from the neighborhood would turn around to stare after her (it's almost straight out of Homer), how she moved freely, not anxiously or hurrying with a net shopping bag like the local women here. How her hair followed in step with her gait.

For the first time the agent forgets himself and speaks at length, as if in a trance, as they walk along beneath the mottled shade of the chestnuts, in the city emptied and bleached by the heat. The pursuer and his victim, finally together.

A year or so after I met up with Gaustine in Zurich, we already had a Bulgarian branch of our clinic. A spacious villa, built in the '30s not far from Sofia, outside Kostenets. I love coming here, I have appointed myself as a supervisor, but in fact the doctors and staff do all the work and, to be frank, they don't have much need for me. I sit and observe my Bulgarian past, which is passing away with these people, who have come here at the end of their lives. Old people have always fascinated me. I lived with them as a child. We grew up with our grandparents, we could talk to them, yet we missed out on a whole generation: our parents. Now, when I find myself joining their ranks, my fascination has another motive as well. How to age in the face of death, ever farther away from life, and how to save that which is unsalvageable? Even as a memory. Afterward, where does all that personal past go?

Becoming attached to people here is painful, because you realize you're becoming attached to someone who will soon leave you. I feel especially close to Mr. N. (His is likely a case of retrograde amnesia.) He has only just come to the clinic, and the agent follows him like a shadow, visiting twice a week. Clearly, he, too, enjoys it or feels some need to do it, because he comes all the way from the city every time and spends the whole afternoon here. In the beginning we sent a car for him, but then he turned it down and started coming with his own. People need to tell stories, I think. Even people like him. Before he couldn't, and now, when he can, nobody cares. Suddenly he has found someone who hangs on his every word. One man who has turned into an ear for all those stories from back then. One man who is ready to hear everything. The man he followed, who was losing his memory, and has ended up being erased twice over.

Tell me who I am.

The agent feels like a person who could be manipulative, he always had such power thanks to his profession, but not such enormous power as he now has. The power to think up the life of another person who no longer remembers much about it. He could feed Mr. N. completely made-up memories. Okay, so he'd still have to take into account some of Mr. N.'s remaining anchor points of memory. And he would never know when some lost detail might float up, and faces or phrases might travel across a fragile neural bridge. But for now, the agent, let's call him Mr. A., does not appear to harbor such intentions. He, too, wants to return to the warm cave of the past.

Once, he tells Mr. N., you came and sat down at my table. At the Ivy Café, which was not far from the entrance to your apartment building, on the same street. I usually sat there to watch who was coming in and out. And one afternoon you came out, walked over to the café, looked around, and sat down at my table. There were other empty tables, the café was almost deserted, but you sat down at mine, you didn't even ask me, "May I?" I was horror-struck, thinking I'd been unmasked. I waited to see what you'd say, going over all sorts of scenarios in my mind. You ordered vodka—at that time we all drank vodka. Vodka with cola, even. In those pretty glass bottles, so, see, we even had cola back then. Anyway. I'm drinking my vodka and waiting for you to show your hand. You didn't say anything. The most agonizing half hour of my life. You glanced at me from time to time. I felt completely unmasked. And even now I wonder, did you know that I was following you? Usually people can sense it. Did you know?

I don't remember. Mr. N. shrugs helplessly.

Mr. N. looks forward to these meetings with great excitement. I get the feeling he is still alive only so he can hear the whole story of himself. I love sitting next to him, sometimes we chat a bit, then we fall silent. I don't know what is going on in his mind, but I suspect he remembers more than he lets on. Maybe he is also playing his own game, that of the forgetful one, the victim, who ostensibly lets the storyteller lead him, and in demonstrating his own total oblivion lulls the storyteller's vigilance to sleep, forcing him to tell everything, complete with all the details he didn't plan on revealing.

Tell me, Mr. N. says, what kind of shirts did I wear, what shoes, did I grin or grit my teeth in a frown, did I look down as I walked, was I hunched over... *was I happy?* he finally blurts out. This startles the agent, he can say everything there is to say about the shirts, jackets, overcoats, cigarettes, beer and vodka that the target ordered, but...

There's no one else who remembers these details, even mistresses and wives forget after a time. Only the secret agent knows the details. Let's try to put ourselves in his shoes. He has to sit there and watch, to describe what he sees. And what he sees is woefully insignificant. Indeed, what could really happen in the day of a man of fifty at that time? He goes out. He walks down the sidewalk. He stops. He takes out a match, cups his hand, lights up a cigarette. What kind of cigarettes does he smoke? Stewardess, of course. What is he wearing? A gray shirt with the sleeves rolled up, pants, shoes, well, lookee here! The shoes are Italian, expensive, with pointy toes, that needs to be noted. What's more, he's wearing a Borsalino. Not many people wear Borsalinos. That gets noted, too. If anyone took the effort to read as literature all those thousands of pages written during the '50s/'60s/'70s/'80s by all the eavesdropping and note-scribbling agents, it would surely turn out to be the great unwritten Bulgarian novel of that era. Every bit as mediocre and inept as the era itself.

17.

Notes on the Impossible Epic

In all ancient epics, there is one strong enemy you battle—the Bull of Heaven and Gilgamesh, the monster Grendel, his mother, and finally the Dragon, which fatally wounds the already aged Beowulf, all the monsters, bulls, etc., in Ovid's *Metamorphoses*, the Cyclops in the *Odyssey*, and so on ... In modern-day novels these monsters have disappeared, the heroes are gone, too. When there are no monsters, there are no heroes, either.

Monsters still do exist, however. There is one monster that stalks every one of us. Death, you'll say, yes, of course, death is his brother, but old age is the monster. This is the true (and doomed) battle, with no flashiness, no fireworks, no swords inlaid with the tooth of Saint Peter, with no magical armor and unexpected allies, without hope that bards will sing songs about you, with no rituals ...

An epic battle with no epos.

Long lonely maneuvers, waiting, more like trench warfare, lying in wait, hiding out, quick sorties, prowling the battlefield "between the clock and the bed," as one of the elderly Munch's final self-portraits is called. *Between the Clock and the Bed*. Who will sing praises of such a death and such an old age?

18

Mr. N.

(continued)

Mr. A. recalls how difficult it was for him to make up nonsense to write in his reports. To a certain extent he was not immune to writer's block. He had expected more from his profession, like in the movies or detective novels, car chases, mysterious visitors, for the person he was following to jump out the window in the middle of the night. He needed a plot, without knowing the word. But there was no plot. And therein lies the deep anti-cinematographic-ness of life. Nothing but leaving home, coming back. Even the target's closest friends had stopped visiting him, so as to spare themselves unpleasantness. Yes, the mistress on Thursday was a promising exception. That was documented, of course. But even that wasn't much of an adventure. Besides, it's a part of everyday life, who doesn't have a mistress (or a lover)?

Sometimes I wondered what to write, Mr. A. admits, because nothing interesting happened. Mr. N. feels anxious that he has caused him trouble, he feels awkward that he lived such a boring life, about which nothing could be written. He should have done something more, you know, daring, he should have shot himself in front of the agent, that would have filled up two pages easily. On the other hand, Mr. N. is interested (or I'm projecting this onto him because

I am interested) precisely in the nothingness of everyday life, in life in all its details. This is exactly what he wants to remember. He has systematically erased every exceptionality, if that is the right word, with which he could describe the arrest, the beatings in the basement of Moscow 5, the wretchedness and the stench of urine in the crowded cell of the Pazardzhik prison, the petering out of his visits, the cessation of the letters coming from the outside. All of that has been ripped out. But alongside that it seems something else has disappeared, the normal things, that which we are made of. All of his documented everyday life before prison was confiscated during the searches, then returned, but since then he hasn't touched it. Two black-and-white photographs as a child, one from his army days, a small photo album from his wedding (he ended up with it after the divorce), again black-and-white, some photo of him walking along the boulevard, caught mid-stride, his overcoat blowing in the wind, he's laughing and making some gesture toward the person taking the picture. And that's it. There is no photograph of the woman who visited on Thursdays, of course.

One day Mr. A. arrives with several letters—Mr. N.'s letters to the woman. How did you get these? he asks. Mr. A. merely raises his eyebrows, surprised at that naïve question. Mr. N. opens the letters and finds they are short. He reads them and realizes that he does not remember them at all. He reads with genuine curiosity, as if he were not the author. And he must admit that he is impressed. They are well written, he'd found the right words, he was romantic without going overboard. Quite persistent and bold in certain suggestions. This is something new. He would have described himself as timid and bashful. The final letter ends with a warning that it would be better for her not to come anymore, since they were surely watching him and some shrimpy stooge in a scally cap was loafing around the café across the street all day. At that point Mr.

N. lifts his eyes apologetically from the letter. Don't worry about it, I'm over it, says Mr. A.

Mr. N. leaves the letters on the middle of the table. He doesn't know whether he can keep them or whether he has to give them back. Understanding his question, Mr. A. nods in encouragement, Yes, they're for you. They continue to speak in the polite *"vous"* form, even though neither one of them has anyone closer than the man across from him now.

Over time the woman from those Thursdays starts dominating Mr. N.'s thoughts more and more. But this, for some reason, scares him more than anything. Her image starts to float up from the nothingness, like photos out of the chemical bath of a darkroom. She wears her hair in a ponytail and has a silver streak in her bangs. Even though this is precisely what he wanted in the beginning, now her appearance starts to seem frightening. The reason for this is simple—he suspects that this woman could crack the dike that he has carefully built up over the years, freeing everything he has managed to keep out. He is not sure he could stand it. On the other hand, if there had been someone who loved him, this meant that he had existed after all, even if he doesn't remember much of himself.

If there had been someone whom he had loved, this could also count as proof of his own presence. But what then?

On his next visit, Mr. A. has yet another surprise for him. He takes a carefully wrapped photograph out of his leather satchel. He hands it to Mr. N. It is a black-and-white photo, strongly contrasted, a deserted street can be seen, and on the sidewalk in the shade of a tree stand Mr. N. and a woman who is leaning toward him, perhaps she wants to whisper something in his ear or to kiss him, it's hard to tell. The shadows of the leaves are falling on her dress.

The most beautiful woman in Sofia, Mr. A. says finally. She didn't belong here, not in this time and this place. I knew a lot of people were dying to be with her. Some of your problems were because of her. Of course, first and foremost you were in trouble because of what you wrote and said in the cafés, especially in '68, about all the events happening then. But also because of her. She was the daughter of an old writer, by the way. He couldn't stand you, may he rest in peace. A talentless hack, from the big-time nomenclature, the joke was that she was his only good work. She knew she had no future with you. Because you yourself had no future. I think that's also why she loved you.

Again the future. If he could have, Mr. N. would have remembered that he had always been indifferent to the future. Conversations about the future under communism inspired him to make snarky comments at parties; the cosmic future also seemed unclear and suspicious to him, the new order, the new people—all of it sounded so distant and hollow. The bright future gives me heartburn, he once told a group of friends. (That, of course, immediately got written down). Shortly thereafter Brodsky, if I recall, formulated it more beautifully, but it was the same idea: "My objections to that system were not so much political as aesthetic." Nevertheless, I prefer Mr. N.'s formulation. His objections to the system were physiological.

19.

There is also a dead, mummified past.

For those of my generation, our first memory of a dead body is a shared memory. It's as if there was an order from the Ministry of Edification (surely there was just such an order) for everyone in the earliest years of primary school to visit the mausoleum of Georgi Dimitrov. To bow before the leader and teacher who so loved children and would take time for photos with them, despite his busy workday. To pay their respects to the hero of Leipzig, who bravely set fire to the German Reichstag, as one of my confused classmates put it, thus calling down a world of trouble on himself, which included his parents being called in, getting scolded, etc. Goebbels himself didn't manage to convict him, yet you have the cheek to call him an arsonist, the teacher shouted at my poor classmate.

Anyway, that first meeting with death stays with you your whole life. The mausoleum guaranteed you a real live experience of death, if I can put it that way. All subsequent deaths and deceased bodies would be compared to that body, they would be copies of that first, model dead body. We knew we were very lucky, as the world is not exactly bursting at the seams with mausoleums and stuffed guys. That's what we whispered among ourselves before we went inside, and good thing nobody heard that "stuffed guy," because we would've caught hell for it.

They brought us there all the way from the other side of Bulgaria. A whole night rocking and swaying on the slowest passenger train so as to avoid having to pay for a hotel in the capital city. In the morning still groggy, sleepy-eyed, directly from the train station we waded into the thick November fog in front of the mausoleum. Fear comes when it's our turn to go in. We pass by the honor guards at the entrance, who stand stock-still. Perhaps they are stuffed as well? Inside, the hallways are darkened, illuminated only by electric torches and cold as a refrigerator. The mausoleum is a refrigerator, of course. Something like our freezers at home which our mothers stuff full of pork knuckle and chicken so the meat doesn't go bad.

We near the room with the body, we can already see the glass coffin lid. Chubby Demby, my friend whom I sit next to in class, had whispered to me outside that if you take a really close look at his eyelids, you can see them twitching slightly. That's what his brother had told him, who'd already passed through here.

The dead man looked like he was made of plastic, his suit coat and pants were more alive than he was, his lapel covered with medals, the hair of his mustache like a clothes brush. Just then, as I passed slowly by his head, I saw perfectly clearly how for a split second his eyelid twitched. Tick-tick, two times, the left eyelid. I could barely stop myself from screaming. It was as if he were giving me a sign, winking at me from his glass-lidded coffin. Be careful, because Comrade Dimitrov sees everything, our teacher at school had warned us, pointing at the portrait on the wall. Yeah, right, he can see, my ass, I had said to myself then, but now he was winking to punish me for my doubts. He really will turn out to *live eternally*, as they were always telling us.

Good thing Demby was there to save me from this early metaphysical fear. I'm not sure whether he saw the wink (or whether the sign was for me alone), but as an amateur biologist who had devoured his older brother's textbooks, he explained everything to me in graphic detail based on the experiments with dead frogs described there. With a frog, even if it's dead and its legs are just dangling there limp, if you give it a little electrical shock, it'll start kicking as if alive. We would do this experiment in sixth grade, he said. So the guy here was dead as a frog and would never be getting back up, he just had muscles that still moved.

I still use this explanation when my fears grow too metaphysical.

20

Mr. N.

(the end)

So how did she end up with me, despite everything? Mr. N. asks.

She was the wife of a friend of yours. He came over to our side, had a few skeletons in his own closet, we put the screws to him a bit. To tell you the truth, he didn't put up much resistance. He was our main source, but you always suspected other people, at least that's what you said on the phone. You tapped my phone? Mr. A. does not even deign to reply. The day your friend got promoted to some big-shot position, she came to you on her own for the first time. It was Thursday afternoon, the first of all those Thursdays to follow.

Mr. N. listens and gradually begins to imagine this woman, with her long hair with the white streak in her bangs, and her careless gait. When she walked down the street, they would all turn around to stare after her. A famous theater director was crazy about her, too; he staged a play and had the actress done up like that—hair in a ponytail, with the white streak . . . Everyone knew who she was playing. The director was immediately sent to another theater, the play was canceled, his marriage was over. That woman brought nothing but trouble, Mr. A. said.

But why does the secret agent Mr. A. keep coming? In the beginning, surely out of curiosity or fear of being blackmailed. He quickly must have realized that there was no risk of anything like that. There is something else. If Mr. N. remembers nothing or almost nothing of all that, then Mr. A. is free of guilt, in a manner of speaking. Without being able to formulate it clearly, he senses that if no one remembers, then everything is permissible. *If no one remembers* becomes the equivalent of *If there is no God*. If there is no God, Dostoyevsky said, then everything is permitted. God will turn out to be nothing but a huge memory. A memory of sins. A cloud with infinite megabytes of memory. A forgetful God, a God with Alzheimer's, would free us from all obligations. No memory, no crime.

So why, then, does Mr. A. come and tell these stories? Probably because a human being is not meant to keep a secret for so long. Secrets, it seems, are a late outgrowth in the course of evolution. No animal keeps secrets. Just man. If we had to describe a secret's structure, it would most likely be uneven, granular, some kind of lump. In Mr. A.'s case, this is not a metaphor. The lump is real, he had been trying to ignore it for several months, but after going to the doctor three weeks ago, everything is now clear. The fact that he is terminally ill frees him from many things, but it also spurs him on toward others. Now the predator begs the prey to hear him out. Age is the great equalizer. They have become brothers-in-arms, they have crossed over to the losing side in a battle whose outcome is clear. Mr. A. can finally tell everything. And Mr. N. can finally hear the whole story about himself.

What happened to her? Mr. N. asks again, less and less certain that he wants to know.

Mr. A. could wriggle out of this a thousand different ways. She was not a target of operational interest and he never entered into communication with her—this was the bit of officialese nearest to hand. Or he could say some other operative agent took over the expansion of the investigation, or so on. Mr. A. is silent for a bit, rolls a cigarette, his hands trembling. Mr. N. seems only now to notice that in recent months his interlocutor has aged visibly, his skin has turned yellow, his face has suddenly grown gaunt. Two or three weeks earlier he had called to say that he couldn't come, he had to go get some tests done.

And then Mr. A. admits everything. How, when they arrested Mr. N., she told her husband that she would leave him that very second if he didn't do something for his friend. How she packed her bags and moved out the next day, how she went around from office to office by herself. She wanted to visit him, but they told her that the prisoner had refused to see her at all. How in the end she reached Mr. A. himself. She came to his home one evening and wanted to talk about Mr. N. She begged him to tell her where he was, to arrange a visit. She would do anything . . .

Suddenly Mr. N. clearly imagines the whole scene between the two of them. With one aberration. The woman's body is naked in the middle of the room, young and beautiful, Mr. A. is standing in front of her, except that he is his current age, a shriveled old man, skin and bones. Suddenly that terrible heartburn comes back, that nausea that was not metaphysical, on the contrary, it had a physical and even physiological dimension. His whole stomach is burning, as if someone had poured vinegar inside him.

I'm sorry, Mr. A. says, sitting there frozen, waiting to see what Mr. N. will say. Whatever it might be, it will be the end of this story.

Mr. N. doesn't say anything. He only feels a terrible urge to vomit. The heartburn is back, his body has remembered and is disgusted. He takes the photograph, stands up, and leaves. If this were a film, against the backdrop of the blank screen as the final credits rolled, we would hear a shot.

It's the afternoon of the world. A man is walking down the sidewalk on the shady side of the street. On top of everything, it's August— the afternoon of the year. The sun passes through the leaves of the

trees, throwing dappled sunlight on the pavement. There is nothing else around, the houses are resting with their baking walls,
somewhere a forgotten radio can be heard playing through an open
window. The scene is simplified, almost like in a movie. A woman
appears from the other end of the street and stops next to the man,
the two of them standing in the shade. (The absolute past is something like that—the afternoon of the world, a hideout in the shade
of a tree.) A bit farther down the street, invisible to them, a man
stands and takes their picture. The photograph is almost a work of
art, it has clearly captured the shadows of the leaves on the sidewalk and on their two bodies, the woman's leaning figure and the
emptiness of the afternoon street. Everything that would happen
after this photograph has not yet happened.

The man from the photograph is now holding the image of himself and the woman in his hands. Of the couple beneath the tree,
only he remains. And the photographer. The photographer is also
the only one who will never forget the scene. Because this story,
he remembered as he told it, was the only story in his flat life. This
woman, also the only woman in his life (who disappeared under
mysterious circumstances), has pursued him since then, along
with this man, who stands here, his memory gone. Some call this
kind of pursuit guilt. But like most others, Mr. A., up until the very
end, will not find the right word.

21.

Floors of the Past

A year before Mr. N. joined us, things with the clinic in Zurich
were going quite well, even outstripping our expectations. Gaustine now occupied the entire top floor of the building, where we

could create all sorts of variants of the '60s. Not long after that, the Geronto-Psychiatric Center that owned the building invited us to further develop our theory in their wards as well, so in practice we had free run of the whole building. We started opening rooms of the past as well as small clinics in several other countries, including Bulgaria.

Alzheimer's, or more generally memory loss, had turned into the most quickly spreading disease in the world. According to the statistics, every three seconds someone in the world developed dementia. Registered cases had surpassed fifty million—in thirty years, they would triple. Given lengthening life spans, this was inevitable. Everyone was getting old. Elderly men would bring their wives here, or vice versa, elderly women with discreet diamonds would lead their partners here, the latter would smile awkwardly and ask what city they were in now. Sometimes sons or daughters would bring in both their parents, who were often holding hands, no longer able to recognize their own children's faces. They would come for a few hours, for an afternoon, to the apartment of their youth. They would enter as if they were right at home. *The tea set must be here, I always kept it here . . .* They sat down in the armchairs, looked through albums of black-and-white photos, suddenly "recognizing" themselves in some of them. Sometimes their companions brought in their own old albums, which we would leave on the coffee table in advance. There were also people who took a few faltering steps and then returned to the middle of the living room, right under the light fixture.

One elderly man whom they brought in regularly loved to hide behind the curtains. He would stand there like an aged boy trying to play hide-and-seek, but the game had dragged on, the other kids had thrown in the towel, they'd gone home, they'd gotten old. And no one came looking for him. Yet he would stand there behind the curtain and peek out timidly to see what was taking them so long. The most terrible thing about hide-and-seek is realizing that no one is looking for you anymore. I don't think he will ever come to that realization, thank God.

Actually, our bodies turn out to be quite merciful by nature, a little amnesia rather than anesthesia at the end. Our memory, which is leaving us, lets us play a bit longer, one last time in the Elysian fields of childhood. A few well-begged-for, please-just-five-more minutes, like in the old days, playing outside in the street. Before we get called home for good.

And so, the past and Gaustine gradually took over the remaining floors of the clinic. We needed to differentiate the '40s and the '50s. We had started with the '60s as if we were subconsciously preparing rooms for ourselves. But ninety-year-old patients also wanted their childhood and their youth. Thus, World War Two moved into the ground floor. Which turned out to be a good choice, first, because it saved them the trouble of climbing the stairs. And second, the basement below could be used as a bomb shelter, and that made our re-creation of the decade truly authentic. Most people had memories of hiding precisely during bombing raids.

Should we awaken fear, the memory of fear? Classical reminiscence therapy insisted on positive memories. According to Gaustine, however, every awakened memory is important. Fear is one of the strongest triggers of the memory, and so we should use it. Of course, these trips to the basement were rare, but they always produced results. Shivering and shaken up, that's how people came out of the bomb shelters, scared and alive.

The '50s sprawled on the floor above. Here was the dominion of Elvis Presley, Fats Domino, Dizzy Gillespie, Miles Davis, here you could hear that whole astonishing mix of jazz, rock-n-roll, pop, and the now old-fashionedly symphonic Frank Sinatra.

Here were *North by Northwest*, Hitchcock, Cary Grant, *Nights of Cabiria*, Fellini, Mastroianni, Brigitte Bardot, Dior . . . The world was recovering from the war and wanted to live. In one part of the world, that was easier to do. For the other part, we had a separate zone at the end of hallway, several apartments for the Eastern Bloc countries. One for the '50s for Eastern Europe, and the other—a separate room for the Soviet '50s (well financed, by the way). Similarly, the Chinese '50s were established. The past is also a financial investment. The Cuban revolution and Castro did not receive a separate hacienda, but nevertheless half of the people wandering around this section were wearing Che Guevara T-shirts and they would stop in front of the portrait of El Comandante. The hallway between West and East was divided in the middle by an "iron curtain," a massive wooden gate, which was always locked and which only clinic personnel could pass through. You never knew what those on the one side might think up.

It only took one escape attempt from the Eastern hallway, a guy who tried to jump over the top of this mini–Berlin Wall (there was a few feet of empty space between it and the ceiling), but fell and broke his leg. After that casualty, one of the orderlies patrolled the Eastern side in old military uniforms.

Memory loss was affecting ever younger people, thus the need for a '70s floor was also growing, so the fourth was dedicated to that. And the '60s was moved down to the third. The attic was left for the 1980s and '90s—they would be needed someday.

22.

A Dentist's Memory

He doesn't remember faces, nor does he connect them with names. Open your mouth and let's take a look, aha, now I recognize you, you're the one with pulpitis on the lower sixth on the left, Kircho, wasn't it?

Surely it's possible to create an archaeology of teeth and to clearly establish each decade according to the different kinds of fillings and materials used. Oh-ho, my dentist always says, your teeth are a brief history of the '90s, the chaos back then, the crisis, those heady first experiments with metalloceramics, mass use of root canals, posts put in crooked, a complete nightmare. If dentists were archaeologists . . .

At the dental clinic in the town where I grew up, in the hallway over the doors to the offices they had hung photos of the whole Politburo, who knows why . . . Even as kids we knew the term "politburo," a fact which is revolting in and of itself. I was able to recognize some of the faces; their portraits were all over the place, they were often shown on television. So you'd be sitting there trembling in this marble corridor with identical white doors, listening for the grinding sound of the drill. Someone just screamed from inside the rooms. And in this sterile, unfeeling hallway the faces of those guys would be looking down on you. Nondescript, aged faces, unfeeling faces, with no hope at all.

That's how the 1970s were to some extent, marble and old men.

Those faces have been imprinted in my mind forever and, like with Pavlov's dog, the second I hear a dentist's drill, they appear before my eyes like the impassive patron saints of pain. And vice versa, if I catch a glimpse of them in some archival newspaper, I always feel a twinge in my teeth.

23.

Every morning I look through the newly arrived newspapers and magazines. *Time* magazine from the second week of January 1968. *Rosencrantz and Guildenstern Are Dead* by Stoppard is playing on Broadway. The movie theaters are showing Visconti's recently released *The Stranger*. And in almost all sections: *The War*. You'd think the Second World War hadn't ended yet or had broken out again. Of course, it's the Vietnam War. Up in the corner, in a little square, the number of American soldiers killed in 1967: 9,353. Then there are two columns about the events in Czechoslovakia, actually the events are yet to happen, and the title is "A Reason for Hope," about Dubček's election, hope that would soon be shot down as well. But now it's the beginning of 1968, we still don't know anything. History is still news.

Suddenly Bulgaria appears in a single line stating that nearly twenty percent of the cars on the road are chauffeur-driven, i.e., ferrying bureaucrats and head honchos of various calibers. Coincidentally or not, the whole facing page gleams with an enormous red Pontiac, wide as the street itself, an ad for the Pontiac Bonneville of 1968.

At the same time, during the second week of January 1968, a green village Jeep (the local co-op's car, *Time* magazine was right), one of those with a canvas top rather than a hard cover, was bumping down a dirt road toward the maternity hospital in the nearby small town. In that Jeep was my mother, inside my mother was me, the driver was my father. I was on my way to be born.

Just look how those statistics from *Time* affected me very personally: There were no other cars in the village. Perhaps due to the whole stress of finding a car to drive my mother to the hospital, my father withdrew all of the family savings, took out a loan, and bought a used Warszawa, which dramatically increased the per capita percentage of personal automobiles in the village. The Warszawa was a powerful, corpulent, and booming car, not like that red Pontiac, and according to one neighbor the military kept tabs on them, so in case of a mobilization any Warszawa would be nationalized, some light artillery mounted on the roof, which would automatically turn it into a little tank and the driver into a tank driver. This had my father very worried, since it was already May '68, spring had sprung in Prague, and that very same neighbor (agent or joker, we never did figure that out) said that we'd have to go free our Czech brothers. Free them from who? my father asked naïvely. What do you mean from who, from their own selves, the neighbor replied and my father could already envision himself setting out for Prague in his mobilized Warszawa.

Did *Time* magazine have any inking of my father's worries and of my birth (which happened on the way to the hospital in the cooperative farm's rustic Jeep), when writing about hope in Prague and about the deficit of privately owned cars in Bulgaria? Did my father have any inkling about *Time*? Doubtful. Yet despite this, everything is connected. A Jeep, a Pontiac, and Dubček.

Reading magazines and newspapers from forty or fifty years ago. What was worrisome then is no longer worrisome now. News has become history.

Breaking news has long since broken. The paper is slightly yellowed, a faint scent of damp wafts from the magazine's glossy pages.

But what is going on with the ads? The ones we passed over with annoyance back then have now taken on a new value. Suddenly the ads have become the true news about that time. The entrance into it. A memory of everyday life, which goes bad quickest of all and acquires a layer of mold. Of course, the items being advertised are long gone. Which therefore increases their value. A sense of a vanished world that had had a good time, driven a Pontiac, worn white slacks and a wide-brimmed hat, drunk Cinzano, strolled around Saint-Tropez. The very same world that thirty years earlier had waited in line for a special sale on radios in 1939 *so as to tune in live to the upcoming war*, as if it were a baseball game . . .

Incidentally, in 1939, the use of radios sharply increased. That would be the medium of the war. They would declare it on the radio, they would broadcast congratulatory concerts for the soldiers at the front, all the propaganda would pass over short and long waves, they would crow over victories, keep silent about retreats or losses all on this medium, everyone would huddle around that wooden box.

Where did all of that go . . . what happened to the radios and the people around them, with all the full-color inserts in the magazines? The little blond girl from the ad for the children's radio hour is now an old woman in hospice and she probably doesn't even remember her own name.

24.

It was a true revelation for me to look through the half-open door into another room and see an elderly woman, who had arrived with a completely blank face, devoid of any emotion, with an empty gaze, suddenly come to life when she saw the huge wooden radio with the dial of cities on it, and start reading it aloud.

London, Budapest, Warsaw, Prague
Toulouse, Milan, Moscow, Paris
Sofia, Bucharest . . .

Ooh, Sofia, she said, Sofia. In such situations my job was to tactfully draw closer, to strike up a conversation, to be ready to hear a story, to encourage her to remember. She turned out to be an emigrant from Bulgaria. Her father had been a German engineer who had married a Bulgarian woman, they had lived in a nice house with a yard in some village near Sofia, near the mountain . . . she couldn't remember the name anymore. Her nephew, who had brought her to the clinic, stood next to us and could not believe that his aunt was speaking and livening up. That must be her language, Bulgarian, he said.

For a person who had been silent for so many years in a given language, she spoke very well. Of course, her story was broken up by some blank spots in her memory, in her language, but then it would pick up again in another place. She remembered how in the evenings they would gather around the radio for the music hour. As for the news, only her mother and father listened to it. But they would all listen to the concerts for the soldiers on the front and the classical concerts together. She talked about the blinking light on the radio, how she would read out the cities on the dial like a counting-out rhyme, imagining what lay behind each name.

I remember doing the same thing as a child, that dial was my first Europe and I thought that every city had a different sound and if you moved the dial, the condenser, you'd hear the sound of the noisy streets of Paris or people arguing in a London square. Who knows why, but I always imagined that in London there was somebody squabbling . . . The world was closed and those city names were the only proof that somewhere out there beyond the fading, the crackling, the deliberate jamming, those cities existed, and in them some other people with kids were also sitting around their radio, and if I pricked up my ears enough I could hear what they talked about in the evenings.

And the woman kept on talking and talking...And then... the radio ordered us, *schnell, schnell*, we must run, the Russian troops, I *kleine Mädchen* of nine, a blue cardigan, *rote buttons*... Mama...a little bunny here, she pointed at the upper right-hand side of her cardigan, Mama had sewed a *Kaninchen* there...we have to run, Daddy is German, German, they'll kill him...and Grandma yelled...here bad, bad, run...last train and quick, quick, schnell, airplanes, shooting *krrrrrrr* train stops, down, we lie...grass, grass...

Grass...

A long pause, as if she had lost her train of thought...

Grass...

Again a pause, then suddenly the memory comes back, swooping over her head like an airplane...Her face is twisted in fear, she raises her arms...

(Is it possible, I think I know this woman from somewhere...)

Her nephew hugs her...I'm not sure she even notices him, he is absent from this memory, she is now in 1944...her language becomes completely broken, more German words slip in...*Achtung*...The train is carrying the last German employees, refugees, families...the planes are dropping bombs, the train stops, they have to jump out and lie on the ground. The scent of soil, bullets around her, her mother's body, she doesn't mention her father... but a cow appears, walking toward them, it breaks into a run, stops and looks around, then starts running again, frightened by the bombs and the shooting...Get out of here, little cow, the woman yells, the girl yells, Get out of here, cow...they're killing you...

but the cow clearly doesn't hear, *mooo*, right at the girl . . . and then a piece of shrapnel (I'm filling in the unclear parts of the story) hits the cow in the rump, she starts bleeding and limping *mooo, mooo, mooo*, the woman moos, Hey, cow, hey, cow . . . she gets up and starts running toward the cow, her mother pulls her down sharply and she falls . . . where, where . . . *mooo, mooo* . . . oh, cow, oh, cow, you not dying, I saving you . . . the cow is lying in front of her, shaking its head . . . and eyes . . . It has eyes and cow cry, the girl-woman is saying, it's crying, crying, and she's crying . . .

Tante, tante, her nephew keeps saying in German, with all the awkwardness of a person witnessing a taboo scene, calm down. Do something, he turns to me, she's crying . . .

She's remembering, I say, that's why she's crying . . .

Hilde! All of a sudden the name comes to me. Hilde, I say loudly, grasping the woman's hand. The nephew is stunned, How do you know her name?—they are here for the first time, and I wasn't the one who did her intake registration. She raises her head and looks at me. She won't recognize me. Twenty or so years ago I was sitting in her living room in Frankfurt, my wife and I had stayed at her place for two nights, a friend had put us in touch. I wrote something about her back then. Hilde, the woman who saved Germany.

She doesn't recognize me. I hold her hand and speak to her in Bulgarian, I tell her that I see that cow, it is now grazing at the right hand of God, because it wasn't alone when it died, it had seen a young girl talking to it . . . that is a happy death. Other cows now die unhappily, but that one had been embraced, so everything is okay now, she is okay. I realize that I am not speaking to the elderly woman, but to that nine-year-old girl, and she quiets down, sits on the sofa, lets her head loll back, and falls asleep.

25.

Hilde, Who . . .

I'll wait for you at the aerodrome Hilde said on the phone. Her voice was bright, her Bulgarian was from the '40s. There are words that suddenly open unexpected doors into other times. For a moment I wondered whether, when we met up at the Frankfurt airport, which was indeed an aerodrome, it would be 1945 or 2001. (That's when this conversation took place.) As if, from this moment on, that "aerodrome" would be the "madeleine" of my memory, which would tie me to Hilde. Along with two more things that come up in this story—a cooking pot and the most average, ordinary factory-made bread.

Of course, Hilde was waiting for us right on time at the aerodrome, splendid in her early seventies. Outside Bulgaria's borders, people age more beautifully and more slowly, old age is more merciful elsewhere.

Here is the place to mention that Hilde was born in Bulgaria and managed to catch the last train out before the Red Army rolled in. Her family wanted to stay, her father, a German geologist, was not involved with the military, but they warned him that nothing good awaited him there. Hilde fled with her Bulgarian mother and her younger brother. Her father stayed behind to finish up a few things on the house and was supposed to catch the train a week later. They shot him the next night . . . Hilde was nine. They traveled almost a whole week, the train was constantly being bombed. She remembered clearly the scent of grass and dirt as they lay beside the rails. She told us all this as we sat in her living room, which, for its part, had remained forever in the '60s, with its floor lamp and worn armchairs with wooden armrests.

Then I remembered to take out the factory-made bread she had asked me for on the phone. I must admit that this request had puzzled me. I had to go around to several stores until I could find ordinary factory-made bread in Bulgaria. Who even buys it anymore? Hilde carefully took the bread, she was evidently deeply moved, and went out into the hallway so I couldn't see her. She returned a short while later and said that she remembered the taste of that bread from her childhood. She cut three slices, sprinkled them with a little salt, and handed one to me and one to my wife. I've never seen anyone savor more a slice of simple factory-made bread with salt.

After that she took us to the kitchen and showed us something very special. She opened up the lower compartment in the sideboard and took a pot out from way in the back. It was an enormous, heavy pot, fashioned from rough, solid metal. As if tanks had been melted to cast it, I thought then and even said it aloud. Hilde smiled and said that I had no idea how right I was. This pot was the first and most valuable thing the devastated German state had given out to families. One big cooking pot apiece made of melted-down weapons and munitions. We survived thanks to this pot, Hilde said, you could even boil stones in it.

And I imagined the young Hilde amid the devastation of the '40s and '50s in Germany, clearing away the ruins alongside the other women, searching for whole bricks, building, sewing clothes for her brother, waiting for a few potatoes, sitting in the dark to save electricity. Without complaining, like a person whose lot it was to rebuild a nation that had been razed to its foundations.

We sat in her humble apartment and I thought that someday I

must tell the story of Hilde, who, without even realizing it, rebuilt Germany. With a heavy, beat-up cast-iron pot and the memory of a slice of factory-made bread with salt.

26.

Gradually Gaustine's clinic found its fans. Over several years rooms and houses of the past began popping up in various places. In Aarhus, for example, they used an ethnographic village made of old-fashioned houses to show schoolchildren and tourists how their forefathers had lived, how they had raised geese, sheep, goats, and horses. The geese, sheep, goats, and horses were not from the nineteenth century.

This piqued my curiosity, so, using a literary festival in Denmark as an excuse, I went a few days early and took a train to Aarhus. I had asked a Danish friend of mine to call in advance to let them know that as a writer or journalist I was interested in this social project, and so on. Clearly she went above and beyond the call of duty, because when I got there a pleasant young woman was waiting to show me around.

Actually, this place didn't have much in common with Gaustine's clinic. It was a museum like any other museum, but twice a month they closed a bit earlier to the general public and in the remaining hours welcomed groups from retirement homes, primarily those suffering from dementia. Some of these men and women, depending on their strength and their memories, would go into the farmsteads, feed the ducks and goats, water the gardens, or sun themselves in the yards. There were also others for whom such activities meant nothing, who had no memories of village life and farming. Those they would take directly to an apartment preserved just as it had been in 1974. I liked that bit with the exact year, although it wasn't clear whether this apartment hadn't been the same in both 1973 and the following year, 1975. It's doubtful that the kitchen table, the refrigerator, and the upholstered couch in the living room would fade in one year like tulips. I snarkily pointed this out to my guide, of course.

The young woman was pleasant. She calmly and in that typically northern way put up with my suspicions, questions, and direct, typically southern jokes. In the apartment, the women headed straight for the kitchen, she said. As if switching on some hidden compass. These women who found it difficult to navigate their own apartments, here instinctively knew their way around—a conditioned reflex that had transformed into instinct. They were attracted by the scent of the spices and would open up jars of basil, cloves, mint, rosemary, burying their noses inside, no longer remembering the names, mixing them up, but knowing what was what.

They set off after the now-lost scent of freshly ground coffee, the girl went on, we have stockpiles of the exact kinds that were popular during the fifties and sixties. They like to grind it themselves. They often keep turning the handle of the grinder after the coffee is ground.

I thought of how the recollection of scents is the last to leave the empty den of memory. Perhaps because it is an earlier sense, so for that reason it is the last to go, departing like a little beast, sniffing with its head to the ground. I clearly pictured those women eternally turning the handles of square wooden coffee grinders or the tall cylindrical ones of tarnished silver with copper handles. It should be a scene from the seventeenth century, worthy of the brush of those old Dutchmen Vermeer, Hals, and Rembrandt, detailed realism and sublime everyday life rolled into one. The endless spinning of a coffee grinder, the scent which you imbibe with your nose, some things don't change over the centuries. I imagined them grinding up the years, the seasons, the days, and the hours like coffee beans. When they turn the handles of these coffee grinders, the Girl with a Pearl Earring (that's what I called my guide, who introduced herself as Lotte) said, it's like they really go into a different time. We also have a library with books from the sixties and seventies, but letters no longer mean anything to most of them. Sometimes they look at the children's books, enjoying the pictures and that's it.

Actually, it turns out that right at the beginning of the seventeenth century, a Dutchman, Pieter van den Broecke, managed to transport several coffee seeds across the seas to raise the first plants in Europe. His successor was none other than Carl Linnaeus, who was enchanted by these bushes and took over their care. And Linnaeus himself in his old age also began to suffer from progressive memory loss. He who had given names to the world, who had ordered and classified the unorderable, suddenly began to forget exactly those names. I can imagine him sitting over some forget-me-not and trying to remember the Latin name that he himself had given it.

We strolled past the houses from different eras, stopped into the post office from the 1920s to note the end of an entire industry of anticipation, of the delayed gratification of messages that traveled for days. We crossed paths with noblemen from bygone centuries, with milkmen, with shepherds without sheep, we nodded at the shoemakers sitting in front of their shops, in one spot kids in shorts, suspenders, and flat caps were playing leapfrog, and at an intersection a beggar had meekly laid out his torn hat. Most of them are volunteers, my guide noted, or history students or retirees. They don't get paid anything, yet more and more turn up every year. Sometimes homeless people come as well. And what do they dress up as? I livened up at this idea. We give them warm, clean clothes from a certain epoch. But most of them don't want to change their clothes. They want to stay as they are. And as they themselves say, there've always been vagrants, right, what century do you need us for?

And they're right, of course, I think afterward. The homeless have no history, they are . . . how shall I put it, extra-historical, unbelonging. To a certain extent, that is what Gaustine was, too.

Finally we sat down in the most popular chain pastry shop from the '70s, where they made their cakes, meringues, and croissants from scratch with flour, vanilla, lemon rind, cinnamon, and all the other ingredients from that time, using cake molds and icing from back then, as Lotte emphasized. We sat there and drank some brand of hot chocolate that had been popular in its day, from porcelain cups with a gold rim. The waitresses of the '70s whirled past us, and there was something very familiar about them which sent me back—one of my first almost erotic memories was connected with those high white shoes that came up over the ankle.

Lotte, I asked without beating around the bush, what decade would you choose—the sixties, the seventies, or the eighties?

She fell silent for a moment and gave the best answer that can be given to such a question: I'd like to be twelve years old in each of them.

That would be my answer, too.

27.

Yes, the experiment in Aarhus worked, but it still had the feel of a museum, like a trip to Disneyland on Sunday. Gaustine's experiment had a different aim.

Let's go down to '68, he suggested when I got back.

It was nice, that "Let's go down to '68," something like Orpheus's descent into the Underworld. The '60s were simply on a lower floor. We sat down in the two lemon-yellow armchairs. He'd found them on sale, for what seemed like a ridiculous price to me; they'd been cleaning out the apartment of some rich local Warhol wannabe.

He took out a pack of cigarettes, Gitanes this time, lit one up, and the spicy smoke slowly wafted around the room. He opened a bottle of *Seagram's Extra Dry—The Perfect Dry Gin*, as the ad on the last page of *Newsweek* put it, *you bring the olive, we'll do the rest.*

So tell me, he started in . . . is Denmark still a prison?

I replied it was more a museum now and told him in detail about the houses from different eras, about the apartment from 1974, about several more rooms that Lotte had shown me, preserved just as they had been when inhabited by ordinary families, with their stories, albums, suitcases, clothes hangers, bread boxes, vase of fake flowers on the fridge. One apartment was that of Turkish emigrants, a man of fifty and his sons of around twenty, *Gastarbeiters*; the ashtrays were overflowing with cigarette butts and the smell still lingered. I wondered if they replaced the butts now and then.

The problem with that is, Gaustine began . . . he uttered the words carefully, as if trying to formulate at the moment what he had been thinking about during the night. Did I tell you that Gaustine suffered from insomnia? I could hear him when I slept at the clinic, he would walk around, stop, make tea, or go out to smoke. He was like Funes the Memorious. Once I suggested to him that if we managed to re-create the shape of the clouds on the morning of April 20, 1882, for example, we would have reached the point of perfection. And also how the dog looked in profile at 3:14 in the afternoon. Gaustine joined the game.

According to Gaustine, the problem with the Danish model was that temporarily entering into a regime of reminiscence, visiting a past from two to five in the afternoon, and then coming back out again into some now-unfamiliar present was too jarring and painful. Like opening a door between two seasons or moving from summer straight into winter. Or constantly going from dark to light or from youth to old age, without any transition. Staying for only a few hours opens that window of the past for too short a time. He poured himself more gin from '68 and said that as he saw it, the moment had come to take a step further, to try something more radical.

In brief, his idea was to create a whole city set in a specific time. But a real city, not one of those simulations with a single street and a few fiberglass houses. It'll first be in 1985, let's say. That's where we'll start. I replied that I didn't recall there being anything noteworthy about that year, unless you count the fact that, I added mentally, that was the year my class finished high school and was sent to do our mandatory military service. A year in the shadow of the following one, when we had Chernobyl, silence, radioactive rain, a deficit of iodine, which we secretly stocked up on . . .

There doesn't need to be something unusual about the year, Gaustine replied. Time doesn't nest in the unusual, it seeks a quiet, peaceful place. If you discover traces of another time, it will be during some unremarkable afternoon. An afternoon during which nothing in particular has happened, except for life itself . . . who said that? Gaustine laughed.

You, I replied.

You're always trying to attribute to me everything that pops into your mind. But perhaps you really did swipe this in particular from me. And so the city will first begin in 1985—Gaustine was getting worked up now—we've got to turn that year inside out, make it totally gnarly, as they said back in 1985. We'll be fine with Gorbachev, Reagan, and Kohl, they've left clear traces. But let's find out what they called something cool, what the slang was, which actors everybody was going nuts over, what posters they hung up, which housekeeping magazines, the TV guide, the weather forecast, the whole run of *Ogoniok* from that year. How much did broccoli and potatoes cost, the Lada in the East and the Peugeot in the West. What were people dying from and what did they fight about at night in their bedrooms? We'll reprint day by day all the newspapers from that year. Then we'll do the same for 1984 . . .

Doesn't 1986 come next? I asked.

I don't know, maybe first we'll have to go backward, he replied. On the one hand, having lost their memories, our patients will keep going further and further back, they'll keep remembering ever-older things. After 1985 for them will come 1984, then 1983, and so on . . . I know you're not such a fan of the '80s, but you'll just have to put up with them. You'll restore them, fill them up with stories. What made people sad during the '80s? We can, of course, stay for longer in the same year, we can repeat it. Then we'll do the 1970s as well, that will be a different neighborhood.

But new forgetters will come, for whom the '90s are also the past, I cut in. I guess we'll have to keep all decades available. The past grows like a weed.

In any case, once we reach the '70s, Gaustine continued, it'll be more colorful there, psychedelic, you've got experience from the clinic. Of course, the clinic will seem like child's play in comparison with these cities. People will be there twenty-four hours a day, seven days a week, 365 days a year. Things will happen between them. We don't know how things will go. Then comes the neighborhood of the 1960s, there you'll be in your element. We can extend 1968 to two or three years if you insist, he said with a laugh. Some years last longer than others. We'll also reach the 1950s. There it'll be especially important what side of history you're on, although those were ascetic years for both sides.

And what will we do with the 1940s, I asked, with the war?

Gaustine got up, went over to the window, and after a full minute replied: I don't know, I honestly don't know.

To hear the phrase "I don't know" from him happened only once in a hundred years. Gaustine knew everything, or at least he never admitted anything to the contrary.

Then, in the afternoon of 1968 or 2020, it was one and the same afternoon at the end of the day, Gaustine hinted at that which to some extent would later come about. It seemed logical, yet at the same time so beyond all logic, simultaneously innocent and dangerous—a danger of historical proportions, so to speak. He had taken out an old spiral notebook and was sketching out plans, years, chronotopes, names of cities and countries. The Gitanes smoked away, sometimes he would forget his half-smoked cigarette and light up another, my eyes were watering from the smoke, yes, from the smoke, or so I thought. Gray clouds drifted ominously over the future or the past, whatever we might call it, that Gaustine was sketching out before me. Of course, this is only a metaphor, I thought back then, trying to shake off my sense of foreboding.

What was this whole experiment to him, why did he need to expand the field of the past? He had achieved what others had never even dreamed of. He was one of the first to introduce clinics of the past. Centers based on his experience opened up in various countries. Geriatricians were falling all over themselves to reach him, to work with him, to invite him as a consultant. He never appeared in person, he sent me most places to deliver his refusals, always polite but firm. And although he turned down all sorts of interviews and publicity, his name was mentioned with respect and reverence, just as one speaks of a genius and an eccentric whom few had seen, and this only added to his legend.

28.

The Runaway

I dubbed him the Lonely Long-Distance Runner, a nod to an angry British book from back in the day, which, I must admit, I never did get around to reading, but the title stuck in my head. Lately I remember far more books that I haven't read than those I have. I don't find this an anomaly, it's the same as with the unhappened past.

Anyway, he really had been (or so they tell me) a long-distance runner—physically fit, strong, a former athlete, and it was as if his body didn't want to forget. Once a very lively, very curious man, the disease had eaten away the past thirty-forty years of his memory, although sometimes he would surprise us with sudden returns. The medications attempted to slow down the process, and we attempted to give him back the time that he remembered . . . (Obviously, there is no cure, but a person has a right to happiness even when ill, as Gaustine would say.) It was a battle for the past, a battle for every memory.

Most probably in two or three years the Runner's strength would leave him, his muscle memory would weaken, that sliver of remembered time would grow much narrower or even disappear completely. But he was still in good shape now, even in suspiciously good shape. He lived happily at our Alzheimer's community in the '70s neighborhood, we'd assigned him to the Seventy-Ninth Regiment, as Gaustine and I liked to joke.

He would go to the little library every day to read the new issues of every newspaper from 1979. We had collected issues from the whole year and released them day by day. Only the weather forecast was off sometimes. But then again, nobody expected much from the weather forecasters, so nobody really even noticed it. The Runner read a lot, he got excited over everything that happened. He was a music connoisseur and still couldn't get over the fact that the Beatles had broken up, he was on Lennon's side. The fall of Pol Pot's regime, Pope John Paul II's first visit to Mexico—he followed everything, the year started off well that January. Then he moped around downcast for a time, reading about the Chinese attack on the Vietnamese border. He was as delighted as a child to see the first photograph of Jupiter's rings sent by *Voyager*. He wanted to talk for a long time about what might be found on these rings, where the colors came from. Whether some form of life might happen to be discovered there . . . I tried to share his anticipation and premonition of a miracle, as Gaustine would say, and to feel that same excitement.

Lennon got him more worked up than anything else. At that time the whole world was blasting ABBA and disco, an incontrovertible sign of decline, yet he followed John's every step in the magazines and newspapers. They wrote that he had become a homebody, that he baked homemade bread and dandled three-year-old Sean. The Runner saw nothing wrong with this and when caustic comments from Cynthia, John's ex, appeared in a different paper, saying that actually he just spent the whole day in front of the TV, the Runner got truly angry. Once he came to me with the new issue of *Life*, if I'm not mistaken, and read to me that Lennon recently had been working on his autobiography and had already made tape recordings of his earliest childhood memories from Penny Lane. I can't wait to read that, the Runner eagerly said over and over again.

Once he came and found me in the middle of the night. He shut the door behind him but didn't want to sit down. John Lennon will be killed, he said quickly. Very soon. He was truly worried, in any case he couldn't explain whether he had dreamed it or not. Some crazy guy will shoot him, I've even seen his face. While he's coming home, in front of the entrance to the Dakota. We need to tell the police immediately. He needs to get out of there right now.

I didn't know how to react. Was it a sudden flash of memory (that meant the therapy was working!), or a leak of information from outside? I promised that I would call the police the very next morning. We talked for a while longer and I escorted him back to his room.

The next morning, the Runner had disappeared.

The community had a discreet but formidable security force. For no other reason than that people who have lost their memories often lose their way as well, they are easy targets for incidents when outside the protected zone. The Runner was still in good shape, the security guards said they had only seen at the last moment how he had launched himself over the fence and disappeared.

A patient running away is a rare and unpleasant event for everyone involved. Most of all due to the life-threatening danger to the patient himself. In this case, he had leapt over not only a fence, but thirty or forty years as well. We didn't know what effect this collision with another reality would have. What's more, the incident could eventually lead to an investigation and a closing of the community, to yet another round of arguments with the guild about the advisability of such therapy, whether we had the right to "synchronize" internal and external time, and so on.

All the police in the region were informed of the incident and asked to be very careful with a patient who "inhabited" another time. I played out all kinds of scenarios in my head as I, too, wandered around the nearby city searching for him. I imagined how he would stop the first policeman he saw and share his concerns that we needed to alert the FBI immediately, as well as the police in New York. Why? the policeman would ask. I have a secret message, John Lennon is going to be killed, the killer might already be on his way. Really, the cop would say breezily with his cop-like sense of humor, aren't you a little late, buddy? Well . . . what do you mean, has he already been killed, I'll never forgive myself, the Runner would moan.

I would hate for him to go through all that.

Thank goodness everything ended quickly and in the best possible way. The Runner, whom from then on we would call the Runaway, wandered for a few hours in the nearby city (I was afraid he would go straight to the airport and look for a flight to New York), then he found the police station, where they already knew about the incident. He asked to speak to the boss, who listened to him carefully, wrote everything down, and said he would immediately set the system in motion. In front of the Runner he picked up the phone to speak directly with FBI headquarters. Then he offered to escort him back to the community in the station's nicest (unmarked) car.

I didn't know how to deal with the Runaway. He had come back from "another" world, he had mixed times. In that case the therapy probably should have been discontinued and he should have been released. Or perhaps he would request this himself. I imagined him telling everyone that real time was passing outside, while here we were palming some secondhand past off on them. Upon entering the community, patients (at least those in an earlier phase of their disease) and their families knew that this was in fact a form of therapy. Yet nevertheless for the sake of the purity of the experiment it was better not to let particles of another reality in. The environment needed to remain antiseptic with respect to contamination from other times.

What the Runaway did after his return was completely unexpected. After dinner I heard him telling the others how in the city outside everyone was being subjected to an experiment. They were playing out the future, if you can believe it, guys . . . Some people are walking around with wires in their ears and little TV sets in their hands and they never look up, their eyes are glued to the screens. Either they're filming some crazy expensive sci-fi movie, or they're testing out what life will be like fifty years from now. That was the Runaway's conclusion, publicly proclaimed. He had recently read some prognoses in *Time* and now surely they were conducting experiments. But everything looks so fake that there's no way people will believe it. Good thing they've been strictly fenced off from us, he finished.

Don't worry, he told me later, I didn't tell anyone out there what year it is, so I wouldn't spoil their experiment.

Then he apologized for making trouble, then asked me if I believed they would really take action to protect John.

I thought for a bit and said—yes. I had a whole year until the papers would prove me wrong.

29.

Numbers

You can see where the world is heading, Gaustine said one morning . . . A complete failure, everything we had previously expected for the coming twenty-thirty years has not happened. You yourself know that part of the failure of the future is also the failure of medicine. The world is getting older and every three seconds someone loses their memory.

Statistics were his new obsession. He tracked them, constantly comparing and analyzing the growing curve of various memory disorders, data from the World Health Organization, from the European headquarters and several of the larger national centers. The numbers for the U.S., for example, were truly terrifying— around five million with dementia, another five and a half million with Alzheimer's. Globally there are now more than fifty million, Gaustine would say, and those are only the registered cases, that's a country bigger than Spain, in seven or eight years it'll be seventy-five million, and again that's only the diagnosed cases. In India, for example, ninety percent of those suffering from dementia are never diagnosed, while in Europe almost half aren't. Almost half, can you imagine, that means just double the numbers we have. We are surrounded by people for whom the trigger has already been pulled, they just don't know it yet. You and I could even be among them . . . have you gotten yourself tested?

No.

Me, neither. Some kind of global dementia is coming.

Gaustine knew how to tap into all my hidden fears. Recently I'd had the feeling that every day, names and stories were abandoning me, quietly slipping away like weasels.

That's not all, he went on with his numbers, it's one of the three most expensive illnesses at the moment. The Americans have calculated it, two hundred fifteen million dollars a year, and that was five years ago. That includes medicines, social workers, doctors, home health aides, can you imagine how many aides are needed? Some politicians there will soon think to ride this wave, they'll stir up unrest, nobody wants to pay huge amounts of money for people with *mental disabilities, who are just a burden on society, terminally ill, in need of a merciful death*, they will demand radical health policies, some kind of realpolitik in medicine . . . you've seen this before, that rhetoric was developed and applied back in the 1930s.

Good thing we don't need to re-create the '30s, I thought, even though I'd taken a peek into them. I remembered the cover of *Neues Volk* from 1938, the National Socialists' flagship magazine, with a photo of an "incurably ill" person along with the caption: *60,000 Reichsmarks is how much this person with a genetic disease costs society per year. Dear countrymen, that is your money, too.*

Our patients would be the first on the blacklist. That's how it had begun back in the '30s—with psychiatric wards and geriatric clinics.

30.

Once they brought an elderly woman to the clinic, Mrs. Sh., who refused to go into the bathroom and became hysterical every time she caught sight of a shower. This happened sometimes, in the severe phases of the disease people became aggressive, obstinate, like children refusing to do things that previously had been habitual. In such cases we would find soap and shampoo from the right era, which still held their scents, toiletries, shower caps from back then, thick robes with monograms, mirrors with ivory handles, wooden combs ... Everything that would make a bathroom seem cozy and familiar. But in this case nothing helped. Mrs. Sh. kept trying to pull away, crying and pleading with the nurses to spare her. So Gaustine and I dug through the archives. We searched out the woman's surviving relatives and documents, and discovered, actually I must admit that Gaustine guessed it first, that Mrs. Sh. had survived Auschwitz. She herself clearly had tried to forget and not talk about it. But now, in the late phase of her illness, that which she had tried to erase for her entire life rushed back at her like an oncoming train and she could not escape into other memories. Somewhere Primo Levi wrote that the concentration camp is that inescapable reality which you know that you will sooner or later awaken into amid the dream of life. And that feeling does not fade with the years.

Suddenly it all made sense—her eternal morning questions of whether they had found her mother or whether her brothers were alive. We also understood why she squirreled away crusts of bread and other leftovers from the cafeteria, hiding them in her cupboard. Everything that awakened that memory had to be avoided—showers, the clicking of the nurses' high heels in the hallway. (We switched them out with soft slippers.) The daytime lighting was softened. Part of the cafeteria was divided into smaller, cozy booths, so as to avoid large common areas and the rattling of silverware. Unwittingly you realize how many things in a clinic are potentially charged with hidden violence, as Foucault would say. Nothing would ever be innocent again—bathrooms, cafeterias, the gas stove, a doctor in a white coat who wants to give you a shot, the lighting, the barking of dogs outside, the sharp voice, certain German words ...

This was one of the rare instances in which Gaustine refrained from tapping into a patient's memory.

31.

New and Imminent Diagnoses

Family Collapse Disorder

Somewhere in a Swiss village a father came back home to find strangers inside his house, a woman and two young men who were making themselves comfortable. He locked them inside and called the police. The police came and surrounded the house.

Dad, what's wrong with you? his sons cried from inside.

They say that the coming mass loss of memory could be something like a virus that reaches the hippocampus, destroys brain cells, blocks neurotransmitters. And the brain, that supreme creation of nature, is transformed into a pulpy mass in the span of a year or so. Several world-renown scientists offered bees as an example and warned that what is happening with their mysterious disappearance, so-called *colony collapse disorder*, is actually the same as what the Alzheimer's mechanism does to the human family.

The Skipping Record Syndrome

One morning they wake up after a night of restless dreams and find, while still in bed, that they have undergone a metamorphosis . . .

Time has skipped, like records used to.

A young man and woman, university students, go to bed in the evening and wake up twenty years later. They sense that something is off with their bodies, stiff, painful, they are not exactly arthropods, but it's not much better. Some unfamiliar kids barge into the room, screaming at them.

Mom, Dad, wake up, you've been sleeping all day . . .

Who are you, what are you doing here? the couple in the bed asks . . . Get out of here!

Where the hell is my hair? What did we have to drink last night, we were at a party . . . Do you remember what you dreamed?

No, not at all.

Me, neither.

Hm. Wait a second, there were some people, they were congratulating us for something, then . . . no, it's all a blur. You try to remember.

I was supposed to go back to my parents' place—I'd just taken my final exams for junior year.

We were in the same major, right?

I was supposed to call them to let them know I wouldn't be coming home. She looks at her watch. Should I call them now? What year is it?

Where the hell is my hair, for Christ's sake? He again touches his bald head.

We'd been going together for a few months. That night when we got drunk, you said you wanted to get married.

A person says all kinds of stupid stuff when he's drunk.

Well, clearly we did . . .

I don't remember a thing. This isn't that old apartment of ours.

We must've gotten married. We must've found jobs. We surely had friends. I don't remember a thing, zilch. Maybe we took vacations at the sea, we must've gone to the seaside. Do you know our kids' names?

No, goddamn it, I have no idea about any kids.

We've got to go to a doctor.

To a doctor? And what will we say?

Well, that we woke up today and it turns out that twenty years have passed.

Did you see the calendar?

Yes, I did, it's 2020. Two thousand and twenty. I mean, that's a whole other century.

Wait, when were we juniors in college, when was that party?

It must've been 1998.

Okay, right, so we got drunk after that exam in, what was it again . . . and you stayed over at my place. We did whatever we did, then fell asleep. But back then I was twenty-three and had hair, goddamn it.

You also didn't have that . . . you were thinner, is what I'm trying to say.

You were different, too.

So what would we tell the doctor? We woke up this morning, and the last thing we remember is going to bed in June of 1998. We've slept for twenty years. Well, you shouldn't have slept that long, the doctor will say. Any other symptoms? Well, just that I've gone bald, you'll say, while I've gotten old. And we don't remember a damn thing. Absolutely nothing.

They pull the covers up over their heads and fall asleep again, in hopes that this time they'll sleep backward and wake up in that old apartment.

32.

Protected Time

The next step came when Gaustine decided to open these clinics of the past not only to patients, but to their friends and family, too. Then we had people showing up who wanted to live in certain years, without having any connection with a patient at all. People who didn't feel at home in the present time. I suspect that some, if not most of them, did it out of nostalgia for the happiest years of their lives, while others did it out of fear that the world was irrevocably headed downhill and that the future was canceled. A strange anxiety hung in the air, you could catch a whiff of its faint scent when inhaling.

I wasn't totally sure it was ethical to admit technically healthy people to the clinic. Was it ethical to mix them in with the patients? Or perhaps the right to the past is inviolable and it should be valid for everyone, as Gaustine liked to say. People wanted it, and if not here, they would find it elsewhere. In fact, all sorts of quickly cobbled-together hotels for the past were starting to pop up.

Gaustine didn't share my equivocations and began gradually opening up the clinics to a broader set of clients. For a person whose obsession is the past, every such expansion of the field was a welcome one. Nevertheless, Gaustine did it carefully. I am not sure that he had a strategy or that he was looking to make money off of it. (Although there was definitely a niche for it.) If you ask me, he was looking for something far greater than the solidly backed paycheck of the past. He wanted to enter into the clockwork of time itself, to nudge some gear, to slow it down, to move the hands backward.

Gaustine's idea went even further. He didn't intend for you just to drop in for a couple hours a day, like at a gym, but rather to stay . . . he didn't say forever, perhaps a week, a month, a year. To live in that place. I say "place" and immediately see how out-of-place that word is. Actually, Gaustine wanted to open up *time* for everyone. Because that's exactly what this was about. Where other people were thinking about space, square meters or acres, he was measuring years.

The point of the experiment was to create a protected past or "protected time." A time shelter. We wanted to open up a window into time and let the sick live there, along with their loved ones. To give a chance for elderly couples, who had spent their whole lives together, to stay together. Daughters and sons, more often daughters, who wanted to spend another month or even a year with their parent, before things completely went to seed. But they didn't just want to stand next to their beds in a sterile white room. The idea was for them to stay together in the same year, to meet up in the only possible "place"—in the year that still glimmered in the parent's fading memory.

33.

The Last Game

I was walking along on a warm June evening in 1978. A song floated from somewhere on the street. "Hotel California" by the Eagles flowed out of everywhere back then. Gloomy and intoxicating, in some places it would stop making sense, then it would come back again, that guitar coda at the end truly hypnotizing. Those boys were the real deal. The music magazines foretold a brilliant future for them. Thirty-odd years later, out of all their albums only that song would remain.

... some dance to remember, some dance to forget ...

All the tables were filled at the restaurants that lined the central street. The final game of the World Cup poured from some potbellied Bakelite TV. They were broadcasting live from Buenos Aires. I stopped and watched. Holland vs. Argentina, Europe vs. Latin America. I knew very well how that match would end, for it was the first one I had ever watched with my father forty-some years ago. Because of the Argentinians' constant dirty tricks, we were rooting for Holland, but they were clearly going to lose. In the ninetieth minute Rob Rensenbrink would get the ball after endless passing, he'd take a shot . . . and hit the goalpost. We'd bet on the losing team. We should be used to it by now, because Bulgaria always loses; besides, we're not even playing in this game. But you never get used to it. Plus, Holland was playing beautifully. It's not fair, don't the good guys always win? I pound my small fist on the table. I'm trying to be even angrier than my father. My father turns to me and says: *Look, old man* [that's what he called me], *life is more than a single loss.*

There are things you remember your whole life. Perhaps because fathers at that time—and my father was no exception—generally spoke down to children. So when my father told me *life is more than a single loss,* it was an usual event. It must be a fatherly commandment. I never did quite figure out whether he meant that life would be full of losses and this was just the first of them, or that life was always more than any one loss. Maybe both.

The restaurant is buzzing, everyone is keyed up from the game. There at the end table a tall, thin man of eighty is sitting, with pure white hair and light eyes. He doesn't take his eyes off the television, but it's as if he is not taking part in the general excitement, at least not visibly. He doesn't blink and he doesn't move. I make my way over to him and sit down. May I? I ask. He looks at me without turning his head and his lower lip quivers almost imperceptibly.

The game is already nearing the end of the second half, the score is tied. The stadium is going nuts. The goalpost shot has yet to happen. Overtimes have yet to happen. Everyone is chanting Kempes's name. Now here's the ninetieth minute. A beautiful parabolic shot, everyone at the tables bristles, Holland's fans get up out of their chairs ready to cheer, the ball flies menacingly toward the Argentinian goal, lands on Rensenbrink's foot, a shot . . . Ah! Aaaah! . . . The goalpost. The shout that had been prepared for a goal in the end collapses into a drawn-out sigh . . .

I glance at the man next to me. Actually, the whole time I've been trying to watch the game through his eyes. When Rensenbrink's shot comes, he just clenches his right hand into a fist on the table. So he is excited after all. The score is still tied, the tension is mounting, the commentator is hoarse. This is followed by a break of a few minutes, during which time the spectators order more beers. I look at the people's faces. I wonder whether all of them are watching the game as if for the first time. Or do some of them nevertheless know, do they remember? Their companions surely must. But actually, what does it matter, it makes no difference, everyone's faces are anxious and lit up. We don't know how a match that ended forty years ago will end. I, too, try to watch it as if for the first time. Maybe this time a miracle will happen. Everything is possible, everything is once again imminent.

The morning papers will be bought up right away, they'll have the first analyses, the first photos from the game. The same ones from forty years ago, just reprinted on new paper that still smells like ink. They'll be talking about that game for a whole month, about Kempes's goal during overtime. About the Dutchmen's refusal to appear at the awards ceremony, about Cruyff's refusal to play on the tulips' national team, which predetermined the outcome of the World Cup, about the Argentinians' dirty move in delaying the game due to concerns over a cast on the wrist of one of the Dutch players . . . About all of those details that history is made of.

But right now I'm not interested in history, I'm interested in biography. People don't hurry to leave, they stay, finishing their beers, commenting, fuming. Those who were rooting for the Argentinians don't dare celebrate. I sit at the table next to the man. It's dark, people start getting up and leaving. A cold wind picks up.

I take him by the arm and say in a quiet but clear voice: *Look, old man, life is more than a single loss.* He turns to me very slowly. He looks at me, and I'm not sure what he's seeing, what is racing through his drained memory. Forty years have passed since we watched that game together.

If I'm not in his memory, do I exist at all?

A minute passes. His lips move and he repeats voicelessly, only with his lips, but I understand, that is the password, two syllables: *Old man* . . .

This is our final conversation. He does not recognize me anymore, everything progresses terribly quickly. His brain has surrendered, the provinces of the body rise up in rebellion. I've brought him to be here with me in the community that Gaustine just opened.

Of course, before that I checked to see what was available in the country I come from. The clinic I went to—supposedly to "visit a relative" so they would let me in—was horrific. Most patients were tied up so as not to be unruly, they rolled their eyes frantically and howled softly like animals, their voices hoarse from screaming. I think it was the most horrifying thing I have ever seen in my life, and I've seen some truly horrifying things. What do you expect? an orderly snapped at me as he passed me in the hallway. I'm alone here with thirty people, I can't keep them in line, but at least they don't suffer for too long . . . I raced outside and shut the front door, where I saw an ad for a funeral home with several telephone numbers printed on a normal sheet of paper. I remembered its name: Memento Mori.

I snatched up my father and against his will brought him to Gaustine's clinic in Switzerland. A human being has the right to die like a human being. For the last three years, when he was still in his right mind, he constantly wanted to "leave." "Leaving" in his language means that we should help him die. He wrote this on all sorts of scraps of paper, even on the wallpaper in his room. While he could still write.

Ten months later I give in and decide to check out the possibilities for euthanasia. Just to look into it.

34.

A Guidebook for the End

We have never before suspected that memory loss could be fatal. Or at least I never suspected it. I've always taken it as more of a metaphor. A person suddenly realizes how much memory they are carrying around in their body, wittingly and unwittingly, on all levels. The way that cells reproduce is also memory. A kind of bodily, cellular, tissue memory.

What happens when memory begins to withdraw? First you forget individual words, then faces, rooms. You search for the bathroom in your own home. You forget what you've learned in this life. It's not much anyway and will run out soon. And then, in the dark phase, as Gaustine calls it, comes the forgetting of that which accumulated before you even existed, that which the body knows by nature, without even suspecting it. Now, that's what will turn out to be fatal.

In the end the mind will forget how to speak, the mouth will forget how to chew, the throat will forget how to swallow.

Legs will forget how to walk, *How does this work again? Goddamn it . . .* Someone has remembered for us how to lift one foot, to bend the knee, make a half circle and then set it in front of the other foot, then to lift the other one that is now the back foot, again a half circle, then set it down in front of the other one. First the heel, then

Time Shelter

105

the whole sole, and finally the toes. And again you lift the other leg which is now lagging behind, you bend the knee . . .

Somebody has cut the power to the rooms of your own body.

The last phase of the illness did not exactly fall within the scope of our clinic, although people did die here, too. Most went to hospices and spent a bit more time on life-support systems, despite signs that the body was now refusing to support life. It kills itself piecemeal, organ by organ, cell by cell. Bodies get fed up, too, they get tired, they want a rest.

Only in a few places around the world can this desire of the body be heard. Besides being a paradise for the living, Switzerland is also a paradise for the dying. For several years in a row, Zurich has invariably been the best city for living in the world. It probably is the number one best city for dying, but the shocking thing is that they don't actually make such rankings, at least not officially. The best cities for dying. Of course, the best for those who can afford it. Dying has gotten to be quite expensive. But was death ever free? Perhaps with pills it is slightly pricier, it's harder with a gun, at least until you get your hands on one, but there are far simpler and perfectly free methods—drowning, jumping from a height, hanging. One woman I know told me: I feel like jumping off the roof, but when I think how messed up my hair will get as I'm falling, and who knows how wrinkled my skirt will get, full of stains and everything, and I start to feel ashamed and give up on the idea. After all, they still take pictures of you in those cases, right, people watch . . .

Now, those are the signs of a healthy body—it feels ashamed, it foresees what might happen, it thinks about the future, and even after its death, it is vain. The body that truly desires death no longer experiences vanity.

In short, if you manage to kill yourself, it's a freebie of sorts. But what happens when you no longer have the strength to kill yourself, and not just strength but you no longer even remember how to do it? How do you leave this life, goddamn it, where have they hidden the door? You've never had firsthand experience of it, or maybe you have once or twice, but they were unsuccessful attempts. (Actually, it is precisely the unsuccessful suicide attempt that is a real tragedy, the successful one is merely a procedure.) How, for the love of God, does a person kill himself, the fading brain wonders, how did they do it in books? There was something about the throat, something happens with the throat, air, you stop the air or water gets in and fills you up like a bottle ... or the sharp edge cuts, I think there was a rope involved, but what do I do with that rope ... ?

Then comes assisted suicide. What an expression. Things have gotten so bad that you can't do anything without an assistant, you can't even die.

And in this hopeless situation, a service appears. If you are in a position to order and pay for such a service yourself, you're in luck. If not, you've just created a whole lot of worry and expense for your nearest and dearest. The question is how they, in paying for your murder, can avoid feeling like murderers. Indeed, human civilization has advanced quite a bit when you now have to justify a murder. Don't ever underestimate civilization in that respect. It'll always think up a nice word for it. Eu-than-a-sia. It sounds like an ancient Greek goddess. The goddess of a good, beautiful death. I imagine her with a slender syringe in her hand instead of a scepter. "Euthanasia is a death caused for the benefit of the person whose death is being caused." Now, there's the awkwardness of language, which must justify the act and so it spasms, twists, biting its own tail in the end. I'm killing you for your own good, you'll see (how could you not?) that it'll be better for you and the pain will be gone.

I assume that in this country the practice has been going strong since World War Two. Euthanasia suits it. Illegal at first, then semi-legal. Everyone closed their eyes to it, like so many other times, and gave the private clinics an opportunity to welcome people from Europe who were headed toward death. From one part of Europe, to be precise. For those from the other part, my part, this, too, was denied to us. We didn't even have anesthesia, never mind euthanasia. Death under communism was no indulgent affair in silk sheets. Besides, nobody would have given you a passport and visa to leave the country with a one-way ticket, without a guarantee that you would return. You go, die, and automatically become a defector, for which you are sentenced to death. In absentia and posthumously.

Switzerland as euthanasialand. If you're looking for a good destination for dying, we can help you. The funny thing is that this death business has not officially entered the guidebooks, the tourist handbooks. All guidebooks are created with the illusion that a person is alive and traveling. This is a given. Death does not exist in the world's guidebooks. What an omission!

And when the time draws near for a person to set off? When he is already a traveler in the other sense of the word? Why are we still waiting for guidebooks for such travelers? Or perhaps they already exist, who knows?

Sterbetourismus. I'm almost positive that the word was first thought up in Switzerland. The data indicates around a thousand foreigners per year, mainly Germans, but quite a few Brits as well. And not only the terminally ill. Elderly couples who have decided in advance to leave together, if one of them is terminally ill. I can imagine how they arrive, mild-mannered and slightly awkward, holding hands. And just like that, holding hands, they go through the whole procedure. They don't want to lose each other somewhere in those boundless Elysian fields. It's not like they can arrange a time and place to meet up.

The cost. What is the cost, after all? I dig through the sites. Around seven thousand francs for the prep work. With a burial and all the formalities—ten thousand francs. Surely if you hire a killer it would be more expensive, and far less comfortable, to boot.

Perhaps couples get some kind of discount. But then again, seven thousand francs isn't much for a country like this. So that means they make their money off turnover. When you think how everything has gotten more expensive . . . Clearly the price of life has fallen, while everything else has gone up. Even though death could never really keep its prices high throughout human history, while in the twentieth century it was outrageously cheap. Yes, indeed, they surely count on a high turnover.

On the other hand, how much could it really cost, fifteen grams of pentobarbital powder? You can get it in Mexico from any vet if you tell them you're going to euthanize your elderly dog.

I carefully study the website of one of these organizations, supposedly a nonprofit. The site is quite simple, in green. I have never imagined green as the color of death. The slogan up on top is *To live with dignity, to die with dignity,* and seems more fitting for an order of samurai, which I guess makes some sense. A simple photo of the whole team, which inspires a quiet horror—all of them smiling widely, nice white teeth and open arms. How big was the team? Twelve, like the apostles. I wonder if that was deliberate, I doubt it. In 2005, however, one of them turned out to be Judas and leaked insider information, calling the organization a "well-paid death machine."

There are no reviews, just as there are no money-back guarantees.

This process is absolutely risk-free and painless, this is what the medical brochure they give me says. But isn't it life-threatening? What are they trying to say, goddamn it, that you won't get stomach issues, constipation, blood pressure crashes, or risk addiction?

There is also a discount during the summer months. Clearly people prefer to die primarily in the winter. I wonder whether these discounts cause more people to decide to go for it. For your swan song, there's really no reason to be a cheapskate, you can allow yourself a certain luxury. I assume that the brokers and discreet managers of death (surely they must exist, disguised as tourist agencies) take advantage of this. A long black limousine, to have room for the stretcher if you are bedridden, which whisks you off along the highways of Europe. If the patient so desires and is in a suitable condition, we stop for the evening in Austria, then spend the afternoon at the Zurich Lake. On the way back the limousine transforms into a hearse and takes the urns straight back, with no stopovers on the return trip.

Sterbetourismus is for people of means, the poor don't use euthanasia.

After the whole slaughter of the Second World War and the death industry in the camps, it is much more difficult for Europe to permit the business of offering good death. Thus neutrality by necessity turns Switzerland into a delicate monopolist. As Gaustine would say, whatever you grab in Europe today, it'll always lead you back to World War Two. Nothing was the same after 1939.

I went to see the building where they carry out the ritual or procedure, and it was completely unremarkable. It looked more like a big two-story shed with plastic siding on the exterior. The décor inside was humble as well, judging from the photos on the website. A bed, a nightstand, a painting on the wall, and two chairs. Some of the windows look out toward the lake.

I tried to read everything coldly and technically, so I wouldn't think about the main thing. Funny, but the whole time I was imagining myself, and not my father. The technology was clear, but still, how do you deal with the feeling of guilt? My father, seeming to sense this, delicately helped me. Just as parents subtly sacrifice themselves for their children their whole lives. He passed away on his own. I was with him in his final hours. I held his hand and I wondered what he would like to sense once again with his last cells of memory if he could. I lit up a Stewardess cigarette from our '70s stockroom with Eastern supplies. My father was the most beautiful smoker I ever knew. I tried to imitate him when I secretly lit my first cigarettes. I now took a drag off the Stewardess in his place, and noticed how his nostrils twitched slightly and his eyelids registered the change. Then he went quiet.

Now the last person who remembered me as a child is gone, I told myself. And only then did I burst into sobs, like a child.

35.

Where does this personal obsession with the past come from? Why does it pull me in, like a well I have leaned over? Why does it seduce me with faces that I know no longer exist? What is left there, that I didn't manage to take? What's waiting there, in the cave of that past? Could I beg for just one trip back, even though

I do not have Orpheus's talent, just his desire? And I wonder, will those things and those ones I manage to lead out be murdered by me with a single look back along the way?

I find myself turning back to the *Odyssey* more and more often. We always read it like an adventure novel. Later we came to understand that it was also a book about searching for the father. And, of course, a book about returning to the past. Ithaca is the past. Penelope is the past, the home he left is the past. Nostalgia is the wind that inflates the sails of the *Odyssey*. The past is not the least bit abstract; it is made up of very concrete, small things. When, after he spends seven happy years living with the nymph Calypso, she offers him immortality if he will stay with her forever, Odysseus nevertheless refuses. I've wondered about that myself, come on, let's all be honest and say whether we'd turn that offer down. On the one side of the scale you've got immortality, an eternally young woman, all the pleasures of the world, and on the other you've got going back to where they hardly remember you, impending old age, a house besieged by hoodlums, and an aging wife. Which side of the scale would you choose? Odysseus chose the second. Because of Penelope and Telemachus, yes, but also because of something specific and trifling, which he called hearth-smoke, because of the memory of the hearth-smoke rising from his ancestral home. To see that smoke one more time. (Or to die at home and disperse like smoke from the hearth.) The whole pull of that returning is concentrated in that detail. Not Calypso's body nor immortality can outweigh the smoke from a hearth. Smoke that has no weight tips the scale. Odysseus heads back.

Immediately after 1989, a political emigrant, a defector who had been sentenced to death in absentia, returned to his hometown. He hadn't been there for forty years. The first thing he wanted to see was his family home, which had been built by his grandfather. A nice big house in the center of Sofia, nationalized over the years, had been the Chinese embassy, then stood empty . . . As they showed him around the various floors, he recalled each room one by one, but nothing in particular spoke to his heart. *These rooms did not speak to me at all*, he said the next day. *I asked them to take me down into the basement, the "ice room" had been down there, that's what we called it, the place where various goods were stored in the cold. I took a deep breath and it was as if all the scents from that time hit me at once. It was only then that I burst into sobs and realized that I was home, I'd come back. Because of the ice room, and nothing else. That ice room melted my heart.*

What I wouldn't give to find out how Odysseus's story continued, after his return home, a month, a year or two later, when the euphoria of arrival had passed. His favorite dog, the only living creature that recognized him immediately, without the need for proof (unconditional love and memory) would have died. Did he begin to have regrets and pine for Calypso's breasts, for nights on that island, for all those wonders and adventures on his long journey? I imagine him getting up out of his marriage bed, which he himself had crafted, in the middle of the night, sneaking out so as not to wake Penelope, sitting on the doorstep outside, and remembering everything. That whole twenty-year voyage had become the past, and the moon of that past attracted him ever more strongly, like at high tide. A high tide of past.

One night, now old and flabby and starting to forget, he leaves his home secretly. He's sick of everything, so he heads back one last time to see the places, women, and wonders he had once encountered. To go back again into his drained memory to see how it had been and who he had been. Because thanks to the bitter irony of old age, he has begun to transform into the Nobody, the name he had once cleverly used when introducing himself to the Cyclops.

Telemachus finds him in the evening, collapsed by the boat, only a hundred yards from home, with no idea what he is doing there and where he had been heading.

They take him back to a house with some woman he no longer remembers.

36.

What thievery life (and time) is, eh? What a bandit . . . Worse than the worst of highwaymen who ambush a peaceful caravan. Those bandits are interested only in your purse and in hidden gold. If you are docile and hand these over without a struggle, they leave you the other stuff—your life, your memory, your heart, your pecker. But this robber, life or time, comes and takes everything—your memory, your heart, your hearing, your pecker. It doesn't even choose, just grabs whatever it can. As if that's not bad enough, it mocks you on top of everything. It makes you so your tits sag, your butt grows bony, your back becomes bent, your hair thins, it goes gray, it puts hair in your ears, sprinkles moles all over your body, puts age spots on your hands and face, makes you prattle on about nonsense or fall silent, feeble-minded and senile, because it has stolen all of your words. That bastard—life, time, or old age, it's all the same, they're the same scum, the same gang. In the beginning at least it tries to be polite, it thieves within limits, like a skillful pickpocket. Without you noticing, it picks off the small things—a button, a sock, a slight shooting pain in the upper left side of your chest, your glasses a few millimeters thicker, three photos from the album, faces, what was her name again . . .

You lock the door, stop going out, stuff yourself full of vitamins, discover the fully proven magic of deepwater seaweed from that lake, what was the name again, that makes you young again, calcium from little crabs from the clean northern seas, the wonderful properties of Bulgarian yogurt or rose oil, you boil marrow from cow bones over low heat, which is a source of collagen for your connective tissue, you follow the lunar cycle of Deunov's wheat diet, then you venture further into the labyrinth of the soul, Castaneda, Peter Deunov, Madame Blavatsky, you vanish into the mysticism of ancient teachings, Osho, you make (unsuccessful) attempts at reincarnation, the primal scream, counting backward, breathwork in some neighborhood gym, you stare at parallel bars, Swedish walls, the pommel horse as they talk to you about the illusion of the physical body and lead you into the astral plane, while before your eyes you keep seeing that gym equipment they tormented you with in school, and you tell yourself, now that's the small joy of old age, you won't have to climb up on the balance beam or the Swedish wall anymore, your astral body doesn't have to worry about that, and later, while you are struggling to stand up, you quickly realize that all other bodies have left you, except your own physical one— that limping old donkey that you sink alone into the darkness with, no longer afraid of any bandits.

37.

We are constantly producing the past. We are factories for the past. Living past-making machines, what else? We eat time and produce the past. Even death doesn't put a stop to this. A person might be gone, but his past remains. Where do all those heaps of personal past go? Does someone buy them, collect them, throw them away? Or does it drift like an old newspaper, blown by the wind along the street? Where do all those familiar and unfinished stories go, those severed connections that still bleed, all those dumped lovers; "dumped"—this word isn't a coincidence, a garbage word.

Does the past disintegrate, or does it remain practically unchanged like plastic bags, slowly and deeply poisoning everything around itself? Shouldn't there be factories for recycling the past somewhere? Can you make anything else out of past besides past? Could it be recycled in reverse into some kind of future, albeit secondhand? Now, there are some questions for you.

Nature annihilates historical time or processes it, just as trees do with carbon dioxide. The glaciers at the North Pole were not particularly touched by the Thirty Years' War. But everything is recorded within them, in the ice and in the permafrozen ground. Melting strips bare the corpse of the past, the mammoth of the past arises. And times and eras will be mixed, somewhere in Siberia seeds that lay frozen in the ground for thirty thousand years are starting to sprout. The earth will open its archives, even if it's not clear whether there are any readers for them.

Now, with the arrival of the Anthropocene, for the first time the glacier, the turtle, the fruit fly, the gingko biloba tree, and the earthworm sense with such force that something in human time has shifted. We are the world's apocalypse. In that sense, we are also our own apocalypse. How ironic—the Anthropocene, the first era named for man, will likely turn out to be the last for him.

— *Gaustine,* On the End of Time

38.

Gaustine gradually began to change. For him the past had transformed into that white whale, which he pursued with Ahab's blind passion. Step-by-step, certain principles, certain inhibitions began falling away, as they would only turn out to be obstacles to his larger aim. I have to hand it to him for two things, though. First, that he realized this and tried to control it. And second, he wasn't chasing some outsized ambition, but rather a slightly old-fashioned and romantic idea (if we take revolutions as old-fashioned and romantic) about a reversal in time, about some shifting and searching for a weak spot, via which the past could be "tamed," that's exactly the word he used.

After our first meeting and his later disappearance into 1939 (according to his chronology), Gaustine had studied psychiatry and memory disorders, as if to rationalize his own obsession. And indeed, the Gaustine whom I met later could appear to be perfectly normal. Only sometimes, in the very depths of his eyes, in casual phrases or gestures, something from other times would glimmer for a moment. It seemed to me, however, that in our final months together at the clinic, it found a way to overpower him more often, to overpower even the science with which he had safeguarded himself. I saw him resisting, trying (with ever greater difficulty) to maintain the calmness of a person who lives in the here and now, while the past is simply a project, a type of reminiscence therapy, which he had developed to an unforeseeable extent.

Once or twice, when I tried to remind him about our first encounter as students by the seaside, and his letter from the eve of September 1, 1939, Gaustine's face would abruptly shift and he would change the subject. As if that guy there had been some other person or it had been a momentary lapse of reason, which he had since overcome and did not wish to be reminded of. I imagined for a moment how he must wake up every morning, he, the same one from all those eras, and before his first coffee, while still in bed, he would let his mind construct that day's world and himself in it: It is such-and-such a year, in such-and-such a place, I am psychotherapist, a specialist in memory disorders in the clinics of the past, which I myself created, the day is Saturday, let's not forget the year.

Every obsession turns us into monsters and in that sense Gaustine was a monster, perhaps a more discreet one, but a monster nonetheless. He was no longer satisfied by his clinic with its rooms and floors, those campuses from various decades that were growing and multiplying were not enough. I imagined how one day whole cities would change their calendar and go back several decades. And what would happen if a whole country suddenly decided to do so? Or several countries? I wrote this down in one of my notebooks, telling myself that if nothing else, a short novel could come out of it.

II

THE DECISION

What was it, then? What was in the air? A love of quarrels. Acute petulance. Nameless impatience. A universal penchant for nasty verbal exchanges and outbursts of rage, even for fisticuffs. Every day fierce arguments, out-of-control shouting-matches would erupt between individuals and among entire groups . . .

—Thomas Mann, "The Great Petulance,"
from *The Magic Mountain*, translated by John E. Woods

1.

And then the past set out to flood the world . . .

It spread from one person to another like an epidemic, like the Justinian plague or the Spanish flu. Do you remember the Spanish flu of 1918? Gaustine would ask. Not personally, I would reply. It was terrible, Gaustine would say. People simply dropped dead on the streets. You could get infected by everything, all it took was someone saying "Hello" to you and by the next evening you'd be dead.

Yes, the past is contagious. The contagion had crept in everywhere. But that wasn't the most frightening part—there were some quickly mutating strains that demolished all immunity. Europe, which had thought that after several serious lapses in reason in the twentieth century it had developed full resistance to certain obsessions, particular types of national madness, and so on, was actually among the first to capitulate.

No one died, of course (at least not in the beginning), yet the virus was spreading. It wasn't clear whether it was transmitted by aerosols, whether the very spray of spit when somebody shouted, *Germany* (or *France* or *Poland . . .*) *über alles, Hungary for the Hungarians,* or *Bulgaria on Three Seas,* could pass on the virus.

It was most quickly transmitted through the ear and the eye.

In the beginning, when people turned up on the streets in some European countries dressed in their national costumes, this was more or less considered an extravagance, a touch of color, perhaps a holiday of sorts, perhaps the beginning of carnival season, or a passing trend. Everyone smiled as they passed by, some joked about it or whispered among themselves.

Somehow imperceptibly people in native costumes began to take over the cities. Suddenly it became disconcerting to stroll around in jeans, a jacket, or a suit. No one officially banned pants or modern clothing. But if you didn't want to get dirty looks or to arouse the nationalists' suspicion, if you wanted to save yourself some headaches or even an ass-kicking or two, it was better to just throw a woolen cloak on over your clothes or slip on lederhosen, depending on where exactly you happened to be. The soft tyranny of any majority.

One day the president of a Central European country went to work in the national costume. Leather boots, tight pants, an embroidered vest, a small black bow above a white shirt, and a black bowler hat with a red geranium. The clothes fit him like some erstwhile *czardas* master who had since let himself go, but who was already ready to leap up with surprising nimbleness the second he heard music from a wedding. This look was a hit with the people as well as with the TV stations, and he began to dress like that every day.

European MPs also quickly fell in with the new trend, and soon the European Parliament began to resemble some German New Year's special from the '80s, as a Euronews journalist put it, recalling the *A Kettle of Color* program on television in the GDR—a shared and unifying memory for several generations of East Europeans.

The deputy prime minister of a southeastern country also put on a pair of full-bottomed breeches with decorative braid, a wide red cummerbund, and a shaggy shepherd's hat, which was trimmed with popcorn like in the olden days. The minister of tourism donned a heavy red tunic and an embroidered shirt with wide sleeves. The coins adorning her costume gleamed like real gold and there was a rumor going around that she was wearing part of a Thracian gold treasure kept in the state vaults. Gradually all the ministers started wearing native costumes, and in the end meetings of the Council of Ministers resembled a village working bee. We're breaking up the working bee, the prime minister would say instead of the official "The meeting is adjourned." It was slightly embarrassing at first when the minister of defense showed up on horseback in a revolutionary uniform, girded with a long saber and with a silver-handled Nagant revolver tucked into his wide leather belt. The horse would stand all day tied up next to a row of black Mercedes in front of the Council of Ministers, and a cop would give it a bag of oats and sheepishly clean up the dung.

A few websites tried to poke fun at this, but their voices were so weak and even irritating against the background of the general euphoria that they quickly shut up.

A new life was beginning, life as a reenactment.

2.

One evening two quiet electric Teslas would pull up in front of the clinic on Heliosstrasse, and three men in dark blue suits would get out to see Gaustine. One of the men, the chairman in blue, had come there before, since his mother was a patient. Later he stopped by a few more times on his own to hold long conversations with Gaustine. His visits were discreet, incognito, he was one of the big three in the European Union.

That evening the whole triumvirate came. Gaustine would invite them into his favorite study from the '60s. They would stay there all night, talking, raising their voices, and falling silent.

The past was rising up everywhere, filling with blood and coming to life. A radical move was needed, something unexpected and prescient, which would stop this irresistible centrifugal force. The time for love had ended, now came the time for hate. If hate were the gross domestic product, then the growth of prosperity in some countries would soon be sky-high. A certain delay, a way to inhibit the process and gain some time—that evening the three men in blue had come searching for something of the sort, it seemed to me.

When we talk about Alzheimer's, about amnesia and memory loss, we skip over something important. People suffering from this not only forget what was, but they are also completely incapable of making plans, even for the near future. In fact, the first thing that goes in memory loss is the very concept of the future.

The task was as follows. How can we gain a little more time for tomorrow, when we face a critical deficit of future? The simple answer was: By going backward a bit. If anything is certain, it's the past. Fifty years ago is more certain than fifty years from now. If you go two, three, even five decades back, you come out exactly that much ahead. Yes, it might already have been lived out, it might be a "secondhand" future, but it's still a future. It's still better than the nothingness yawning before us now. Since a Europe of the future is no longer possible, let's choose a Europe of the past. It's simple. When you have no future, you vote for the past.

Could Gaustine help?

He could create a clinic, a street, a neighborhood, even a small city set in a specific decade. But to turn a whole country or an entire continent back to another time—this is where medicine becomes politics. And the moment for that had clearly arrived.

Could Gaustine have stopped them?

Did he want to?

I can't be sure. I suspect that he had secretly been dreaming about just such a development, that he even, forgive me for saying it, innocently suggested this idea to his acquaintance in blue. There's no way to know for sure. Or there is, but I don't want to know. Actually, the three of them wanted advice, expertise, some kind of instructions, but clearly the decision had already been made. Besides, Gaustine didn't hold the exclusive rights to the past. Not for a whole continent.

In fact, it didn't seem like such a bad idea, plus anyone could see with the naked eye that there was no other way out. The past was already bursting through all the barely plugged bullet holes in the hull of the present in any case. They needed a farsighted move to take control of the situation, to give it some kind of shape and order. Fine, since you want the past so badly, here's the past for you, but let's at least vote on it and choose it together.

A referendum on the past.

That's what they would talk about that night. Or that's how I would invent it, outside, in the entryway, with my notebook.

3.

I have a dream . . . My dream is that one day the sons of former victors and the sons of the former vanquished in the Referendum of the past will be able to sit down together at the table of brotherhood . . . My dream is that all of us can live in the nation of our happiest time . . .

I observed how Gaustine stormed into action, without leaving his '60s study. Of course, he never gave a single public speech. But in everything the three men in blue said, you could hear his voice, words, and intonation, borrowed from everyone from Socrates to Martin Luther King.

To me, this seemed to be a project in which everyone was investing different dreams.

That was also why it would succeed in the end.

And why it would fail spectacularly.

4.

All elections up until this point had been about the future. This would be different.

TOTAL RECALL: EUROPE CHOOSES ITS PAST . . .
EUROPE—THE NEW UTOPIA . . . EUROTOPIA . . .
A EUROPEAN UNION OF THE COMMON PAST.

Those were the headlines in European newspapers. If nothing else, Europe was good at utopias. Yes, the Continent had been mined with a past that divided it, two world wars, hundreds of others, Balkan Wars, Thirty-Year Wars, Hundred-Year Wars . . . But there were also enough memories of alliances, of living as neighbors, memories of empires that gathered together supposedly ungatherable groups for centuries on end. People didn't stop to think that in and of itself, the nation was a bawling historical infant masquerading as a biblical patriarch.

It was clear that a simple agreement on a unified Continental past was impossible at this stage. For that reason, as was to be expected, following good old liberal traditions (even though an election on the past is a conservative act) it was decided that each member-state would hold its own referendum. Due to the extraordinary nature of the procedure and so as not to lose time, alongside the question of whether there should be a return to the past, voters in favor also had to indicate which specific decade they chose. After that, temporal alliances would form, while further down the line it would even be possible to vote for a unified European time.

Everyone accepted the Memorandum for the Recent Past, which clarified the process for holding the referendum in EU countries. Everything somehow took place more quickly and easily than expected.

And afterward they would agree on the various ... *pasts*.

(Hm, this word isn't usually used in the plural, well, what do you know. The past is only in the singular.)

5.

There are more and more signs of the coming of the past as I write this book. The time is near.

In Cuba they have banned the removal of old cars from the sidewalks because the tourists come specifically for them. Some countries are well supplied with history: Soviet Moskvitches and American Buicks sit there and rot next to each other, with bent wheel rims and flaking paint, while their rusting skeletons crumble, washed clean by the rain and dried by the Caribbean sun (like that marlin picked clean in *The Old Man and the Sea*).

I wonder, when the Second Coming finally arrives one day, whether old cars will also be resurrected.

TODAY IT SAYS IN THE paper that Germany has brought back typewriters to some of the top-secret government departments, in order to guard against leaks of information after a spy scandal a few years back. You can't hack and drain a typewriter. I find this piece of news very telling. Back to the Brave Old Analog World.

IN THE UK MILKMEN ARE enjoying a resurgence and more and more people are ordering milk in glass bottles, delivered to their doors in the morning.

THE NEW ISSUE OF THE *New Yorker* has reprinted (for the first time) one of its old covers from 1927. What would happen if on one and the same day all the newspapers and magazines decided to reprint their old issues from a certain day fifty or sixty years ago? Would the wheel of time creak?

THERE'S NOW A RADIO STATION that plays whole days from different decades, with news, interviews, the entire program for a given day.

6.

The very definition of the recent past turned out to be the subject of more than a few arguments, and for that reason a compromise was reached in which the borders were left flexible. Countries just needed to remain within the confines of the twentieth century.

There was something romantically doomed about such a referendum, especially given the recent fiasco with Brexit, but in the end, shouldn't people get to decide for themselves where they wanted to live? Things imposed from the top down never worked anyway and only provoked irritation. The referendum was a terrible idea, but a better one, as they say, has yet to be proposed.

This will be our final attempt to survive in the face of an impossible future, the chairman in blue was saying, we must choose between two things—living together in a shared past, which we have already done, or letting ourselves fall apart and slaughtering one another, which we have also already done. Both options are legitimate. Remember that great line from Auden, *We must love one another or die.* He paused briefly and repeated it, deliberately lowering his voice, *We must love one another or die,* knowing full well that he was coining a slogan for the media to seize the next day.

I heard Gaustine behind every word. These people had finally learned to speak, or, rather, to listen.

7.

Sometimes names really are correct by nature, as is argued in Plato's *Cratylus.* There is something telling in the very etymology of the word "referendum," if we drill down to the Latin provenance of the verb *re-ferro,* which means to go back, to carry back.

Turning back was loaded into the very word, and nobody even realized it . . . A referendum on the past. Do language games, with their etymologies and tautologies, sometimes hint at more than we think? And through the trumpets of tautology, does the revelation of a new apocalypse arrive?

8.

First, a country that had always wondered whether or not it was part of the Continent set itself apart. Great Brexitania, as we called it then.

Literature is to blame for everything, I told Gaustine once.

As usual, he laughed.

More specially, *Robinson Crusoe*, I went on. The confidence that an island can give you everything you need to survive, sustenance, all of that comes straight from Defoe. I'll be fine on my own, Robinson declares, God is with me. We'll be fine on our own, his descendants say, God save the queen (but even without her, we'll be fine).

Yes, Gaustine agrees, it would've been better if they'd read Donne instead of Defoe.

And suddenly, with his seventeenth century voice ringing out—I swear it was in that English from back then, declaiming that which we remember better thanks to a novel by Hemingway—he said:

> No man is an Iland, intire of it selfe; every man is a peece of the Continent, a part of the maine; if a Clod bee washed away by the Sea, Europe is the lesse, as well as if a Promontorie were, as well as if a Mannor of thy friends or of thine owne were; any mans death diminishes me, because I am involved in Mankinde . . .

That's the problem—Defoe defeated Donne, Gaustine said with a melancholy that could sink the whole British navy.

We were silent for a time and he repeated in his voice from the seventeenth century: *any mans death diminishes me*...Funny, we've always just skipped over the title: "Devotions upon Emergent Occasions." And now the occasion is emergent.

Once again Great Britain presents a troublesome case. Given Brexit, it should remain outside the referendum. But a pro-European movement immediately reared up on the island, insisting that the UK should by rights be included in the referendum on the shared past, since during that very same past it had been part of Europe and the union. Every nation, just like every person, has its moments of madness, the movement declared, let's give ourselves a historical second chance to shake off this madness.

The argument about a "historical second chance" was an exact quote from the preamble of the memorandum. But Brussels had gotten tired of British dithering in recent years and preferred to take a salubriously firm position. It refused the request.

9.

While these conversations were taking place, however, another miracle occurred. Switzerland, which has always been something like a hidden island within Europe, suddenly expressed the desire to join the Referendum on the Past. This was truly unexpected and headquarters in Brussels did not know how to respond for some time. All sorts of suspicions were whirling around as to why Switzerland would so blithely agree to violate its own traditions. Had it discovered a crack, a weak spot in the project that it could cleverly take advantage of? In the end, as part of a cautious agreement with several additional clauses, it was allowed to take part. Switzerland was an island, but it was also Europe in miniature. Where else could you see Germany, Italy, and France rolled into one? Thus, beyond the suspicions, there lay something very natural in its desire to try, albeit with a certain autonomy, to join the referendum.

10.

A Critical Deficit of Meaning

The acute phase of the disease is characterized by a sharp, strangling pain in various points on the body, which hampers precise diagnosis. Many patients report paroxysms in the late afternoon between three and six o'clock.

Difficulty breathing is one of the most commonly mentioned symptoms. A feeling of suffocation. *I don't have any strength, or any desire, to take a breath. I exhale and don't know if there's any point in inhaling again . . . I stopped buying calendars for the new year* [N.R. 53, housewife].

A sudden rush of senselessness, while I'm sitting on the couch— that's one of the best descriptions given by a patient. Empty fields within the memory, holes where you try to remember a source of joy. *This is exactly where the photographic negative has been overexposed* (according to one person's complaint), *the power has gone out* (according to another).

Beyond the individual diagnoses a tendency toward collective fear and rejection of the future, futurophobia, has been observed.

The aftereffects of the syndrome—melancholy, apathy, or

intense clinging to the past and the idealization of events which happened in a different way or more commonly never happened at all. In comparison to the past, the present pales, patients claim that they are literally seeing in black-and-white, while their memories are always in color, albeit in the paler hues of a Polaroid. Frequent dwelling in an alternate, made-up everyday life.

— *Gaustine,* New and Imminent Diagnoses

11.

Yes, the referendum was a radical idea and everyone had pinned their hidden hopes on it. For Gaustine, it was, of course, a passion. It looked so simple. That which was valid for an individual patient at the clinic would now be valid for everyone, for an entire society, if we could still use that concept.

The men in dark blue suits were counting down the final seconds before the chain reaction of disintegration in Europe would be set off.

As for the rest of the world? If the referendum turned out to be a success and things went well, then others could draw on the experience, if not—serves those Europeans right in any case, they had gotten too full of themselves these past twenty centuries or so . . .

Europe was no longer the center of the world and its people were intelligent enough to realize this. There is always something tragic about such a realization, whether it be about a person, a nation, or a continent. It usually comes at a later age, when there's not much that can be done. But at least you can try.

12.

One day Gaustine called and asked me to stop by the clinic.

I was walking toward Heliosstrasse. The April sun shone softly, yet without warmth. Here and there a few trees had begun blooming. A vague scent of soil and barns seeped in even here, in the city. That's how it smelled in the village, when my grandfather was shoveling manure out of the barn onto the garden in front of the house. That scent is gone now. Everyone uses synthetic fertilizer, so the soil smells like penicillin. Even now the scent of real manure takes me back . . . there, forty years ago and two thousand kilometers to the east. Switzerland was the ideal Bulgarian village of my childhood, the village that never existed.

In the meadow in front of the clinic the late hyacinths blazed in pink and blue, the narcissuses vainly swayed in the light breeze coming from the lake. I like this pre-May lull, before everything bursts out twittering, buzzing, and going crazy with color.

However, the forget-me-nots sprinkled throughout the meadow in front of the clinic were the most striking. Here of all places, forget-me-nots. (With surprise and slight bitterness I discovered that the Latin name of that little flower was not nearly so romantic—*Myosotis*, which literally means "mouse ears.") I preferred the legend according to which Flora, the goddess of flowers, when giving out names to various plants, walked right past that humble blue flower and then heard a soft voice behind her: "Don't forget me! Don't forget me!" Flora turned around and called it forget-me-not, endowing it with the ability to invoke memories in people. I read somewhere that the blossom of the forget-me-not cures melancholy or, to put it more officially, has an antidepressive effect. Moreover, its seeds can stay in the ground for thirty years, sprouting only when the conditions are right. That flower remembers itself over the course of thirty years.

I entered the clinic. Gaustine had invited me to the 1940s, on the first floor. He was drinking Calvados and smoking some German trophy cigarettes. An old map of the front hung on the wall, where flags indicated the movements of the various armies. On the large, heavy table of burnished cherrywood several detailed prototypes of the Spitfire were lined up, that favorite monoplane of the Royal Air Force from the 1940s, fast and hardy. A Messerschmitt and a Hurricane were keeping them company. They stood there exquisitely, on a stand, as if they had just returned from battle. Gaustine was dressed in a green military shirt with the sleeves rolled up, resembling an English officer responsible for the landing at Normandy, who has just found out that the expected meteorological conditions have suddenly changed. I was seeing him for the first time in uniform. Perhaps he didn't want to spoil the atmosphere of the decade.

I got the feeling that he was struggling to concentrate, like a person trying to step out of the river of a different time. (I'd noticed such efforts a few times before.) The referendum would begin in just a week. He knew that I was getting ready to go back to Bulgaria, for he himself had insisted upon this. He told me that he wanted to withdraw for a bit during this time, that he would observe developments from afar. Suddenly he strongly reminded me of that young man whom I had met thirty years earlier, with that same sense of othertimeliness and a lack of belonging. It seemed to me that he was walking slowly toward his 1939, where he had disappeared then. We exchanged a few more words, and agreed that when everything was over, we'd meet up again. At six before the war, right? I joked. (I don't know why I said "before," in *The Good Soldier Švejk* it was "after.") He turned around sharply and stared at me intently for a full minute. Yes sir, at six before the war . . . he said, accenting the "before."

I'm not sure it was a good idea to— I started in hesitantly.

You're never sure, that's why you need me, Gaustine interrupted irritably. You need somebody to do what you don't dare.

It's easy for you, because when things get rough, you just change times, whereas I have to stay here . . .

But I fight for every time as if it were the only one, while you, in the only time you have, act as if you've got another hundred possible times.

(He's right, he's right, goddamn it!)

But you're a . . . you're a projection, you're a monomaniac, except that you're a serial monomaniac, you just don't remember your previous manias. You can't just play with the past. Don't you remember all those other projects from the last novel . . . the cinema for the poor, where we were supposed to retell movies before they were shown for half the price, without having seen them ourselves, we just about got our asses kicked, what about our projections of clouds on the sky, or the Condom Catwalk . . . All those things were total failures, you're the prince of failures . . .

That's enough, Gaustine said coldly. We aren't the ones who thought up referendums.

But we also didn't try to stop them.

And should we have? He said quickly as I headed for the door.

I don't know, sir, I replied dryly, taking in his green shirt and trying to get into the tone of the '40s. He didn't laugh. We shook hands coldly and I left. I had the sense that I would lose him again . . .

III

ONE COUNTRY TAKEN AS AN EXAMPLE

We used to pay too little attention to utopias, or even disregard them altogether, saying with regret they were impossible of realization. Now indeed they seem to be able to be brought about far more easily than we supposed, and we are actually faced by an agonizing problem of quite another kind: how can we prevent their final realization?

—Nikolai Berdyaev, *The Philosophy of Freedom*

Returning

Folk music is playing softly on the airplane. The stewardesses are rushing around before takeoff in stylized native costumes, their hair in braids, their tunics shortened above the knee. The only male flight attendant looks slightly ridiculous in his modified breeches and vest. The pilot's voice comes over the loudspeaker.

We are proud to welcome you on board the Bulgarian national air carrier . . .

I notice the little changes to language. Until recently they said "we are happy to welcome you." Where did this pride come from all of a sudden? The airline is certainly not one of the best, it is a public secret that it will soon be heading for bankruptcy. The airplane starts rolling away from the gate as those safety instructions that we are all sick to death of begin. I put in my earplugs and only watch the stewardesses' movements. Without sound their gestures resemble a strange conjuring ritual, the gestures of tribal sooth-sayers. The strange thing is that they keep doing it. There is no evidence that anyone has ever been saved during a plane crash thanks to having put on their oxygen mask that automatically drops down from above or by having pulled out *the life vest from beneath your seat* and by blowing the emergency whistle. Perhaps a joint prayer would do more good.

The plane I am on resembles one of those fixed-route taxi-vans so ubiquitous in Sofia. I wouldn't be surprised if they soon start allowing standing-room-only passengers. A few years ago I flew on some domestic flight from Belgrade to Montenegro standing up as if on a bus, hanging on to a metal bar. The driver, pardon me, the pilot, was just an arm's length away from me. There was no door, just a threadbare curtain that was unhooked on one side, so he and I shot the breeze a bit. At one point he lit up a cigarette and I was praying he didn't open up the window to ash outside, and thus wreak havoc with the cabin pressure.

With age the fear of flying grows. Clearly it accumulates with the hours and miles you fly, too bad you can't cash it in, too. A Frequent Frighter card would be a good idea.

After the safety ritual the plane takes off relatively smoothly, perhaps the stewardesses' conjuring did have an effect after all. The upholstery is threadbare, the seat pockets are ragged, the in-flight magazine is crumpled from the nervous fingers of dozens of passengers. The Bakelite body of the plane creaks softly. The smoking sign only shows how old these machines are, from the era when you could still smoke on board.

Suddenly a fly lands above me, right next to the call button. A fly in the airplane. (A friend once sent me a poem with that title, knowing of my passion for flies, and now look, the poem is coming true, in a manner of speaking.) I have a special relationship with this creature, which most find annoying, thus its presence here makes me happy. I wonder if it's a Bulgarian fly; the plane had come from Sofia earlier that day. Or perhaps it's a misguided Swiss fly (actually, do they allow flies into Switzerland at all?) who mixed up the flights. A fly who shall remain a foreigner its whole life in an obscure Balkan country that proclaims itself the Switzerland of the Balkans.

Do flies have nations? What are the characteristics of the national fly? Does it feel devotion and nostalgia for its homeland, could it develop some primitive form of patriotism? What would happen if we were to put that nationalism under the microscope of natural history?

The fly and the nation, now, there's a serious topic for you. In the framework of historical or natural time, the nation is only a speck of dust, a microscopic part of the evolutionary clock, far more ephemeral than the fly. In any case, the fly surpasses the nation time-wise hundreds and thousands of times over. What would *Homo nationalisticus* be, if it could slip into the taxonomy of living creatures?

Genus—*Homo . . . sapiens . . .* I'm afraid that even at this level the nationalist will jump up, who are you calling a *Homo*? Where are you putting me?

Where did we start from? From the fly. And where did we end up? At the elephant of nationalism.

A fly, my seat neighbor squeals, stating the obvious and interrupting the newly built evolutionary chain in my head . . .

The stewardess rushes over. Can I help with something?

An unregistered passenger on board, I say, he flew away just now.

The fly, however, makes a circle and naïvely lands in the same place. Get out of here, I tell it in my head, but with an unexpectedly quick grab, the stewardess catches it in her hand. Do they get special training for that?

Please let it go, says the women next to me, who had outed the fly only a few moments earlier.

Yes, I would also ask you to let it go, I join in, it isn't bothering anyone.

Everything teeters on the edge between irony and seriousness.

Is it with you? the stewardess fixes me with a stern gaze, taking up the game. Good God, if stewardesses, those ironclad creatures, have a sense of humor, there is hope for the world yet.

It's with me, as a pet, I reply. That's not a problem, is it?

It just needs to be in a cage or in its owner's lap, she recites. And delicately opens the bars of her long fingers.

My neighbor turns to me a bit later. Thank you for stepping in. A woman of a difficult-to-determine age around fifty, with narrow blue eyes and freckles.

Oh, I am a great friend of flies, I say casually. I'm something like their historian.

She smiles, giving herself time to assess whether I am some kind of maniac or just a man with a strange sense of humor. Ultimately, she seems to go with the latter.

I didn't know flies had a history.

Quite a bit longer than ours, I reply. They appeared several million years before man.

It's strange to see a fly at this altitude, she says.

Actually, it shouldn't be all that strange. The first living being sent into space was none other than a fly, *Drosophila melanogaster*. Its name is longer than the fly itself. Right after the war, with the then-prized rocket V-2.

I thought it was the dog Laika.

That's what everyone thinks. There is a great injustice in that. Before the dog Laika there were quite a few other dogs, there were monkeys, snails . . . All of them remained anonymous. Like the poor fly, who sacrificed itself first, after all. But flies don't have names, and therein lies the whole problem. If you don't have a name, you're dropped from history.

But why exactly a fly? my seat-neighbor asks.

Now, that's a good question. Because they are short-lived and die quickly. The rocket flew for only a few hours, at an altitude of a hundred kilometers, on the very border of space, incidentally. So they needed a creature with a quick life cycle. It needed to be born,

develop, attain sexual maturity, conceive, give birth, and die . . .
The simple fruit fly possesses all these qualities. Besides that, the
death of a few flies is far more acceptable than that of a dog, mon-
key, or cow, don't you think? People are very impressed by size.

I look around and notice the subject of our conversation has
wisely hidden somewhere.

At that time they start passing out "Bulgarian Rose" wet wipes—
now, there's something that hasn't changed since my first flight so
many years ago. The scent of rose oil wafts amid the clouds. The
airplane prepares for landing. Mount Vitosha is visible, as is the
outline of Sofia, the neighborhoods with their concrete panel-
block apartments, then Alexander Nevsky Cathedral, the green
rectangle of Boris's Gardens, and the strip of Tsarigrad Road down
below. There, somewhere to the right of the highway, is a neighborhood called "Youth," where I used to live in some other lifetime.
Suddenly the woman next to me, we never did introduce ourselves
by name, starts to cry, quietly, calmly, without hysterics, as she
turns her head toward the window. I'm sorry, she says, I haven't
been back in seventeen years.

The plane lands softly, followed by the passengers' inevitable
applause. Some foreigners, unused to this ritual, always look
around rather puzzled at that moment. The woman next to me
starts clapping, too.

Be careful, the pilot might take that as a plea for an encore and
take off again, I joke.

Over the loudspeaker they welcome us to Bulgarian territory
with pride, inform us of the outside temperature, and play the song
"One Bulgarian Rose" by Pasha Hristova, who died, by the way, in
a plane crash on this same airline at this same airport.

2.

The jostling and cutting in front of the passport control booths is something of a trademark for this place. Luggage delivery will take forever, then the taxi driver won't return your greeting and will drive off angrily, the pedal to the metal, once he realizes that the address you give him is not on the other side of the city. He'll crank up the music and light up a cigarette.

And yet this time there is something I wasn't expecting. The first driver I head toward is wearing a wide red sash around his waist, a white shirt with a vest over it (in complete contrast to his Bermuda shorts below), and the handle of a dagger peeks out of his sash. Things have really gone too far—too far back, that is. I think how much better suited that costume would be to a horse cart or a carriage with two and not ninety horsepower, which is how much the secondhand Korean Daewoo he's driving is. At the last moment I decide not to take the cab (taxi drivers with daggers have never been a weakness of mine) and turn toward the neighboring taxi stand. There at least the drivers are dressed normally. I open the door of the first car and ask whether the cab is free. It's free, the driver says with a laugh, and while I'm still getting settled in he says: You've heard that old joke, right, where back in the day a Cuban student in Sofia would stop taxis, open the door, ask if they were free, and when they'd say they were, he'd just shout: "Long live freedom!" and send them on their way. I chuckle, even though, yes, I had heard it before.

Something is a bit off with this car, too, but I only figure out what it is as we drive off. As we slowly pull away from the airport, I see that all the cars are from the socialist era.

Moskvitch, I nearly shout, in a tone that combines a question, suspicion, sincere surprise, and confusion.

Moskvitch, the driver proudly confirms, a twelve. It's forty years old, but a solid machine. They don't make 'em like they used to, he says, starting up the car on the second try, which for a car of this venerable age is a brilliant start(er). It reeks terribly of gas, clearly the insulation has long since given up the ghost.

I recall that my uncle used to have a Moskvitch like this. He said it with the accent on the first syllable because he thought it sounded more Soviet that way. If we truly have body memory, then my body from 1975 surely remembers even now how the seat dug into me, that stink of gas and vomit. I always traveled with a plastic bag. I feel sick now even thinking about it. I also note the small portrait of Stalin above the rearview mirror.

It's my buddy on the night shifts, the driver says, catching my gaze. Old Uncle Dinko is all for the 1950s.

I remember how at one time all the buses had photos of Stalin—both before and after the cult of personality, they never disappeared from the drivers' cabins. Even later, in the '80s, those Georgian mustaches would be peeking out from beneath Sandra and Samantha Fox's full-color breasts.

Do you remember Samantha Fox? I suddenly ask.

Ooh, I think I've got a lighter with her on it somewhere here, I collect them, he says, reaching over and opening up the glove compartment, where at least a dozen different lighters and as many boxes of matches are rolling around inside. I prefer these. He takes out a Zippo engraved with Che Guevara. But otherwise these girls are mighty fine, too. He lowers the sun visor and on the back beam the Golden Girls of Bulgarian rhythmic gymnastics from the '70s, who were part of our very own permanent and always permanently suppressed adolescent sexual revolution.

Leaving Sofia Airport in the puttering Moskvitch, the last thing I notice is an enormous billboard for one of the leading mobile operators. They offer a patriotic package with thirteen hundred free minutes—one for each year since the country's founding—access to all Bulgarian historical films, and a portable flag with a collapsible handle, which will fit easily into your toiletries case.

3.

Just like every time I come back, melancholy inevitably settles in. Before, the sorrow was lighter, like a walk through a sparse forest in which invisible cobwebs sparkle. I loved walking through the park, in the upper part, passing by the lake with the lilies. The time I spent there so many years ago in some other life has melted away without a trace. Is the light still the same, at least? The leaves on the trees, which I waded through in late October with a certain girl, strange that I remember only autumns, anyway, those leaves had already turned at least thirty times since then. Do things remember us at all? That would still be some sort of compensation. Does the lake, with every frog and lily in it, preserve our reflections somewhere? Has the past itself—have our younger selves—turned into frogs and lilies?

I didn't find the answer that afternoon. I found only late yet tolerable melancholy and cold April air. For a moment I felt like calling that girl. Then I imagined her—with two kids and a husband; a woman who has long since tucked our story away somewhere on the top shelf between the empty spice jars and a notebook full of recipes from her mother. What would I actually want from her—reconstruction, reenactment, recollection? A recollection of what—the elusive color of her eyes? Or was the desire more egocentric—to make sure that I had existed, so she could tell me what had happened to us, a few memories, nothing more? To give back to my memory a few walks, a few words we had laughed over back then. Souvenirs of the past. The dark entryways we hid in. The park. That one time behind the monument to ... who was it commemorating again? The city suddenly transforms, it has a different topography for lovers ... We imagined an apartment for ourselves, which didn't really exist. We fantasized what would happen to us there, how we'd come home to it. *Yesterday I stopped by there,* she would write to me on my old Nokia, *and I forgot my sweater. Let it stay there and remind you of me. Did you water the orchid? They are very fussy. The cat and I are alone, come on over ...*

Can a person be gathered up like that, piece by piece, through the memories of others, and what would you get in the end? Would some Frankensteinian monster emerge from all that? Something patched together from absolutely incompatible memories and ideas from so many people?

... Well, you were always laughing ... You were totally antisocial, sometimes you'd go days without saying anything (that's my wife, I recognize her voice) ... You were so sweet, so, how can I put it ... romantic, we'd lie on benches and imagine how we would get to be a hundred years old, like turtles, and we'd still be together, in a house with light blue shutters, by the sea ... Jesus Christ, how you could curse, when you got pissed off, watch out ... Skinny, super-skinny ... You got to be pretty heavy ... I was always asking you not to walk so fast ... You limped ... Tall ... Hunched over ... And when I saw your blue eyes ... hazel or green, they changed their color depending on the season . . . in a red jacket . . . That green leather jacket . . . You were always forgetting names, and once . . . You always had a lit cigarette in your hand . . . I can't imagine you ever smoked . . . There were a few words you never remembered, and when you'd be telling a story and get stuck on something, I'd list them off for you . . . Spaced out, very spaced out . . . A person who never wasted any time . . . Then you saw some book on my bed, that very first night, we had just gotten undressed, you turned around and said no way, I've got to go, I can't sleep with someone who reads Coelho, and it was a completely different author, a Portuguese guy with a similar name, we had a good laugh about it then . . . You were gentle . . . A bit rough in bed . . . We had such nice pillow talk afterward . . .

Is all of that me?

4.

There's something, a draft and grief, which instead of weakening seems to grow stronger with the years. And it is surely tied to the ever-quicker emptying of the rooms of my memory. One who opens door after door, going from room to room in the hope, the hope and fear of finding himself in one of them—there, where he is still whole.

Isn't this draft pulling toward the past in the end an attempt to reach that sound place, no matter how far back it might be, where things are still whole, where it smells of grass and you see the rose and its labyrinth point-blank? I say place, but it's actually a time, a place in time. Some advice from me: Never, ever visit a place you left as a child after a long absence. It has been replaced, emptied of time, abandoned, ghostly.

There. Is. Nothing. There.

A man sets out to pull himself together by returning to the places where he grew up. He gathers up all the addresses of the girls and women he has been in love with from kindergarten until now. He won't ask anything of them, he only wants to see them, to tell them that he has carried them in his head his whole life (he wanted to say in his heart, but that seemed too sentimental) and that only they have remained in the end. The doctors have given him a few months at most. Like a miser, he splits them into days and hours, as if breaking large bills into small change. It seems like more to him that way. He still has three months, which means at least 91 afternoons, he loves afternoons and . . . multiplied by 24, that means about 2,184 hours. That still seems like too little to him, so he multiplies by 60, then ends up with more than 130,000 minutes. Now, that's better, he has never felt like such a tycoon, he can spend them down to the last minute. He travels all day on a bus to the little town. The house he lived in is no longer there. Most of the other addresses have changed. The girls have long since become women, they've married other men, how awful. Who knows why, but he thought they would lie there bleeding in the middle of their relationship that had been cut short, still pining over him like Chekhovian heroines.

In the end he nevertheless finds one of the great loves of his life in that little town. They had been fourteen. They had pretended to get married; he had stolen a ring from his mother (who had practically torn the house apart looking for it). She had been a tall, dreamy girl, that's how he remembers her, like a young Romy Schneider. As he nears the house, he catches sight of an elderly woman with frazzled, tied-back hair lugging a tub of wet clothes. She's not here, he says, she must have moved. But he still decides to ask, this woman might know something.

It's her.

Nothing is left of that girl. He doesn't know what to say. We know each other from such-and-such... She doesn't make the connection right away. Several lifetimes have passed since then. She guesses, says the wrong name. Then it is as if something opens up in her memory. At that moment an old man in a tank top comes out, her husband. What's going on? he asks, gripping his cane, seeing his wife talking to a strange man through the fence. What do you want? He can't say what he wants, he hasn't managed to explain why he is here.

She keeps silent, too.

Nothing, our man says, nothing, I'm just buying old junk, pictures, embroidery, watches, radios, old stuff. Go on, the old man says, get on your way now, go on, now, we ain't got nothing old, nothing new, either...

The woman still stands there like a statue, hasn't even set down the tub. The man hides in the shade on the sidewalk across the street. From somewhere he can hear a radio giving the level of the Danube River in centimeters, that abracadabra of his entire childhood. So it's three in the afternoon, he tells himself, he doesn't need to look at his watch. He slowly sets off down the street, the soles of his shoes sticking to the asphalt melted by the heat; he is shrinking while they scatter from his pockets, tinkling softly and gleaming like coins, all those (no longer needed) minutes that were left to him.

The things I do not dare to do will transform into stories.

5.

For an afternoon, I stop by the city where I used to live. I go back there every time I'm in Bulgaria, even though I know that nothing remains of that time, that neither the park, nor the little square by the covered market, nor the street I grew up on remember my footsteps.

On the trunk of a chestnut by the post office I see a sheet of paper affixed with four tacks, upon which the following is written in large letters. I have copied it down exactly:

TRADE
Big L-C-D tellevision
32 inches works good 8 years old
For 30 liters of rakia
Yambol, phone number: 046 . . .
15 feb.

I stand in front of this message, true marginalia taken from the tree of life, or rather, pinned to it with tacks. Now, there's part of the Bulgarian epos for you, a piece of it, the mystery of the Bulgarian voice, quiet, inscrutable, and suddenly erupting with its most sublime dream.

A TV in exchange for brandy.

There are dreams and horror here, horror and dreams . . . February, it says down at the bottom. Only in February could this cry arise, with all its tragedy . . . The rakia is gone, but the winter is still here. Now, there's the whole existential novel of a people for you. The jeep of life, that old battered jeep with the canvas roof, or no, the Moskvitch of your life has gotten stuck at the end of winter, darkness has fallen, the jackals are howling, and you are out of gas. Fuck this life, you say, pounding your fist. Fuck it, fuck you, you even took my rakia. (Nobody's taken it from you, you drank it yourself, but that's how people have talked around here since time immemorial, somebody has taken something from you or let you have it.)

And now you're sitting in the middle of nowhere, in the jeep or

Moskvitch that is your life. And you decide, to hell with shame, you're going to post an ad, you can't take it anymore. You take a sheet of paper, a notice from the bank warning that if you don't pay off the interest by . . . You don't have any rakia, and they're wanting interest. You flip it over and look for a pen. You think about asking your son to write it, because it'll come out nicer, with fewer mistakes, but you feel too ashamed to ask him. That's the only thing you're still ashamed of. Finally you sit down and write it yourself, with all the spelling errors and missing commas. You grab a handful of tacks and go to the neighborhood all the way on the other side of town, for the second time you're a bit ashamed. And what are you offering in exchange for the rakia— you're offering your most precious possession, of course. Measure for measure, meaning for meaning. The television or the rakia, that is the question. The television is transcendence, a false transcendence, of course, but nevertheless the final dream of the beyond. Your grandmother had an icon, your mother had a little portrait of Lenin, and you have your TV. But what good is your TV if you don't have rakia? The TV simply cuts life, like pouring water into your rakia . . . They're already selling electronic ciga-rettes, tomorrow you're going to be shoving electronic rakia in my hands, fucking electronic motherfuckers . . . Well, now, that's what the TV is, electronic rakia . . . so there, take it back, a 32-inch screen for 30 liters of rakia, a liter an inch, I've giving you a deal. Thirty liters of rakia for a month more of life, maybe even a month and a half if we're economical about it. Only rakia is hon-est, goddamn it. It doesn't lie to you like the TV, it doesn't try to pull the wool over your eyes, it doesn't blather on and on. It hits you in the nose, burns your throat real good, then it goes down and warms up all that stuff down below that has long since gone cold. Rakia is the Bulgarian sublime, the Bulgarian television at long last.

I wonder whatever happened to that guy, I think as I curse inwardly. Shouldn't I call the phone number to check? This isn't just a want ad, it's a cry for help. It's the end of April. Not a single one of the tabs at the bottom with the phone number has been torn off. I go back to Sofia that same afternoon.

6.

I don't have anyone to call, so I'm wandering through the windy streets of Sofia. I stop in front of a pet store.

During my first year at university a friend of mine and I bought a pair of parrots as a present for this girl in our class. But won't they be squawking all day? I asked. What do you care, my friend said, you're not gonna live with them, right? The birthday party that night was dreadful, some sort of row erupted, it even came to blows, her ex-boyfriend was pounding on the door—the 1990s . . . I remember clearly that as I slunk away I said to myself: Now there's one woman I'll never live with. A year later I was standing in that same room, changing the parrots' water as they screeched hideously. In the mornings we'd throw an old towel over them so they'd think it was nighttime and we could get at least an hour of peace. We named the female parrot Emma Bovary—at that time we were reading Flaubert at the university—while we called the male one Pechorin, who knows why. Emma was constantly attacking him, and poor Pechorin, who supposedly had all sorts of Princess Marys wrapped around his little finger, would just sit there disheveled and pecked, pressed against the thin bars of the cage.

I now realize that I've never had as many friends as I did then. That studio apartment was always full of people. I remember how one night, in the wee hours around four a.m., when everything had been drunk and smoked up, we suddenly got ravenously hungry.

There was nothing in the refrigerator; those were the hungriest days of the 1990s. I went out with two of the other guys to look for something, as if we could kill a rabbit or doe in the empty city. It was dark, formless, and empty, only packs of dogs roamed the streets. And then, like a miracle, a white Nissan puttered up, stopped nearby, unloaded three crates of yogurt in front of the local store, and drove off. Our generation hated yogurt (on principle), because that's what they used to make us eat every morning for breakfast as kids. We looked around, nobody showed up, so we grabbed two cartons of yogurt apiece, left all the change we could find in our pockets, and ran back home.

Everybody was waiting for us, starved. I will never forget that picture, the empty bottles and cups on the table, ten identical little nickel-silver bowls set out in front of each of us, all of us twenty-odd years old, and slurping up our yogurt like angels. I don't know whether angels eat yogurt, but that's how I've remembered us, with white yogurt mustaches, happy and innocent ...

Soon after that we would go our separate ways, grow cold, forget one another; the rebels would grow tame as teaching assistants in the universities, the sworn bachelors and party animals would be pushing baby carriages and zoning out in front of their TVs, the hippies would get regular haircuts at the local barbershop. The parrot Pechorin would die one morning, and Emma Bovary would shriek and hurl herself against the bars, crazed with grief. She wouldn't outlive him by a week. The other Emma (yes, that really was her name) and I would break up a few months later. Neither of us would die of grief. I would start my first novel, so I would have somewhere to go home to when I was going crazy, a novel about homeless people.

The truth is, there is no way I can call any one of those erstwhile angels, not even Emma, especially not her. It's awful that I can't for-

get them and (I would never admit this to them) that I miss them.
I miss myself, too.

7.

The two big rallies for the primary political forces are scheduled
for the last Sunday before the referendum. Bulgaria is abuzz with
all kinds of movements championing the various decades. Their
arguments range from free medical care to the taste of tomatoes
and grandma's chicken stew. I doubt that the referendum will bring
back the taste of stew. It's as if some people think that bringing
back the recent past will also automatically take them back the age
they were then. The red light goes on and suddenly you are fifteen
or twenty-seven again.

All of that feeds into the propaganda, of course. In the end most of
the polls show two main movements to be considerably ahead of
the rest. On the one hand, there is the Movement for State Socialism (SS), which holds echoes of State Security, but was better
known in short as Soc—which wanted to bring back the time of
mature socialism, more specifically the 1960s and '70s. At its core
stands the Socialist Party, even though the Soc movement's supporters in the referendum outnumber the political party's shrinking ranks by several orders of magnitude. In that sense it would be
truer to say that the party itself is trying to get an infusion of fresh
blood from the movement.

The other movement, whose results are projected to be almost
neck-and-neck with the SS, is officially named Bulgari-Yunatsi, the
Bulgarian Heroes, known colloquially and unofficially as simply
the Heroes. It's difficult for them to point to a specific period, to

the decades they would like to return the nation to, since mythology can't be split into years. Great Bulgaria is an eternal dream and reality, at least according to their speeches. Since, according to the guidelines of the referendum, the earliest possible time frame is the beginning of the twentieth century, the Heroes, illegitimately expanding this deadline, have chosen a late, idealized Bulgarian Revival Period, whose apex is the April Uprising of 1876.*

Can an uprising that never fully happened become sublime and emblematic? Actually, what could become sublime and emblematic but the unhappened? Is this not the only thing that has the potential to happen and to create things as we would like them to be, unimpeded by facts? To be reenacted, as it were, on the basis of memory and imagination? Here everyone is born with (or inherits) the experience of the unhappened.

I wonder which of these two straws—Soc or Heroes—our man with the rakia, rakiaman, would clutch at. Between this Scylla and Charybdis, the little boats of the smaller movements tried to survive.

8.

Meeting with K.

Unlike my previous, almost anonymous visits here, which were tied mainly with the clinic, this time I want to talk to someone about the situation. I finally call a friend from my university days, who has become a professor in the meantime. We haven't spoken

---

* During the April Uprising of 1876, Bulgarian rebels rose up against the Ottoman authorities. Although the uprising ultimately failed, it remained as a key event in the Bulgarian national memory and mythology.

in several years, I don't even know if his phone number is still the same. I am about to hang up when his sleepy voice says, "Hello," into the receiver . . .

It seems to me that, besides surprise, his voice also holds a certain joy. That rush of joy when you see or hear from someone you haven't run into in a long time is not a given in Bulgaria. I remember during my first couple visits back here when I'd meet a friend or acquaintance on the street, I'd rush to hug him, and he would look at me bewildered and grunt out something along the lines of, Oh, hey, what're you doing here? What's more, K. himself suggests we meet up this evening at a pub on the roof of the State Archives. Here in Bulgaria you can still make plans for the same day.

In the late 1980s K. was a young teaching assistant. We loved him because he was different from the others. We had dubbed him "Kafka," Junior Assistant Kafka; I suspect he had nothing against it. He was (and still is) gruff, systematic, something that was quite useful to our confused minds, filled as they were with chaotically read books. Our conversations with him also ended in intense disagreements, often going beyond the pale of civility; he would get fired up, he was caustic, he would interrupt. An academic brawler, but therein lay his charm. We weren't extremely close friends, but we'd drink together and argue through the pubs and seminars of the 1990s, whose like has never been seen again. All of our encounters began with goodwill on his part, passed through long conversations, and ended in rows. A week later he would call and ask with sincere astonishment, Why haven't you called? Uh, well, we're in a fight, I would reply. Well, yeah, so what better time to have a drink and make up?

Our fights were just an excuse to make up, which would lead to a new argument, which in turn would be a new excuse, and so on. That's how everyone lived in that wondrously simmering time.

Maybe that's why I call him now. I'm hoping that he has remained the person who can still formulate things with the clear categoricalness of a Protestant pastor. I have never liked and never availed myself of such categoricalness, perhaps that's why I always need someone like him. And maybe that's why nobody likes him. I like people that other people don't like. (Actually, my first introduction to K. came at that same seminar by the sea in the late '80s where I also met Gaustine for the first time. And I must say that to K.'s credit, he was the only person besides me who was interested in Gaustine; he tried to invite him to his gatherings, but Gaustine, of course, never showed up to a single one.)

We're sitting on the roof of the Archives at dusk, *in the hour of the blue haze*, I quote the famous Bulgarian poet Yavorov, watching how in the distance Vitosha darkens to a deep violet. *Like a violet island in moon-silver waters*, K. takes up the game with another poet. I realize that this city is already more literature than anything else to me, I know it only through books and only as literature does it still attract me. Sofia of the 1930s and the early 1940s, those must have been its strongest years. Somewhere close by here, the first neon advertising sign flickered on outside the office of the French airlines in 1931. Neon immediately entered urban poetry. I imagine those glowing letters, seen for the first time by an eye that has traditionally been entranced by the moon and stars. The rise of neon amid the dim light of the streetlamps clearly must have been shocking and moving, then it quickly became trivial. A long time ago, it now seems like a different lifetime, I had studied the advertising, cinema, and radio from that time, I had looked through the illustrated weeklies, the broadsheets, the film magazines, and handbooks about how to construct your own radio receiver. The whole poetry of that era was teeming with everything from condensers, antennas, neon lights, advertising logos, Bayer and Philips', Lucky Strike, and White Horse to the names of films and the lion from Metro-Goldwyn-Mayer... I take up this topic, even though I've come to talk about something else. We get carried away, the quotations are flying fast and furious. Do you remember that... what about this... *And the ads for Bayer and Philips' bloomed like in paradise?* Hm, K. stops to think about this last quote, and I am truly delighted to have caught him not knowing something. I give up, who is it...? Bogomil Raynov as a young poet, I say, before he became a satrap.

If I were to take part in the referendum on the past here, I would pick the 1930s (despite what comes after them) or I'd truly be torn between the 1930s for the literature and the 1960s for the vague feeling that I remember that decade in detail.

I ask K. which decade he would choose. He doesn't rush to answer, as if he has to decide once and for all at this moment. We order another rakia and as the waiter walks away, K. says slowly: I'm debating between the 1920s and the 1950s, although the polls show they have the least support.

It's understandable that no one wants them; both were pretty bloody.

I know his research on the poetry from the '20s. There are several brilliant Bulgarian poets from that decade. The best of them literally paid with his head, shattered by shrapnel on the front, patched together in Berlin, only to disappear six years later, found in a mass grave and only recognized by his glass eye. It's well known that our inept homegrown police of all eras have always shown unerring taste in poets and writers—they always manage to kill the most talented and leave the most mediocre.

I understand K.'s choice of the '20s, the literary historian in him wants to go back to his subject matter. But why the 1950s? I ask point-blank. Those are dark times, rough, merciless, a time of terror and labor camps, stilted aesthetics in the style of that commie dogmatist Todor Pavlov.

In the '50s my father was sent to the camp in Belene, K. begins, and he was never the same again. He also never spoke a word about it afterward. In school I was immediately designated as "unreliable." When they talked about enemies of the people, the teachers would point me out directly as the son of an enemy. I was the ideal example of how forgiving the people's power was, that they allowed even kids like me to live and study alongside everyone else.

One day the doorbell rang; I was seven. I looked through the spy hole and saw some frightening bearded man with slumped shoulders outside and I automatically turned the key in the lock one more time. My heart was about to burst. Come on, open up—the man outside knew my name. We don't open the door to strangers, I shouted at him from inside. Don't you recognize me, I'm your father, he said softly, as if he were afraid the neighbors might hear. I looked out through the spy hole and he seemed to be crying . . . That's not my father, I told myself, but since he's bawling, he must not be a robber, either. But I didn't open the door. My mother was at the factory, she'd be home in a few hours. He stood there on the wretched landing, his clothing fusing with the dull beige of the stairwell. I asked him how he would prove that he was my father . . . I thought that question would throw him off balance completely. He told me that I have a scar on my left eyebrow from when I fell once in winter when I was little. He told me to open up the wardrobe and I'd see a coat with metal buttons, he'd left it behind when they'd taken him in for questioning. He told me that I was constantly asking him about his time on the front. All of this was true, but my father was a different man, much handsomer and younger than this one, and I actually even let that slip. He sat down on the steps and I could see only a dingy cap. Now I realize how stupid and cruel I was. Yet I told myself again, This is not my father, but since he's crying he must be a good person, fallen on hard times, but if my mother finds out that I've made such a person wait outside . . . So I opened up the door. He came inside, but realized that I didn't really believe him, he didn't hug me, he didn't even try to, surely so as not to scare me, and told me that he was going to take a bath. He knew where it was. I heard the water gush out. Thank goodness my mother returned then, she had heard that they had released the prisoners after an amnesty, and she had asked the boss to let her leave early.

We sit in silence for some time, then K. continues. So I would go through the '50s because of my father, he died a year later. We didn't have time to talk about anything, I never managed to pry a word out of him about it.

While K. tells this story, it is as if he has become a different person, he looks suddenly aged, nothing of his former coldness and causticness remains, even his sharp profile has retreated. He has turned into his father, whom he is telling me about, just as sooner or later we all will turn into our fathers.

Then he suddenly gives a start, realizing he has let himself get sentimental. He calls the waiter, we order a second round of shopska salad, that classic Bulgarian invention of Balkantourist from the late '60s. The white, green and red of feta cheese, cucumbers and tomatoes—now, there's clever move, I say to change the subject, serving the Bulgarian tricolor to tourists.

9.

Evening is falling around us. Once, only thirty-some years ago, the red five-pointed star on the party headquarters would have shone on our right. The 1930s-style clean neoclassicism of the Bulgarian National Bank across the way flows smoothly into the Stalinist architecture of the former Balkan Hotel and the Council of Ministers. Several workmen are scurrying around the empty space left by the mausoleum.

What are they doing, they're not going to reconstruct the mausoleum, are they?

In a certain sense, they are, K. replies. You do know, right, that tomorrow the Soc rally will be here. I wouldn't be surprised if they rebuilt it.

With no body inside, I assume.

Who knows? K smiles sourly.

I've ordered a "triple with sides" because of the name, which immediately brought back memories of long-ago summers at the seaside, when my father would proudly order us those classic three sausages with sides, a single portion for my brother and me to share. That's what it meant to be like the grown-ups.

Like from back in the day, the waiter says conspiratorially as he brings them over.

I hope they're a little fresher than that, I quip.

K. looks at my plate with slight disdain: isn't that a little too Soc?

Actually, it's a little too salty, I reply, biting into to one of the sausages of coarsely ground meat just like the ones back then, with little bits of bone here and there that could do a number on one of your fillings. *Ajvar*, boiled beans, and overfried potatoes—the holy trinity of side dishes.

He has ordered *vinen kebap*, a classic dish of pork in wine sauce. The food isn't very good, but at least the portions are enormous.

So you've already realized that it'll be a choice between nationalism and socialism, K. says. That's how bad things have gotten. If you ask me which is the lesser of two evils, I don't know. Not that there wasn't nationalism in late Soc, of course.

Then he goes into his favorite role of professor and the table becomes his lectern. At one point our two plates join the action as well—my trio of sausages with sides is the Soc movement, while his *vinen kebap* becomes the Heroes. He says that we missed our chance to explain communism with all its horrors and labor camps and now a whole generation just takes it as a "lifestyle."

Don't go there, I interrupt him at one point, otherwise we'll end up at that eternal "back in the day we did such-and-such, while kids these days . . ." Everywhere in the world the young rise up against the old, while here the old try to pound down the young. Like Taras Bulba—I created you, I will kill you.

You might be right, he says, we did nothing, absolutely nothing . . . Here where we're sitting right now, at Five Moscow Street, you do know this was the State Security building, and here below us, in the basement that opens up onto Malko Turnovo Street, were the cells where they'd beat prisoners. They're whaling on a few scrawny kids, come on, take off your pants, but without taking off your shoes. If you can't, that means they're tighter than they're supposed to be, okay you're goin' down to Moscow Five for questioning, a few punches to the kidneys so it doesn't show, and if that's the end of it you should thank your lucky stars. What the hell is your problem, motherfuckers, why should my pants bother you, huh? Why are you beating us like dogs, what's the big deal if my pants are too tight or my trench coat is lemon-yellow or my overcoat has wooden buttons, stupid bastards . . . K. is truly livid. People from the other tables start turning around to look at him.

Look, I try to cut him off—

Hang on a second, K. says, weren't you one of the ones who wanted to make a State Security museum right here in the basement below us? Where is your museum now?

I was, I reply tersely. They ostensibly approved the idea, we wrote up fifty pages about what should be in it and how it should be presented, it was all over the newspapers for a while, and then in the end—nothing. The first excuse they thought up so it wouldn't happen was that there wasn't any free space. If the mausoleum were still standing, but now . . . Suddenly all the spaces in Sofia turned out to be taken. And so then we hit on the idea of the basement of Moscow Five. You know how it echoes in there . . . It has some kind of acoustic memory, so many people have screamed in that basement. And it was supposed to happen, but then everyone backed away from it at the last minute, we don't want to divide the people, it wasn't the right moment . . . In short—nothing came of it. You can't make a museum to preserve something that has never left.

We sit in silence for some time, the neighboring tables start emptying out, it's getting cool. Then K. takes up the conversation again. He talks about how people are sick of political parties, they're sick of globalization and political correctness . . .

What's globalization ever done to them, I try to cut in . . . and what political correctness here, of all places, where we curse out people's mothers as a way of saying hello?

Look—K. does not like being interrupted at all—something's not fair and people can feel it. While we intellectuals have withdrawn like . . . we don't even want to risk talking to them.

"Risk" is exactly the right word, I reply. You talk like somebody who should be helping the weak. But you and I *are* the weak, things have been turned upside down, when are you finally going to see that? Those guys with the shaved heads couldn't care less that some bespectacled twerp has deigned to talk to them.

You're not here all the time and you have no right to talk like that, K. cuts in.

We're heading toward a row, just like in the good old days.

Wait a second . . . So if they don't want to hear us out, what do we do . . . go try to talk to them about the liberal discourse? . . . They'll just grin at you, they'll knock your glasses off and step on them and then push you out to find your way home in the dark, in the best-case scenario. Or they'll beat you around the head with a discourse of their own while you search for your glasses. I realize I've gone too far, K. falls silent and somehow subconsciously raises his hand toward his head, as if to check whether his glasses are still there. He hasn't seen this side of me before, but I've drunk down a lot of silence along with several rakias. I went on: What does the nation-state give you? It gives you the security that you know who you are, that you exist among others like you, who speak the same language and remember the same things—from Khan Asparuh to the taste of Zlatna Esen cookies. And at the same time they have a shared dementia about other things. I no longer remember who said that a nation was a group of people who have agreed to jointly remember and forget the same things.

Ernest Renan, back in the nineteenth century, I taught him to you, K. tosses in.

Okay, fine, but what happens now when Europe splits into different times? Nationalism is territorial in any case, territory is sacred. What happens if we pull that rug out from under its feet? There is no shared territory, instead it is replaced by a shared time.

The question is: Can we make that choice, are we ready?

K. murmurs. By the way, what do you think of this whole business with the referendum? He suddenly eyes me sharply over his glasses in that way of his.

The evening wind buffets the napkins, the table is covered in glasses and dirty dishes not yet cleared away. And amid that whole jumble suddenly, who knows why, I recall that distant evening in the late 1980s, that seminar by the seaside, as if from a different lifetime. (K. was also at the table then.) And the small porcelain saucer which passed exquisitely over our heads with Gaustine's creamer.

I don't know, I reply, I don't know anymore.

I don't get it at all, either, K. says.

I realize that I've never heard this exact phrase uttered by him. Things are clearly not okay if the most categorical person I know shakes his head, uncertain.

Explosions ring out somewhere behind us . . . then a firework blooms in a trio of white, green and red, hanging above us for a few seconds.

They're practicing for tomorrow, K. says. Let's get out of here.

My erstwhile friend, the junior assistant, now Professor Kafka. I feel closer to him than ever, in the way a person feels close to someone he happens to be thrown together with during a disaster. The stars above us twinkle coldly à la Kant, while the categorical imperative is rolling around somewhere on the streets. Down below us the workmen continue building the mausoleum of Georgi Dimitrov with some lightweight materials, surely they'll be done by morning. (After all, back in 1949 they built it from real bulletproof cement in only six days. In 1999 it took them seven days to destroy it.)

Passing by them, K. can't help himself and calls out: And who are you going to put inside, boys?

Several of the workmen turn around, give us dirty looks, but

don't say anything. Once we pass by, I hear them clearly behind
our backs: Just make sure it isn't you.

10.

The Soc Parade

I woke up on the next morning with Auden's headache from September 1, 1939. It was Sunday, May 1. The perfect day for the Soc
movement—International Workers' Day, and for the Heroes—the
outbreak of the April Uprising. (Due to Bulgaria's late switch to
the Gregorian calendar in 1916, the April Uprising is now in May.)
Rallies for both of these largest coalitions, only a week before the
referendum.

I decided I needed to take part in both of them, to go undercover
as a supporter and participant so I would have absolutely authentic
insider experience and also so I would have something to tell Gaustine afterward. It wasn't hard to get ahold of costumes for both. A
costume was the password, the membership card. The movements
had even set up their own booths and were selling outfits at a special discount. On the whole, sewing uniforms had become one of
the most lucrative businesses in the country.

Strange as it may seem, under socialism tailors were a privi-
leged class. I remember how, when practicing private professions
was forbidden, in our neighborhood alone lights shone from tailor shop windows in little ground-floor rooms. We would go there,
dragged by our mothers, to get fitted for new suits. The tailor (as if
born bald, just a few strands of hair covering his pate, little round
glasses, a mustache, and shiny cuffs, a truly bourgeois character)
draped the cloth over me, made a few marks here and there with
the chalk, on the second or third fitting I could see how the cloth

was taking the shape of pant legs and sleeves that hung off my scrawny body, stuck together with pins. I was afraid of those pins. You're like a little Jesus on the cross, my boy, the tailor would say with a laugh, taking a step back, squinting his eyes, come on, now, stand up straight, just look what a fine young bachelor you'll make.

And so, between Christianity and bachelorhood, with a detour through the slap factory, we grew up. But my suspicion of tailors, with their bourgeois airs, their piousness and their pins, has remained to this day. I went on a bit of a tangent there, pardon me, but the past is full of side streets, ground-floor rooms, chalked-up patterns, and corridors. And notes in the margins about things that seemed unimportant to us—only later do we suddenly realize that the goose of the past has made her nest and laid her eggs exactly there, in the unimportant.

Anyway, I got ahold of both costumes easily and at a good price. I first put on the Soc outfit. Their rally began an hour earlier than the other. Socialism was fond of early risers. Revolutions, coups, and murders take place early in the morning, before the daybreak. Back then we all got up at the crack of dawn, not for revolutions, but for school; crusty-eyed and sleepy-headed, we would listen to that signal for the radio show *Bulgaria—Deeds and Documents* (annoying due to its early hour) and that children's song *Here at home the clock is ticking, wake up, little children . . .* For years on end to our still-snoozing ears it sounded like *Hearatome theclocky sticking . . .*

So there I was at seven-thirty in the morning, already at the underpass in front of the former party headquarters. That was the rallying point for the demonstration. I was wearing a long red tie, which hung down to my navel, its bottom part flared. I looked ridiculous in my mousy gray suit with faint stripes and pocket flaps. As a free bonus, I had gotten a real men's cloth handkerchief with blue edging and a little comb to put in the inside pocket of the jacket. I must admit that they had thought of everything down to the last detail. If they win, I said to myself, we'll have to restart production of handkerchiefs and little combs. And the whole haberdashery of that era. "Haberdashery," when's the last time I thought of that word? When things come back, language comes back as well. My shoes were shined, my socks were dark green for some strange reason, probably taken from some military warehouse. I had brought my flat cap just in case, but for now I was holding it in my hands.

Despite the early hour the square had begun filling up with early-rising Soc sympathizers. Everywhere the once-ubiquitous "comrade" could be heard . . . At first I thought that there was still something facetious in the use of that appellation, which my ears had long forgotten, but I don't think there was. I remembered how, since my father's first name is Gospodin, which in Bulgarian means "Mister," and his last name is Gospodinov on top of that, when some acquaintance called out to him on the street "Heeeey, Mister, Missssster!" everybody would freeze. Who are you calling "mister," comrade? some watchful citizen would butt in. Yet "Comrade Mister" sounded equally ridiculous.

An old man with a white beard had sat down to rest on the stones in front of the Archaeological Museum and was now struggling to get back up, without success. He was clutching his little flag in one hand and his cane in the other, and he didn't think to set down his flag so as to steady himself. I went over to help him.

Are you here for the demonstration, grandfather?

Indeedy, for the demonstration, sonny boy. I'm from the Fatherland Front, been a member all my life. Back in those days they whooped me good lotsa times, 'cause I was always pokin' my nose where I shouldn't, but I still wanna go back then if need be. 'Cause that there socialism might've been a load of hooey, but at least I got its number, it'd fool me once, but I'd fool it twice, we always found a way to work things out, but in these here new times, they rob you blind just by lookin' at you. Run you right over like a freight train, *fyooom* and that's it, you're standin' there stripped down to your underpants and no one gives a hoot.

He brushed the dust off his trousers and looked at me, his eyes narrowed. Well, now, if we turn back time, will I get all them years back, too? They can whoop me all they like, as long as I'm twenny-somethin' again.

I laughed, patted him on the shoulder, and Grandpa Mateyko (I will call him that after the Elin Pelin story about the old peasant who winds up in heaven) thanked me for the help and minced over toward his region.

Comrade . . . an older woman wearing a "party vanguard" armband and carrying a red Partizdat notebook came over to me and asked, Which party organization are you from?

(Oof, seriously? . . . Am I really going to blow my cover at the very beginning of my mission?)

I'm asking which precinct you're from.

From the Lenin Precinct, I replied automatically, expecting the woman to call over the militia officer standing nearby (yes, they had found old "people's militia" uniforms for the security guards) to haul me off the square.

Contrary to my grim expectations, she instead beamed and nodded.

People have already forgotten the real names of the precincts from back in the day, she said. I am from Kirkovski. What is your name so I can register you?

I mumbled something like Gaustinov, which the woman dutifully took down.

You can take a red flag and free carnations from those tables there, she said, pointing them out to me before going on her way.

I've seen this picture hundreds of times, I've buried it somewhere in the basement of my mind and now it is floating up before my eyes like a ghost, but one of those ghosts which you know are made of flesh and blood and which won't disperse if you stick your hand through them. And in that sense, if they are real, then you yourself are the ghost.

Men, women, the masses, the people ... Men in identical mousy costumes like mine, here and there some dark blue or black blazer. A sea of women's trench coats, beige, in the style of the late '70s, if I'm not mistaken. As if the Valentina Fashion House or the Yanitsa Center for New Goods and Fashions had again started up their production lines. Actually, I wouldn't be surprised if they had. I also noticed some more distinctly dressed women, with slightly different patterns, clearly the comrades of the higher-ranking members of the party committees; the signature of the first secretary's granddaughter was evident, she herself was a designer and "real fashion dictator," as the left-leaning sector of the media had written ad nauseum. The women sported bouffant hairdos, teased up early in the morning with plenty of hair spray, à la Valentina Tereshkova, the first woman in space; incidentally, those vintage hooded hair dryers at the salons were strikingly similar to the space suits of the first Soviet cosmonauts. I wouldn't be surprised if during an emergency all the women at a salon could just blast off directly with them. The crowd was scurrying around, women were kissing each other on the cheek, then spending a long time wiping the lipstick off each other's faces. The men were smoking, clean-shaven, with the sharp scent of cologne, eyeing their female colleagues.

I must admit there was joyful excitement in the air.

I stuck out, awkward and alone, without a flag or carnations, so I set off toward the stands. They're all gone, comrade. The woman shrugged helplessly. They promised to restock us . . .

Good God, how nice and familiar all of this was. Clearly I must have looked pretty crestfallen, since a man in the line behind me held out a pack of cigarettes: Would you like a smoke?

Stewardess! I exclaimed in utter sincerity. The memory of my first cigarette at age nine, which is also the memory of my first theft (of my father's cigarettes), of my first lie, my first feeling of being a man, my first revolution—how many things lay hidden in the tobacco of a single cigarette.

The man clearly misinterpreted my reaction and took another pack out of his inside pocket: I also have HB, from the hard-currency store.

I laughed, and only then really looked at him. He was wearing a poisonous yellow tie and his suit coat was slightly unusual, it differed from the masses around us. Suddenly something clicked in my brain, clearly it also clicked for him at the same instant. That well-known genre of reacquaintance ensued, considerably more trivial than in the time of the *Odyssey*: Is that you . . . But you . . . I thought you were living abroad. Come on, now, abroad isn't the underworld, people do come back.

Demby, my classmate from way back when, who also was my fellow student at the university for a brief stint, realized in the nick of time that literature was a dead-end street and disappeared somewhere into the parallel world of the early '90s.

We hadn't seen each other in thirty years. Last I heard, he was selling real estate and airplane parts, and opening a chain of Rosa Bella patisseries. In exactly that order.

Once he had called me to think up an advertising slogan for his chain of cake shops. Come on, he said, aren't you a poet? I wasn't a poet at all, of course, I was a sophomore in college studying literature and I was every bit as broke as my major and year demanded, so I immediately took him up on his offer and came up with something along the lines of "Our sweets can't be beat," which he absolutely loved, while I earned my first honorarium of sixty leva, thirty two-leva bills; I got the feeling they had just been taken out of the sweet shop's till and were still sticky with buttercream.

Demby, with whom I had weathered all the idiocies of adolescence, was the slyest dog at our high school, one of the most likable scammers you will ever meet. We were mutually surprised to run into each other here. All around us trumpets started playing, people were lining up in rows. Demby suddenly remembered he was in a hurry and stuck his business card into my hand: I'm here for work, he said, but let's get together when things are less rushed, and then he disappeared into the crowd. I glanced at the business card before tucking it away: Deyan Dembeliev, telephone . . . Just a name and phone number. Only extremely famous or extremely modest people could use such cards. Demby was not the latter.

Suddenly the square was transformed and the buzzing crowd started falling into formation as if on cue. Clearly there was some sort of problem with the sound system, you could hear one of the sound guys say, *Shit* . . . and it echoed across the whole square. Then, as if to cover up this gaffe, the strains of "The Internationale" blared out: *Arise, ye workers from your slumber* . . . In the very front on a platform towed by electrocars stood gymnasts in shorts, ready to make a pyramid on cue. Next to me girls waving kerchiefs and flags practiced a composition, at a certain sign they squatted down and with their bodies and flags created a face that was sufficiently vague so as to pass for Georgi Dimitrov and Lenin at the same time. I recalled that every time we were gathered around a table, an aunt of mine would proudly recount how as a student in 1968 she had been part of Lenin's mustache—at the National Stadium for the opening of the Youth Festival, in front of forty thousand people, you can't imagine how exciting it was. I also remember how every time I heard that story, I was overcome by such an urge to laugh that I always had to run into the kids' room so as not to risk a slap from my mother. My poor aunt, her whole life she dreamed of a career as an *artiste*, as she herself put it, while the role of her life had been as a hair in Lenin's mustache.

The idea for the rally to take the form of a socialist-era demonstration was not bad, but it had certain drawbacks since the space was limited. We only needed to walk about 200 or 250 meters until everybody ended up between the mausoleum and the National Gallery, which had once been the tsar's palace, which had once been the Turkish town hall. The MC's voice crackled from the speakers. Had they taken the trouble to find old speakers, so we could purposely experience that same crackling and popping like back in the day? If that was the case, then serious brains and cash were behind this movement. It was an open secret that the money came from Russia, which was gradually and very clearly turning back into the Soviet Union, returning, via referendums, if we can use that word in this case, its once-lost territories.

The MC's voice floated over the square, deep and emotionally charged. They had found an old actor with the same poignance from back then, you couldn't help but get goose bumps. Those same words about the blood of thousands of heroes, the difficult yet sole path toward the bright future, ebullience and audacity, audacity and ebullience . . .

The people around me, just like back then, hardly tried to crack the meaning of what was being said, and it wasn't possible in any case, but the very abracadabra of the utterance, the intonation and the pathos, was the little red light, sufficient to unlock the digestive juices of the past. I found a spot in the back row of the Fatherland

Front block. I caught sight of Grandpa Mateyko and we nodded at each other.

The parade set off. A brass band was at the very front, followed by a small team of cheerleaders. I never understood when socialism started allowing such erotica, clearly the senile geezers from the Politburo gave their lecherous approval sometime in the '80s. Those very same geezers, who had once ordered the police to stamp girls' thighs with permanent ink if their skirts were too short, suddenly approved these Lolitas in revolutionary uniforms.

Next the gymnasts, on their moving platform, made a living five-pointed star with their bodies, then it was the turn of the girls who had been practicing making Lenin/Dimitrov's head with their flags. This was followed by several electrocars pulling huge floats with Styrofoam constructions and portraits. And bringing up the rear were the common laborers, us with our carnations and little red flags. (I never did manage to outfit myself with either one of these attributes.) Our corps ended up at the very back of the square, by the gallery/palace/town hall, but on the upside from there you could see the whole picture. And the mausoleum, above all. As whole as whole can be, rebuilt, it was the high point of the event. You could sense real excitement ripple through the ranks as we stood in front of it. Those workers the other night really did do a good job. The mausoleum gleamed like the real thing, whiter than ever before. The soldiers in front performed the ritual changing of the guard. On cue the demonstrators began chanting three times: "Glory, Glory, Glory" . . . I wonder when they had rehearsed, chanting so perfectly in sync doesn't happen just like that. In any case I clearly had missed the rehearsal and joined in slightly out of tempo, but hey, we were from the Fatherland Front after all, the bottom of the barrel. At that moment officials began climbing onto the stage, waving just like they used to, only with their palms, from the wrist. There's choreography here, I thought. It's all been worked out in advance. I'd like to know who their screenwriter is.

Suddenly, as if on cue, the chanting died down and the MC's voice once again carried over the square. Let us welcome our leader and teacher, Comrade Georgi Dimitrov... There must be some mistake in the script, I thought. Perhaps we'll honor his memory, but to welcome him back, that's going a little far ...

And then, in the silence that had fallen, a fanfare rang out, the roof of the building opened, two flat panels slid to the side, and from the inside of the mausoleum Dimitrov's funerary bed slowly began rising, looking exactly as I had seen it as a child, with the red plush shroud beneath it, with flowers around the waxy body ... and the waxy body itself. The sarcophagus hung above the stage and those standing on it; a woman at one end quickly made the sign of the cross. The square froze. I was afraid the mummy would roll off his pedestal and fall on the heads of the officials below. I think they were afraid of the same thing. After that, the two panels soundlessly slid back together. And then—a quiet shudder of horror ran through the crouching rows because, no, say it isn't so, the mummy discreetly raised his palm, only his palm, and delicately waved. Barely visibly, almost imperceptibly. I saw several elderly women clutching at their hearts and being quickly escorted away. Immediately Dimitrov's voice joined in, some old recording saying that the path we are walking *ain't* smooth and level like the cobblestones in front of Parliament, but thorny ... These people never did learn to speak properly.

It was horrifying, I must admit that even I felt my heart skip a beat. When the recording ended, the leader of the movement came forward, a red-haired woman of around fifty, in a quintessential suit, slightly gathered and cinched at the waist, a red fichu around her neck and a red carnation in the breast pocket of her jacket. She signaled to the crowd to quiet down and began with that opening: *Dear daring comrades and compatriots . . .* Four *r*'s in as many words, clearly this was the hidden code of socialism. The more *r*'s, the better. It is surely not coincidence that they recommend that dogs' names include the *r*-sound. So they respect you when you give them commands.

11.

Collective Amnesia and the Overproduction of Memory

The more a society forgets, the more someone produces, sells, and fills the freed-up niches with ersatz-memory. The light industry of memory. The past made from light materials, plastic memory as if spit out by a 3-D printer. Memory according to needs and demand. The new Lego—different modules of the past are on offer, which fit precisely into the empty space.

The uncertainty remains as to whether what we are describing is a diagnosis or an economic mechanism.

—*Gaustine*, New and Imminent Diagnoses

12.

The Uprising

I didn't wait around to hear the rest of the speech in front of the mausoleum. It was getting late, and I still had to catch the Heroes' meeting, which was beginning five hundred meters farther down the street in Boris's Garden. I slipped away through the little park behind the town hall. I had rented an apartment nearby, where I changed from my suit coat and slacks into breeches and an embroidered vest; I kept the white shirt on, white shirts are always in fashion, wound my sash around my waist, swapped the cap on my head for the kalpak, and voilà—now I was a young hero. The puttees that wrapped around my calves and the handmade moccasins gave me a bit more trouble, but they also brought certain relief after the hard and unbroken-in oxfords. I made my way past the university, headed down through the Knyazheska Garden with the monument to the Red Army, which was now surrounded by a cordon of left-leaning volunteers who had been guarding it around the clock lately due to a recent spate of pranks. All it took was half an hour's work with spray paint in the dead of night, and the Russian soldiers would wake up the next morning as Batmen and Supermen. Actually, that was the only good thing that could still happen with that monument. I headed past the stadium and entered the recesses of Boris's Garden, which had formerly been called "Freedom Park," and before that Boris's Garden, and even earlier than that the Pepiniera or the Nursery.

Here every place is formerly something else.

I entered Boris's Garden. If one of the patriots gathered here had read that before the liberation this was exactly where the Turkish garrisons had stood, and soon thereafter a Turkish cemetery, surely they would have looked for a different rallying point. But nature has no memory, nor do people, and so Boris's Garden echoed with heroic songs at that near-noon hour, or, as they would have said back in the day—at twelve o'clock Ottoman Standard Time. As I walked past Ariana Lake, one of my moccasins came untied and I almost fell on my face.

How goes it, *bacho*, elder brother, are you in need of help? a young lad said, bending down over me.

I'm well, *brate*, brother—I tried to get into the language as well—thank you, and Godspeed.

It was a nice philological exercise. I could get into that sort of thing. Everything always comes down to language in the end. There it was "comrade," here it was "*bacho*," and language endured everything like a beast of burden, it didn't revolt. Because it remembered the time before we existed. Or because it has no memory.

Lassies decked out in traditional finery with flowers behind their ears passed me, giggling. The coins adorning their costumes shone in the sun, their ornate silver belt buckles gleaming before them. From their costumes you could tell they were from different regions of Bulgaria, the red kirtles and black embroidered aprons of the girls from Thrace, the black tunics of the maidens from the Shoplukregion around Sofia, the beautiful satiny bodices of the Rhodope lasses . . . Many companies for making men's and women's clothing, which had now renamed themselves as "studios for homespun," were sewing breeches, vests, tunics, and rebel uniforms at full steam, including for children, as if we were preparing for a new April Uprising.

It was a fine day, the May sun was shining softly, and you could say that the trees, too, had put on their native costumes, so as not to be left out of what was to happen. On the broad meadows of Boris's Garden, people were sitting in small groups. Some had spread blankets on the ground and were pulling out chicken, hard-boiled eggs, *ajvar*, whatever they had brought along.

There were men of every caliber—from smooth-faced young boys to fellows of an undefined middle age (but with well-defined potbellies) to white-haired old men. These latter were the most sympathetic, some of them were so old that it seemed as if they had never shifted to Western dress. Every man had either a saber or an old dagger or a pocketknife.

Most of them were wearing roomy breeches decorated with black braiding and deeply pleated backsides, a revolver and a dagger with a bone handle tucked into each sash. More or less every single one of them had an old rifle—Berdans flashed past, you could also catch sight of flintlocks, Krnkas from the Russo-Turkish War, and here and there some Chassepots from that same era. The more amateurish among them, having no other weapons, had come with Flobert air rifles with the buttstocks painted in the colors of the rebel banner. (Just look how your tongue begins to slide and before you know it has slipped on breeches as well, going from word to word.)

To the right, next to the stadium itself, there was a small band of cavalry taken straight out of Zachary Stoyanoff's 1884 *Pages from the Autobiography of a Bulgarian Insurgent,* or rather, the movie version of that book. Thirty or so horses with rebels mounted on them, each with a lion on their kalpak and a feather, turkey feathers, it seems to me. One of them, it must be Benkovski,* had tied up his horse and was bantering rather cheekily with some lass carrying a green rebel standard.

I wanted to mix in with some group, to hear what people were saying. I was curious, while my ironical attitude was slowly evaporating. This was my homeland, "which nationalism has stolen from us," as K. would say. I remembered sweating in grade school under my astrakhan hat, which crushed my ears, while my woolen cloak bit into my neck so badly that for a week afterward they had to slather the rash with pig lard. Every morning, instead

---

* Georgi Benkovski (1843–1876) was a leading figure in the ultimately unsuccessful April Uprising of 1876 against Ottoman Rule in Bulgaria; he was the head of "The Flying Band" or Hvarkovata cheta of horsemen.

of normal exercises, we had had to do various folk dances in the schoolyard. They always put me at the tail end of the line, but I still managed to throw off those around me. That's how it was, but didn't I secretly want to feel like one of the whole for just an hour, to laugh out loud at the jokes, to feel other bodies like mine, with whom I supposedly shared common memories, common stories? . . . And weren't they here precisely for that, to be with someone who was as confused as they are, yet proud, someone who hates Turks and Gypsies with the same passion that he loves tripe soup and *imam bayildi*, the magnificence of the Bulgarian Khans, Turkish coffee, the anthem "Get Up, Get Up, Young Balkan Hero," but also the pop-folk hit "White Rose," someone who loves to doze a bit in the afternoon, to sit down in the evening with a little shot of rakia, to turn on the TV, to let fly a juicy curse or two, to yell toward the kitchen, *Woman, where the hell did you hide the saltshaker?*, he likes for everything to be neat and clean at home, that's why he dumps his ashtray into a little plastic bag, then throws the bag outside, over the balcony railing, so that tomorrow when he's walking down the street and the wind picks up the bag and sticks it to his forehead or when he steps in dog shit, he can say, *Damn, but isn't Bulgaria a pigsty*, and again let fly a few choice curses. Who ever said that swearing is the Bulgarian satori, the Bulgarian Zen, a flash of enlightenment, a shortcut to the sublime . . . ?

Thank God the bagpipes started up with a squeal and pulled me out of these dark thoughts . . . People jumped up and ran to join the *horo*, the traditional round dance. I stepped away and saw an old man under a tree, this rally's Grandpa Mateyko, exactly the same as the other one I had seen at the demonstration this morning, so I headed over to him. I even wondered if it wasn't the same old man. He was trying to light his little pipe with tinder, hitting the steel against the flint to give off a spark. There was something of the whole of Bulgarian literature and folktales in that gesture.

How goes it, grandfather, may I sit down a bit in the shade with you? I said.

Good day to you, my son. Go ahead, sit down, the shade is for all of us, he replied without lifting his eyes.

Did your heart leap when you heard the bagpipes? I said, teasing him a bit.

Aye, my heart leapt, but my legs won't follow, the old man replied. My heart says, Giddyap, legs, but they'll hear none of it. And my ears are deaf as doornails, as well, and my eyes can't see. I'm like Balkandzhi Yovo* himself, the old man said with a laugh. The years are the biggest Turk of them all, they've taken everything from me. Without even asking. I used to spin songs, but my *gadulka* burned up, so now I just play on a pear leaf, but nowadays you can't even find a pear tree anymore. I can sing you the songs of Botev and Vazov from beginning to end. I'm from Baldevo, have you heard of Baldevo?

I knew of the beggars of Baldevo, who were the descendants of Tsar Samuel's blinded soldiers who scattered across the land after the grimmest of Bulgarian defeats in 1014 and became wandering *gusla* players and singers on the bridges and squares. To earn a crust of bread with songs about misfortunes and blinded soldiers. The old man was visibly delighted that someone had heard of this.

Well, I'm from their stock, he said, and now look, with time I, too, have gone blind like one of Samuel's soldiers.

Have you anyone to help you? I asked.

I do, my granddaughter brought me here, she's surely joined the

---

* Reference to the poem by Pencho Slaveykov (1866–1912) in which the Ottomans repeatedly ask Yovo from the Balkan Mountains to give up his beautiful sister Yana. After each refusal, they punish him.

horo. Once she's had her fill of dancing, we'll head home. This hullaballoo they're kicking up, I don't much like it, nor the rifle shots.

A gentle soul, he reminded me of my grandfather. Thank goodness we have such old men, who have miraculously survived.

The *horo* was truly thundering, growing ever larger. It had begun from the upper walkways of the park, had wound around the lily pond, and was now heading down toward Ariana Lake and the entrance to the garden. Soon it reached Eagles' Bridge itself. I don't know if they had a permit to block traffic on Tsarigrad Road, but who would have the guts to stop them? There was something telling about the emptiness of the highway that led to that outsized Bulgarian dream of yore. The song "A Din Rising near the Bosporus" tells us of Tsar Simeon before the walls of Tsarigrad, a city that would never be his, a city the Greeks called Constantinople. But just the fact that the Byzantine emperor Romanos *trembled* was still enough for the long-suffering Bulgarian soul. Besides, every day buses dumped Simeon's descendants out onto the Kapali Carsi Market. Why bother conquering a city when you can bargain for it?

Indeed, the *horo* was growing by the minute, leaping over the guardrails of Tsarigrad Road and again winding through Eagles' Bridge and into the park.

Eee-hooo-eee-hoo-hoooo, the dancers whooped and hooted. . . . If someone were to give the command, "Onward! To Tsarigrad!" at this moment, the dance line would head there, to the east, like a dragon, snaking along the highway the whole way, until it finally halted before them there *Tsarigrad Palaces*, surrounding its walls on all sides and splashing straight across the Bosporus. And when the noose tightened around the city, when the bagpipes wailed and the *horo*-siege surrounded it, wouldn't the city fall? Of course it would fall, and it would join the *horo*, to boot. The *horo*, now, there's the secret Bulgarian strike troops, the Bulgarian Trojan horse.

Georgi Gospodinov

Young Heroes disguised as *horo*-dancing revelers, but with pistols tucked in their breeches. There's an Odyssean slyness here, Clever Peter* and Wily Odysseus rolled into one.

Suddenly there was a noise above Boris's Garden and a shadow slowly floated over the trees, even though there wasn't a cloud in the sky. Everyone immediately looked up. A Bulgarian flag, carried by three hundred drones, as they wrote in the papers afterward, was flying in the heavens above us. The largest Bulgarian flag ever unfurled, a candidate for the *Guinness Book of World Records*. (Here Wagner's "Ride of the Valkyries" would have fit perfectly, even though the organizers had chosen "Izlel e Delyo Haydutin," the Bulgarian folk song that had gone into space on *Voyager*, instead.)

There was something strange about the whole sight, reminiscent of a postapocalyptic film. The drones buzzed solemnly, pulling the flag, the end of which was not in sight. Down below some people with breeches and rifles from the nineteenth century hurled their hats into the air and shouted hurrah . . . When the drones had covered the whole patch of sky above the park with astounding accuracy, they paused over the heads of the flabbergasted people.

A sky made of silk so grand, that is my fair homeland . . . Someone started singing a socialist children's song from the improvised stage, but no other voices joined in and he awkwardly fell silent. Then one of the leaders of the movement grabbed a megaphone and gave the password: *Bul-ga-ro young hero!* The chant was taken up immediately; it echoed off the hills and valleys, slammed into the buildings on the other side of Tsarigrad Road, and returned amid the trees of Boris's Garden. *Bul-ga-ro young hero!* . . . people shouted, their eyes gazing up at the drones as if greeting them.

One bold lad not far from me could no longer contain himself.

* A classic trickster character from Bulgarian folktales.

He lifted his Mannlicher and let off a joyful shot into the sky, just as he'd seen people do in the movies. Knock it off, you're gonna punch holes in the flag, an older compatriot sitting next to him, perhaps the leader of their rebel band, immediately scolded him. The lad blushed and lowered his rifle, but the signal had been given and around us shots rang out from rifles and revolvers ("levorvers," as they once wrote, and how nice that sounds). Several drones were hit, and they sputtered and fell into the crowd below. Thank God there were no casualties. It was strange to witness the murder of a drone, like seeing a goose shot in flight; no feathers went flying, but still you get the sense of a shot-down bird.

Right at that moment, as if on cue (no one ever did figure out whether this was part of the scenario or if it was due to the sudden shooting), the drones opened their pincers in perfect sync and disappeared to the west, while the flag, left hanging on its lonesome in the air, seemed surprised for a moment before slowly starting to fall; it descended somewhat silkily, embracing the trees, the bushes, the slides, and the stone elephant on the playground, the pond with the lilies, the benches, the gazebos, the monuments to poets and generals, Benkovski's cavalry, and the people with all their riflery. Those people at the edges of the park managed to escape, a few of the more frightened women and children also took off running immediately, but most people remained standing underneath it. Where there were tall pines and chestnuts, something like enormous circus tents were formed, while on the slopes and meadows the fabric settled flat on the ground and the bodies of those pressed beneath it could be seen scurrying around, and here and there people screamed that they were suffocating, so someone was forced to slice through the sacred cloth with a knife. Boris's Garden was covered with the largest Bulgarian flag ever made, more than three square kilometers, as if wrapped by Christo, whom most of the young heroes otherwise lambasted.

Thank God I ended up near the tall chestnut that Grandpa Mateyko had been sitting under. There was air here, it was even pleasant, except for the intense aroma of the cloth and hand-wipes. It turns out the flag had been spritzed with rosewater and Boris's Garden was now transformed into the Valley of Roses, to the horror of those wheezing and hacking beneath it. Those daggers and sabers at long last came in handy for the liberation of the suffering people. Screams, coughs, and curses rang through the air, people called out their lost loved ones' names. All of this spoiled the planned re-creation of the outbreak of the April Uprising. The cherrywood cannon never did end up firing; they had a hard enough time getting it to fire back in the day, and now under the cloth it would only asphyxiate the populace. Of the cavalry only a few horses could be seen, frantically racing around in a circle crazed with fear and at risk of trampling their fallen riders. From the very hill that was supposed to have represented Shipka Pass and from which for the sake of historical accuracy they were supposed to hurl *stones and wood*, only muffled groans floated, along with a lonely voice reciting the famous poem over the loudspeakers.

The uprising was headed for disaster, just as it had historically. And this made the reenactment absolutely authentic.

13.

The May twilight was delicately trying to conceal the remnants of the rebellious afternoon, the scraps of flag on the chestnuts in Boris's Garden, empty bottles, newspapers, wrappers . . . I don't know who cleans up after every revolution.

I walked up Krakra Street toward the Doctors' Garden. I didn't feel like going home yet, so I went into the café at the Union of Architects, a place where I used to spend almost all my afternoons at one point. They had a cozy little courtyard with a garden, the perfect place for reading and reflecting, unless you run into a chatty friend, of course. I called Gaustine's phone number at the clinic. I wanted to give him a brief report. It rang and rang, so I hung up. I told myself it would be better to write him, since he didn't like phones in any case.

Then I decided to call Demby. I took out his card and dialed his number. Again it rang and rang with no answer. I texted him that it was me and suggested we meet up. A minute later I got a message. Demby apologized, but he'd had a really rough day and invited me to meet him for a coffee at his office in the Central Bathhouse the next day instead.

The Union of Architects' courtyard was rather quiet. After a whole day of demonstrations and uprisings it was as if nothing had happened. Several elderly aristocratic-looking couples were gathered at a larger table in the corner, demurely celebrating something—an anniversary, perhaps a diamond one, or simply the fact that they were still alive. Not far from me a young couple were kissing. Now, there are things that don't change, I thought, trying not to look in their direction. I also tried to imagine how this café and its courtyard would look if the Heroes won. Would they lug the cherrywood cannon up to the entrance, would they switch out the glass cups for clay ones, those traditional Bulgarian ceramics? Would they cover the tables with folky red woven cloths? Would the pleasantly spacey waitress be forced to don a tunic with decorative coins and tie a colorful kerchief on her head? Would the soft jazz be replaced by folk music? Would at least a couple neutral places remain for citizens exhausted by history?

Perhaps, in place of all the wonderful polyglot flowers that grew here, they would plant the new sort of tulip known as the

National—with blossoms of white fusing into green and red. After many attempts, a gardener had succeeded in isolating this variety. To force green into the petals of a tulip was to do violence to its essence, which has preserved green for the stem and leaves, but not for the flowers.

People believe that no matter what happens, the inviolable consolation of nature will remain. There will always be spring, summer, and fall, replaced by winter and then in turn by spring. But even this is not guaranteed. Incidentally, according to the Celts, one of the first signs of the apocalypse is the mixing of the seasons.

At that moment shots rang out clearly somewhere nearby. After a whole day of clamor and commotion, this did not faze me at all, but I thought I heard a round of machine gun fire, and the sirens of ambulances and police cars confirmed that something really had happened. High-profile killings in the center of Sofia were the trademark not only of the 1990s and the 1920s, but also of the late nineteenth century. One prime minister was blown up here on Tsar Osvoboditel, another hacked to pieces right over there on Rakovski. Just so you know where you are.

I paid and got up to leave, having had enough emotional upheaval for one day. When I got home, I turned on the news and saw that at the Monument to the Soviet Army there had been a clash between participants in the two rallies. Two of the Heroes had been seriously injured, most likely shot by a Shpagin submachine gun from the era of World War Two, the reporter clarified. The monument was on the border between the two rallies. In the segment, the wounded meekly lay there bleeding. The TV crews had gotten there before the ambulances.

14.

At Demby's

The next day I headed over to the Baths early in the morning. It had rained overnight and in the cool May dawn the city looked completely different from the day before. The sidewalks were like minefields, the paving stones would tilt and spit mud up on your pant legs. This turned walking into a peculiar exercise indeed, full of careful assessments, jumps, hesitations, searches for detours. Not walking, but maneuvering. And so, imperceptibly, with curses and surges, I reached my destination.

The Central Bathhouse, of course, had long since ceased to be a bath, but it remained one of the most beautiful buildings in Sofia, with a light, exquisite touch of Secession on the façade and rounded Byzantine contours. At the moment it housed the Sofia History Museum, but everyone still called it the Bath, in any case and from time to time some NPO would turn up demanding that it be changed back into a city bathhouse, with the large pool in the men's side and the smaller one on the women's. I made my way through the museum galleries, slipped past the golden Louis XVI–style carriage, and past a massive desk—a present to Tsar Ferdinand from Bismarck himself—that rivaled the carriage in size...

Demby's office was on the upper level at the very end of the hallway. A spacious room, chaotically heaped with objects from various styles and eras, as if it were a natural extension of the museum.

What'll you drink? he asked me as soon as he answered the door.

What's on offer?

Everything from coffee to *kumis*.

Kumis? I exclaimed. Mare's milk?

Yes, along with a Proto-Bulgarian breakfast, Demby replied, it's been selling like hotcakes lately. Porridge from millet, boiled bulgur, and a thinly sliced strip of jerky. Try it.

And he whipped a sheet off the little table next to him, where the foods had been laid out.

Dried under the saddle of a horse, I joked, reaching for the jerky.

Well, that's what's written on the package, but I can't guarantee it . . . By the way, in recent years horses have gotten to be more plentiful than sheep, they've even caught up to the number of cows raised here in Bulgaria. Patriotism has turned out to be a force of production.

I chewed the thin slice of jerky slowly and with suspicion. It was tougher than I had expected and had a strange, unpleasantly sweet taste.

Oh, I forgot to tell you, Demby said, seeing the look on my face, that's horse jerky.

I could barely restrain myself from spitting it into a napkin . . .

Well, of course, the Proto-Bulgarians didn't raise pigs and cows, Demby said, they used horses for everything. By the way, that jerky is incredibly good for you, it contains two times less cholesterol and fat, plus lots of zinc, he rattled on like a radio advertisement. It just hit the market recently, Khan Asparuh brand.

He pointed out a calendar on the wall, a gift from the company, which showed Khan Asparuh, the founder of the First Bulgarian Empire way back in AD 681, sitting majestically on his horse, chewing a hunk of jerky as if it had just been sliced off that very same horse. *The taste of Great Bulgaria.* And beneath that in smaller letters: *Made from Bulgarian meat.* Now, that sounded like cannibalism.

A coffee, I requested, without mare's milk, if possible.

I drank it almost in one gulp, to wash away that lingering sweetish flavor of the horse meat. Demby offered me juice from celery and beets, and I accepted. While the blender was whirring, I looked carefully around the room. A big map of Great Bulgaria—I could not remember when exactly it had existed in this form—was hanging to the right of the door. Almost all of Europe was Bulgarian, plus two slices cut from Asia like jerky. In a small glassed-in display case behind the desk stood four extremely odd chalices. I stepped closer and saw that they were in fact skulls, carefully carved out and ensconced in wrought iron to form wineglasses.

The Nikephoros's Noggin* set, Demby called from the far corner of the room.

Several old rifles, Krnkas and Mannlichers, hung elegantly on the wall. Whenever I see a rifle on display, I automatically imagine Chekhov. Right next to the guns—an old wooden radio with a little knitted doily on top of it and a flower vase homemade from an old bottle of Vero dish soap, in which several fake lilies of the valley cavorted. Nothing brings back the past like kitsch.

Look, I know what you're thinking, Demby said suddenly, but these are exactly the type of things my clients like.

I waved off his concerns and continued my tour around the office.

In a glass carafe with a red five-pointed star on the lid floated a brain in formaldehyde, as if stolen from some biology lab. It's Georgi Dimitrov's, Demby noted casually, as he brought over the juice. They preserved it when they mummified him.

---

* Nikephoros I, the Byzantine emperor, was killed in battle in 811 by the Bulgarian Khan Krum, who is said to have made a chalice out of his skull.

At the end of this exposition wall stood a small model of the mausoleum made out of matchsticks, a very detailed work.

That burns easily, I couldn't resist.

Speaking of the mausoleum, what did you think of the demonstration yesterday? Actually . . . my company was behind the . . . re-enactment, he added modestly.

So this was what my old friend Demby had been up to.

So you're saying that you were . . . the director? I didn't know if this was the right word.

I make ends meet. With my company here, I create historical reenactments, that's my main business. I've always loved theater, never mind they didn't accept me into the theater academy back in the day.

I recalled that the demonstration had had some very subtly finessed details and I told him as much, which clearly delighted him.

That bit with the crackling loudspeakers was good, you did that on purpose, right?

What do you think? And that mistake during the sound check and the sound guy swearing . . . People remember those sorts of things. Rest assured that from all those identical demonstrations during socialism, that's exactly what they've remembered, some gaffe. And when you re-create it for them now, it takes them straight back there. And what'll you say about Dimitrov's appearance, hm? Deus ex machina. Before the rally I went down into the basement of the mausoleum. Now, there's a sight to see. When they went to destroy it, they only blew up the upper part, more or less; underneath everything is cracked, the metal reinforcements are hanging down, but the rooms down below nevertheless survived. The room for the mummy, I call it the makeup room, is absolutely unscathed, as is the elevator they used to put him on, a bit rusty, but intact. And it works. Every night they'd bring him down into the freezer, that was Bulgaria's first air-conditioning, from the late

'40s, a huge hall with pipes. Then they'd take him into the makeup room to freshen him up, to slather him with this and that, and then back to the upper world via elevator. It wasn't easy on that poor stiff, going up and down, between this world and that one. Tons of back-and-forth.

If you ask me, that part with the hand wave at the end was a bit too theatrical, I commented, sipping my juice.

What else should we have done? I do theater, not revolutions, he huffed, offended. I couldn't care less about their stupid political movements. They pay up, and I do my thing. It's the new theater, in the open air, with crowds who don't even know they're taking part in a performance. *Tragicomedia dell'arte.* Actually, some of them do know it, he added, they've been called in. I provide extras for rallies and revolutions, in a manner of speaking.

Extras for revolutions? You can't be serious, I said. Wait, don't tell me you're behind the Heroes' uprising, too?

Ah well—Demby hemmed and hawed—I'd rather not discuss it, they called me at the last minute, I had to save them. But when you hand out rifles to amateurs, they end up making a hash out of the drones and of everything—

At that moment his phone rang, and to my astonishment the sound came right from a box which I had thought was purely decorative. It looked like a mini telephone switchboard—a square wooden panel carved at the edges with a heavy black Bakelite receiver, two rows of buttons, and a round rotary dial mounted in the upper corner. They're calling me on the *petoluchka*, the five-pointed star, Demby winked conspiratorially and answered the phone. "The Petoluchka"—that mythical secret telephone network for the crème de la communist crème. Parallel telephones, parallel cafeterias, parallel villas, restaurants, barbershops, chauffeurs, hospitals, masseuses, surely also parallel good-time girls. Clearly there had always been two parallel states.

Sorry, he said, I've got to take this. Give me five minutes and we'll go out for a breath of fresh air.

15.

So these are the dealers of the past, I told myself. Demby has become one of them, a black-market player, and one of the best of them, judging from what he'd later tell me. Actually, it wasn't even a black market, this business was completely legal. He took orders from all sorts of customers, he didn't have any political prejudices. In this case, those from the '60s and '70s paid the best, plus he felt in his element there as well. He always added in a touch of irony. I've pissed on them plenty of times, as he put it. I presume that only he understood these "pissings" and they served mostly as an alibi before his own conscience.

Demby, with his well-tended beer belly, as they called it around here, had actually been chubby since childhood. Everything had always come easily to him, even back in his primary school days. He secretly drew naked women in the back pages of his notebooks, arousing himself in the process, so he'd go and masturbate in the bathrooms. At that time all the books about sex we could get our hands on, and they were a grand total of two—*Man and Woman Intimately* and *Venereal Diseases and Disorders*—condemned masturbation as a dangerous undertaking that led to infamous illnesses. (I only remember that you went blind.) For ten cents, Demby would sell us his drawings as well, so that we, too, marched blindly toward our own blindness, so to speak, adding millimeters to the lenses of our glasses. Besides, the diagrams of copulating couples in *Man and Woman Intimately* more closely resembled a cross-section of an automobile engine, with all those pistons and the like.

I remember that in our final years of high school, Demby had made his attic space into an improvised photo studio/darkroom. I clearly recall the thick curtain over the little window, the red lamp, the trays full of fixer and developer. At that time, developing a photo was a process, hard work, and, let's be honest, a minor miracle. (Where there is darkness, a miracle always lies sleeping.) You dip the photo paper in one tray, then in the other. If you leave it in for longer, the silhouettes get scorched like burned toast, and if you don't leave it in long enough, they come out pale and blurred.

I was his helper and lighting man. I positioned his grandma's old white umbrella and held the battery-powered projector. A few girls from our school passed through the studio. At some point in the session, Demby would send me out, so as not to make the "model" nervous, and they would be left alone in the darkened room. Sometimes even the neighborhood beauty, Lena, who was quite a bit older than us, would drop by. Then Demby would stay in the studio for longer. From time to time he would rent it out by the hour to guys from the neighborhood who wanted to be alone with their girlfriends. I remembered all this because, in fact, Demby took incredible photos. He knew how to measure out the light and darkness with the accuracy of a pharmacist, he played with the shadows, freed bodies from frozen and dull poses. The natural awkwardness of his so-called "models" only added to the eroticism. When he needed quick cash, he could always sell a few photos to the local Komsomol members from our school and neighborhood, who were forever hungry for naked bodies. He said that Komsomol secretaries were always his biggest customers. The deficit of eroticism in late socialism, the early corruption of youth, and the primitive accumulation of capital. Now, there's a possible topic for university economics departments.

Demby could be faulted for many things, but talent gushed out of him with generous negligence. He never wanted to develop this talent, to show off what he had made, to find his way into photographers' circles. Why should I bother, he would say, making his voice sound a bit like an Italian mobster's, I do what I want, I make enough money, and I get the prettiest girls in the neighborhood. I presumed he had maintained this standard of living up until now as well. I wondered whether he didn't sometimes secretly dream of getting out of business and going into art. I asked him. His answer was exactly what I expected: *You've always lived outside the real world.* And he added that one day, when he'd saved up enough money, he'd make only art, he'd even written down his ideas in a notebook. I wasn't sure whether he was making fun of me or if he really did plan on it.

16.

Extras for Revolutions

We crossed Dondukov Boulevard, and then the square in front of the Presidency. We could see how they were dismantling the temporary mausoleum a little farther down the street. On the yellow cobblestones, the heads of carnations were still rolling, along with popped balloons and paper funnels that once held sunflower seeds... The rain had stopped and the day was gradually clearing up. We passed St. Nedelya Church. Twenty-five kilos of explosives under the main dome, plus a bottle of sulfuric acid to asphyxiate any survivors, and at 3:20 in the afternoon on April 16, 1925, Bulgaria became the absolute world record holder for the bloodiest terrorist attack in a church at that time—150 men, women, and children killed. By the radical wing of the same party that now headed the Movement for State Socialism. If someone really wants to go back to the 1920s, they're going to have to tackle this issue as well, I thought.

The whole time, Demby was going on about how the ideologies of the past had changed the nature of the market, bringing back forgotten professions—piecework seamstresses, gunsmiths—and inventing new ones, most likely he meant his extras for revolutions. The market truly was enormous. For example, an endless and unemployed army of actors sitting around provincial theaters suddenly had their moment in the sun. It was precisely professional actors who made up the backbone of every reenactment. There was always a need for either a Thracian king or a fertility goddess, or even a Proto-Bulgarian khan with dramatic cheekbones, while all the blondes were immediately transformed into Slavic concubines in long white robes. There were roles for everyone—Ottomans, Janissaries, bandits . . . Suddenly unemployment in the theater sector dried up. Theaters no longer needed to stage plays and could get by just by renting out costumes and props, old weapons, golden cloaks and Damascene swords . . .

Then idlers of all ages who were hanging around the pubs in the towns and villages suddenly turned into "actors-in-waiting." That is, they were still hanging around the pubs, but now they had hopes, a dream, you could say, that they, too, would be called up to play perhaps a rebel or an Ottoman or even a commie guerrilla. True, Demby admitted, village folks had stopped working the land. Since you could make twenty, thirty, even fifty bucks a day just like that, why roast in the sun out in the fields? If the city council was funding the reenactment, the pay was terrible, but still, even those twenty bucks were nothing to sniff at. But if some local strongman was putting on a private theme party—say, the Battle at Klokotnitsa or Krali Marko freeing three chains of slaves—then the money was better and the job was easier, especially if you were on the chain.

Wait, let me show you something, Demby said suddenly, and stopped.

We had reached the intersection of Angel Kanchev and Patriarch Evtimiy, directly across from where Kravai Café had once been—an underground "cult" place (to use the jargon of the time) in the '80s, where the first shoots of punk sprang up in Bulgaria, in Milena's husky sarcastic voice . . . if they had picked the '80s, they would've needed to restore that place, to revive the legend.

We're going to NPC, he said.

Isn't there any nicer place? I tried to protest. The giant concrete turtle that was the National Palace of Culture, also from the '80s—built quickly, as everything had been for the 1,300th anniversary of the Bulgarian state—stood between us and Mount Vitosha. There was one enormous auditorium for party congresses and a dozen other halls scattered around the various floors. No matter what cultural event you held there, be it a concert or a reading, in some strange way everything always coagulated into a pale imitation of a party plenum. And all the clapping at the end sounded like "wild and unabating applause and cheers of glory to . . ." as they put it in those endless transcripts of party congresses published in *Worker's Deed* daily back in the day.

We went into the building through a side entrance near the giant flagpoles. The security guard nodded at us silently, then Demby used a key card to open some doors farther inside and we headed down to the basement. I had never been there before. We were walking down long hallways reminiscent of bomb shelters—I wouldn't be surprised if that was exactly what they'd been designed to be. Finally, we arrived unexpectedly in front of a large glass door that led us to a windowless hall with a low ceiling. What I saw there was something halfway between gymnastics practice, training of the national honor guard, and rehearsal for a demonstration. About fifty young men and women with athletic figures were practicing various movements. They suddenly raised their right arms, bent at the elbow, fists clenched. And at a barely visible command, they shouted, *Glory . . . Glory . . . Glory.*

I remembered how the previous day at the demonstration I had been struck by the strange synchronicity of the chanting, something difficult to achieve for people who had not practiced and who had just gathered together spontaneously on the square. As if reading my thoughts, at the next command the group suddenly broke up their perfect formation, and (well-rehearsed) commotion ensued. The one giving commands was a short man in military fatigues, I could hardly see him from where we were standing. Somebody in the group shouted, *Resign . . .* and gradually, deliberately disorganized at first, other shouts joined in. From the side it really did look spontaneous and authentic. Faces took on angry expressions for a moment. Then one man bent down, picked up an invisible rock, and hurled it toward an equally invisible building. His gesture was immediately taken up by the others around him. Soon everyone was throwing rocks at the target. I was startled when I heard the sound of breaking windows, but Demby just glanced toward the speakers. A short while later the "police" struck back and clearly started advancing, because the gymnasts, so to speak, went on the defensive. They crouched down, trying to escape the tightening noose, they took out wooden sticks that had been prepared in advance, so that for a short while the scene looked like aikido practice. The commander's voice was harshly barking out instructions and curses, *Not like that, dumbass, kick him in the balls, fall down, now yell, scream, scream already goddammit, the cameras are rolling, so they've gotta hear you . . .* that must have been directed at a woman who was on the ground shrieking . . . Things seemed to be smoothly shifting into a different phase, the victim phase. Suddenly a white-haired man appeared, his head cracked open. I hadn't noticed him before, blood (paint) was running down his temples and dripping onto his T-shirt. He ran his palm over his face, lifted his bloodied fingers over his head, and as if on cue the others began yelling, *Killer cops! . . . Killer cops! . . . Killer cops! . . .*

Get your hand up higher . . . come a little farther forward, the shrimpy commander was shouting, the cameras need to catch you, panic a bit, your head is bleeding, after all . . . go over to the police, yeah, that's it, taunt them, taunt them . . . into coming after you so they're in the shot, too . . .

With a glance, Demby signaled that we could leave if I wanted to, it had gotten pretty stuffy in there.

Those are my people, he said outside, exhaling smoke from his little cigarillo that smelled like cherry. Then he struck a ceremonious pose and quickly launched into a spiel: *The best actors in the world, either for tragedy, comedy, history, pastoral, pastoral-comical, historical-pastoral, tragical-historical, tragical-comical-historical-pastoral, scene individable, or poem unlimited: Seneca cannot be too heavy, nor Plautus too light. For the law of writ and the liberty, these are the only men.* Hamlet, Scene Three, Act Two. I know it by heart, I tried out for the theater academy with it once upon a time, disastrously . . . But now I've got my own troupe . . . Now and then I invite some of the professors to teach them. Those who sent me packing . . . I toss 'em a few bucks.

So these are the extras for revolutions, I said.

Some of them. That was the rehearsal for the protest platoon, but we've got lots of other stuff . . . Lots of other stuff, he said again.

I thought that with a hundred or so people trained like this, or probably even fewer, you could seriously destabilize governments, bring about international incidents, get into the agencies' breaking news. I told him that.

I know, he replied. But why would I do that? There's nobody

to step into the vacuum. I can destroy and turn things on their head, but I can't sustain a new installation . . . or a system, if you will. Whatever comes after that fake coup will sweep us away, too. When there is something like an approximation of a state that nevertheless maintains some kind of order, that's good for us. We work in that alimentary environment. Something like a virus within the body of the state, when the body is weak—that's great for us; but when it disappears completely, we disappear as well. We don't have any political ambitions, Demby said. By the way, I tried some social initiatives along the same lines, he said.

And . . . ?

And, well, diddly-squat . . . (a word from forty years ago, that's what we'd say back in our neighborhood).

And it was an amazingly well-thought-out project, Demby said, and waved his hand dismissively.

17.

It was time for lunch. We sat down on Little Five Corners at a place that used to be called Sun and Moon. At first glance, nothing had changed, even the name was still the same, the young man who came over to give us menus had a lumbersexual beard and resembled the poet-revolutionary Hristo Botev. (Lumbersexuals around here always resemble Botev.) The young man recited the lunch specials: Bulgarian yogurt, Bulgarian lamb with mint dip, Panagyurishte-style eggs from liberated (that's how he put it) chickens, calf-head cheese with Brussels sprouts and Bulgarian spices, spelt rolls made according to a traditional recipe, and for dessert April Uprising cherry cake or Samokov-style crème brûlée. We quickly settled on the Bulgarian lamb. Unlike me, Demby was not impressed by the menu.

It was a brilliantly thought-out project, a real social cause, he repeated. The villages and towns are full of old people, their children have left, some way back in the '90s, others later. They don't come back for years on end, their children's children are born there, abroad. And they're left alone, with nobody around. Intense loneliness, a sickness they don't put down in medical records, but if you ask me there's no more serious cause of death here. When this business with reenactments was just getting started, we went around the country and I got an eyeful of these people. And not just old people, but folks our own age as well. The wife has left for either Spain or Italy, to take care of sick people there, she sends money back home. The husband is left here, unemployed. In the beginning she comes back every two or three months, then every half year, then she quits coming back at all, first, because it's expensive, and then because she's found somebody else there. In the other case it's the husband who's left, but it's the same old story. One is abroad sending money back home, the other is here with the kids, if they have any. A whole generation who only see their mothers on Skype, a whole generation of Skype moms. And so I said to myself, Why don't I make it so those folks can hire someone once a week, for a Saturday or Sunday, a "wife" to cook you up some chicken soup, to go to the café with, to chat a bit. The kids need to sense a woman's touch around the house as well. She doesn't need to look like their mother, we're not going for doppelgängers, but as you know, to the orphan every woman is a mother, every man is a father. I offered fathers as well. At rock-bottom prices, too; I didn't add any markup for myself, I could afford not to.

At first this struck people as so absurd that they couldn't understand what was different about this idea. It was easier for them to hire someone for one night. But sex wasn't part of my package. There were several incidents at the very beginning, customers tried to rape two of the women hired out as Saturday spouses. That was five or six years ago. Now I see that they're doing something similar in Japan. It must be in the air.

It's a great idea, I said with complete sincerity. I know one person who will appreciate it. I was thinking of Gaustine, of course.

He smiled skeptically: In any case a terrible isolation is coming, clearly.

The crème brûlée we ordered for dessert had the same standard taste as all other crème brûlée in the world. Why Samokov-style? I asked Botev as we paid our bill. The cook is from there, the young man replied.

Demby went back to his office to work. In these pre-election days, he needed to make hay while the sun shines, as he put it. I assured him that I would look him up again and that I had an idea for him.

Okay, Joe, come rescue me from here when things get hairy, he called as he walked away.

Joe . . . I had forgotten that we had called each other that in school. "Lemonade Joe," there had been a Czech cowboy film of that name, and we, like the hero, took on superpowers when we guzzled down lemonade. I watched him disappear across Graf Ignatiev Street toward the St. Sedmochislenitsi Garden, and yet again on this visit I felt terribly lonely. Like a superhero who had suddenly lost his superpowers, like somebody who had traveled to the future and everyone he knew was already dead, like a child lost in an unfamiliar city, which had happened to me once, at dusk, as people were hurrying home and no one stopped to help . . . There is always such a moment, when a person suddenly grows old or suddenly realizes it. Surely at such moments you sprint in a panic after the last caboose of the past, which is disappearing into the distance. This backward draft is the same for people as it is for nations.

I needed to get drunk on lemonade right away.

18.

Late in the afternoon I sat out with my laptop on the balcony of the apartment I had rented. It was a beautiful building from the early twentieth century, one of the first blocks of flats in Sofia, actually I think it was the first, if the sign down by the entrance was to be believed. Handsome European construction, the same as what you can find in Prague, Vienna, or Belgrade. The terrace looked over an inner courtyard, clearly a common space, judging by the extent to which it was neglected.

After everything I had seen and heard these last few days and after what Demby had shown me, I wanted to grasp how far the battle for the past had really gone.

The Internet was going nuts. What I had seen on the news and on the street was magnified many times over on websites and social media. Most polls showed almost exactly even results for the two main movements, Soc and Heroes; the differences came down to a fraction of a percent, well within the bounds of statistical error. Of course, we're not counting the sociological studies funded by the movements themselves; ironically, both groups gave themselves an eight-point lead. As for the other parties, the Movement for Reason, which included university professors and intellectuals, K. among them, trailed far behind. As did the Young Green Movement, which the trolls immediately called "Young and Green." These two groups tried to unite into a coalition, which despite not yet having managed to hammer out an alliance, had already been dubbed "Smarties and Greenies." Actually, they were more or less for staying in the present, although their leaders made quite contradictory statements.

I plugged in the keyword "heroes" and one Bulgaria appeared before my eyes. All kinds of clubs for historical reenactments, patriotic associations, small and large communities, propaganda sites, textile workshops for sewing rebel flags, advertisements for native costumes of all possible kinds, tracksuits embroidered with "Liberty or Death," tank tops and other undergarments stamped with the slogan "Bulgaria on Three Seas," patriotic tattoo parlors . . . I remembered what Demby had told me at his office: I'm not one of the biggest players, but the big fish seek me out, because I do things differently, I might be creating kitsch, but at least it is sublime kitsch.

The Facebook pages of such associations enjoyed exceptional popularity. Everyone had revolutionary-inspired profile pictures, with tattoos on their biceps and chests, a few even had the whole poem about the Battle for Shipka Pass on their backs.

Most numerous were the clubs for historical reenactments, every one of them had a few hundred members and volunteers. If you counted up the weapons, the flintlock rifles, the daggers, the scimitars, the pistols and machine guns they had all together, surely it would amount to more than the standing Bulgarian army's arsenal. In a certain sense they could be (and most likely were) real combat units in disguise.

The not particularly discreet support from state institutions was immediately apparent. On the website of the Hajduks[*] Association you could see several men armed to the teeth with daggers

[*] In Balkan folklore, hajduks were Robin Hood–style outlaws during the seventeenth through nineteenth centuries who were also guerrilla fighters against the Ottoman authorities.

and pistols tucked in their belts barging into a classroom filled with frightened children. Most likely this was during the newly introduced class periods for patriotic education, since the teacher, in a blue tunic with a wreath of flowers on her head, was touching the dagger of the most bloodthirsty among them with awe. After that "the children were given the opportunity to see authentic weapons up close," as the caption below the photo explained. An eight- or nine-year-old boy could be seen gripping a revolver with both hands and aiming at the blackboard, another young-hero-in-training of the same age was trying to pull a scimitar from its sheath before the hajduks' grinning faces. All this, even though bringing weapons into schools was officially banned. The website offered special thanks to patriotic firms who had donated funds for the education of young Bulgarians.

On another page the association for reenactments had decided to offer a live performance of the dismemberment of Balkandzhi Yovo, who refused to hand over Beautiful Yana to the Turks. To this end they used a mannequin dressed in a native costume. As far as I could tell, this reenactment had been cut short because several of the more sensitive children had fainted. Otherwise I noted that "Upcoming Events" promised the Hanging of the Revolutionary Hero Vasil Levski and the Massacre of Bulgarian Villagers at Batak.

The sun was rolling red behind Vitosha like the head of a hajduk. As evening fell, the city smelled strongly of roasted peppers, that favorite, most Bulgarian of scents. If I am patriotic about anything, it would be about that scent—roasted peppers at dusk. Somewhere from the other floors, meatballs were sizzling, a TV buzzed . . . Life went on with all its scents, spices, meatballs, and fussing. It was starting to get cold, so I got up, threw on my jacket, and prepared to quickly surf through the Soc Movement as well.

19.

The Soc activists had also mastered the new media, or rather "conquered" it, as they themselves would put it. The specter of communism was haunting the Internet. Old emblems and souvenirs once again became symbols. When did all of this happen? Now, here's a site: "Let's Bring Back Socialism, Druzya," with half of it written in Russian. A video immediately starts playing—archival footage of children ritually "tapping" the general secretary and the geezers from the Politburo with decorated sticks to ensure health during the New Year at the Boyana Residence sometime in the late '70s. The old men are disoriented, they awkwardly pat the children on the head with their bear-like paws and try to kiss them. One little girl wipes her face with her sleeve in disgust and the camera quickly cuts away.

The most striking thing was that the whole site was teeming with poorly rhymed slogans, like from a children's primer. Tons of photos of the Bulgarian communist dictator Todor Zhivkov and Brezhnev, pictures of Stalin, shots from World War Two, photos of Lada automobiles . . .

Every day with iron fists,
The enemy is smashed to bits.

The left's myth remains fundamentally impoverished.

It can keep going, so that the glue of the myth holds, but they have to forget quite a few things. Forget the terrorist attack of 1925 in that church. Forget those who were murdered and buried in mass graves immediately after any coup. Forget those who were beaten, stomped under heavy boots, sent to camps. Forget those who were surveilled, lied to, separated, banned, humiliated ... all must be forgotten. And then forget the very forgetting ... Forgetting takes a lot of work. You have to constantly remember that you are supposed to forget something. Surely that's how every ideology functions.

I really wanted a smoke ... I really wanted to smoke sharp-tasting cigarettes, harsh, like from back in the day. I didn't feel like sitting around the apartment, so I went out. I passed through the little park in front of St. Sofia and came out behind the statue of Tsar Samuel that had been erected a few years ago. The sculptor had put two little LED lights in the eyes, to the horror of passersby and cats. Thank God the lights burned out after two months and nobody had bothered to change them.

If anything can save this country from all the kitsch that is raining down on it, that is laziness and apathy alone. That which destroys it will also protect it. In apathetic and lazy nations, neither kitsch nor evil can win out for long, because they take effort and upkeep. That was my optimistic theory, but a little voice inside my head kept saying: When it comes to making trouble, even a lazy man works hard.

I was strolling around outside, but the Facebook hajduks and communists were screaming in my head, and with the sobering chill of the night air it was growing ever clearer to me—there were two Bulgarias, and neither one of them was mine.

I sat down for a bit near the statue with the glowing eyes which no longer glowed. I must have looked pretty shabby and dejected, like in that old joke: *Are you a writer? No, I'm just hungover.*

A group of teenagers, slightly high, hollered at me: Hey, buddy, don't waste your time guarding Mr. X-Ray Specs. Don't worry, he's not gonna run away! They walked past me laughing their asses off, never guessing that that was the most normal line I had heard this whole week. I would have gotten up and joined them if I could.

It should be my city and my past tumbling through these streets, peeking out from around every corner, ready to chat with me. But it seemed we were no longer talking.

20.

I have determined that communication in this city has been interrupted on all levels. People don't talk across professions; doctors don't talk to their patients, salesclerks don't talk to their clients, the taxi drivers don't even talk to their passengers, people in the guilds don't talk, some writers don't talk to other writers, who in turn don't talk to yet other writers. Families do not talk at home, husbands and wives don't talk, mothers and fathers don't talk. It's as if all topics of conversation have suddenly disappeared like the dinosaurs, mysteriously died out like the bees, they've been annihilated through the ventilation hood in the kitchen or through the little window in the bathroom with the torn screen.

And now they are standing there and they can't remember exactly when and where the conversation left off. At a certain point you fall silent. And the more time that passes, the more impossible continuing the conversation becomes. It's simple, silence begets silence. In the beginning there's a moment at which you would like to say something, you even work it out in your head, take a breath, open your mouth, then you wave your hand dismissively and shut the door from the inside.

I knew some people, a husband and wife, who didn't speak to each other for forty years, nearly a whole lifetime. They had gotten into a fight about something and since they couldn't remember anymore what they'd argued about, the chance of making up was nil. Their kids grew up, raised with their silence, and then they left home. During the rare moments when they would come back, the parents would speak through them, even though they were in the same room. Ask your father where he put the scissors. Tell your mother not to put so much salt in the lentils.

When they were brought to the clinic, they didn't speak at all anymore. It seemed to me that they didn't even know each other.

When people with whom you've shared a common past leave, they take half of it with them. Actually, they take the whole thing, since there's no such thing as half a past. It's as if you've torn a page in half lengthwise and you're reading the lines only to the middle, and the other person is reading the ends. And nobody understands anything. The person holding the other half is gone. That person who was so close during those days, mornings, afternoons, evenings, and nights, in the months and years . . . There is no one to confirm it, there is no one to play through it with. When my wife left, I felt like I lost half my past. Actually, I lost the whole thing.

The past can only be played by four hands, by four hands at the very least.

21.

Chronicle

Here in brief is how events unfolded after that:

Three days before the referendum, the Movement for Reason brought to light evidence of meddling by Russian hackers in support of Soc.

That same night three activists from Reason were beaten in their homes. One of them was K.

Election day passed with a few dozen reports of irregularities at polling stations, which were ignored.

The initial election results showed an almost perfect tie between Soc and the Heroes, within the margin of statistical error.

At press conferences in the wee hours of the night, analysts noted the surprisingly conciliatory tone between the leaders of the two movements and the rapprochement between their positions.

The next day at noon, after the final results of the Soc's razor-thin victory by three-tenths of a percent had been announced, the Soc leader appeared in a red suit, and after vigorously thanking all her supporters, she invited to the podium . . . the chieftain of the Heroes. The shock felt by observers at the press conference was palpable. The general secretary of Soc announced that after a brief meeting, the Central Committee had decided to form a coalition with the Heroes, so as to preserve the unity of the nation. She pointed to the evenly split vote. For the good of Mother Bulgaria and so as to preserve the legacies of Georgi Dimitrov and Khan Kubrat,* she said, raising her voice, at which point together with the head chieftain she picked up a bundle of sticks that had clearly been prepared in advance; they tried to break it but, of course, they could not. They raised it above their heads and uttered solemnly in one voice: Let our people be united like this bundle, in their joys and sorrows, in times of joy and ill fortune!

* Khan Kubrat established Old Great Bulgaria circa AD 632 in what is now southern Ukraine and southwest Russia; all Bulgarian schoolchildren are taught the legend that Khan Kubrat tried to convince his sons to remain united after his death by the demonstration with the sticks. His son Asparuh later founded the First Bulgarian Kingdom in present-day Bulgaria.

It sounded like a justice of the peace's blessing for newlyweds.

All signs indicated that the decision to unite the two movements had been negotiated at least a week in advance (if not even earlier) and was now reconfirmed after the close election results, as predicted. But that wasn't all. Instead of picking a specific decade, Bulgaria, after much dithering, chose a hodgepodge or mixed platter, if you will. A bit of socialism, if you please, yes, yes, that one there with the side of *ajvar*. And a serving of the Bulgarian Revival, but deboned, a fattier cut.

Men in breeches lay down next to women with shellacked hairdos . . .

The second half of the speech was even more radical. After a brief pause, as if after announcing a difficult decision, the general secretary proclaimed that the two leaders had agreed to set into motion the procedure for withdrawing from the European Union and setting out on a new path toward a homogeneous and pure nation, true to the legacies of our hajduks and partisans . . .

None of the outside observers had expected that Bulgaria of all countries would be the first the leave the EU after the referendum. Being first was not part of its portfolio.

The nation nationalized, the fatherland fathered anew. I wrote that online. Less than an hour later I had been reported and my account had been blocked.

I managed to catch a flight out the next day.

The borders were closed two days later.

After a dictatorship of the future, as my friend K. would say, came the dictatorship of the past.

It's nice to know your home country so well that you can leave it shortly before the trap springs.

I had already lived through what was to come.

22.

I could imagine perfectly what happened from then on and sketch it out in my notebook.

Those who had wanted Soc received, as part of their free membership package, a ban on abortions, a subscription to *Worker's Deed*, a moratorium on travel, sudden searches and a deficit of feminine hygiene products. (Those who hadn't wanted Soc also received this.) Various things started disappearing from stores somehow imperceptibly. IKEA left the country and those for whom this had been the site of their Sunday pilgrimages found themselves suddenly bereft. Peugeot, Volkswagen, and all the other Western companies closed down their flagship stores. The Kremikovtsi metalworking plant prepared to fire up again and its chimneys belched out a few salvos of black smoke so as to announce the event. Condoms disappeared on the black market, and with connections you could still find Bulgarian-made ones of light rubber covered in talcum powder. Newspaper cut into little squares replaced the now-missing toilet paper. The erstwhile dissident act of using exactly that scrap of newspaper with the first secretary's picture on it to wipe your ass came back into fashion. Radios again were all the rage, especially the old Selena and VEF sets that could catch the forbidden wavelengths at the very end of the spectrum. Radio Free Europe, which had prematurely been closed down as unnecessary in democratic times, once again opened up its headquarters in Prague. And those who listened to it would once again be rounded up in the early morning by the people's militia in their Ladas.

In the beginning people thought that this was all a game, but the militia quickly managed to explain things clearly and firmly. A fist to the stomach, a dislocated shoulder, broken fingers, billy clubs, and kicks to the ribs—that good old arsenal from before the times of simpering liberalism was back in action. Most likely as a nod to the new coalition, the people's militia now wore shepherds' kalpaks instead of peaked caps. Reviving the network of State Security informers was no problem at all, since it had never disbanded in the first place, it had never become "deprofessionalized," as its members proudly proclaimed. And it would completely naturally pick up from the point where it had left off—or hadn't left off, as it were.

International passports were confiscated. The fences along the national border were reconstructed in record time, actually they had already begun being replaced even before the referendum, due to the migrants. Border guards returned to the once-abandoned outposts. Stores were filled with ready-to-wear clothes of several predominant styles. Quickly the fashion on the streets changed—more and more women were wearing identical suits, the only new things were the stylized traditional tunics. The old Bulgarian brands of jeans like Rila and Panaka reappeared; back in the day we would buy them and rip off the tags immediately, sewing in their place tags from Rifle and Levi's, which we'd gotten God knows where. These were topped with white shirts with Bulgarian embroidery, T-shirts of Khan Asparuh, and wide sashes around the waist.

One of the most unpleasant things for those who had grown unaccustomed to Soc were the newspapers and television from that time. Reading that officious blather was truly agonizing. The television programming ended at ten-thirty in the evening with the news, followed only by the national anthem and white snowflakes on the empty screen.

To the delight of smokers, you could now light up freely everywhere. Unfortunately for them, however, only the old brands of cigarettes were available. Stewardess was every bit as sharp as before, as was BT hard pack, the ladies' slims Phoenix and Femina Menthol had that same slightly nasty sweet aftertaste. While Arda, with or without filters, tore up the lungs of those who had been mollycoddled by Western blends.

Most people, as has always been the case, began adapting unexpectedly quickly, as if they had been patiently waiting for thirty years for those times to return. Old habits turned out to be alive and well. As for those who couldn't get used to it . . . soon disbelieving citizens who were still living under some democratic inertia (including the young) quickly started to fill up the holding cells. The basement at Moscow 5, which my friend Professor K. and I had discussed, started working again at full steam, and not as a museum, of course.

The old jokes were funny once more. And frightening.

IV

REFERENDUM
ON THE PAST

And upon turning back, they saw what was to come . . .

1.

From the airport in Zurich I took a train straight to a monastery half an hour away where I could afford a cell with Wi-Fi (what more could you ask for?) in the guest wing. The Franciscans had been taking in pilgrims for years at rock-bottom prices and I availed myself of their benevolence. I wanted to be alone for a time in peace and quiet to follow online what was happening with the referendum in other countries. And I wanted to finish up these notes, which had initially seemed to me to precede and presage what had happened, but which—as was becoming ever clearer—were actually describing and running alongside recent events. Sooner or later all utopias turn into historical novels.

I saw everything through the computer screen, shut up in this souped-up cell in the ascetic Franciscan monastery with a bell, doors, and windows that were several centuries old. The glass was a true revelation. We've gotten used to buildings and rocks lasting, but for something so fragile to have survived since the seventeenth century is a miracle, no matter how you look at it. Grainy, uneven glass poured by human hands, in which the sand it was made from could be seen. Close to the monastery there was a little farm with a dozen cows, and the cows, too, were no different from those during the seventeenth century. Animals eat up the sense of time. I dutifully wrote everything down in my notebook.

I called Gaustine and let it ring and ring. Afterward, I realized that if he'd gone down to the '60s rooms somewhere, cell phones didn't exist yet. I had to tell him what I'd seen so far. The short version was: a disaster. His darkest fears had come to pass, our darkest fears.

2.

Happy countries are all alike; each unhappy country is unhappy in its own way, as has been written.

Everything was going wrong in the family of Europe ... All was confusion in the European house.

Indeed, the Continent was turned upside down, and every member was unhappy in its own unique way. Incidentally the very word "unique" has multiplied in recent years like the Old Testament flies or Moroccan locusts, such that it has blacked out all other verbal beasts. Everything was "unique." Most of all unhappiness. No nation wanted to give up its unhappiness. It was raw material for everything, an excuse, an alibi, grounds for pretensions ...

Why part with unhappiness, when it's the only wealth some nations have—the crude oil of sorrow is their only inexhaustible resource. And they know that the deeper you dig into it, the more you can excavate. The limitless deposits of national unhappiness.

The idea that nations and homelands seek happiness is an enormous illusion and self-deception. Happiness, besides being unattainable, is also unbearable. What will you do with its volatile matter, that feather-light phantom, a soap bubble that bursts in front of your nose, leaving a bit of stinging foam in your eyes?

Happiness, you say? Happiness is as perishable as milk left out in the sun, as a fly in winter and a crocus in early spring. Its backbone is as fragile as a seahorse's. It's not a sturdy mare you can jump onto and gallop far away. It's not the cornerstone you can build your church or state upon. Happiness doesn't make it into the history textbooks (there only battles, pogroms, betrayals, and bloody murders of some archduke make the cut), nor does it make it into the chronicles and annals. Happiness is only for primers and foreign phrase books, and for beginners, at that. Perhaps because it is the easiest grammatically, it's always in the present tense. Only there is everyone happy, the sun is shining, the flowers smell lovely, we're going to the seaside, we're coming back from a trip, pardon me, is there a nice restaurant nearby...

Swords are not forged from happiness, its stuff is fragile, its stuff is brittle. It does not lend itself to grand novels or songs or epics. There are no chains of slaves, no besieged Troys, no betrayals, no Roland bleeding on a hill, his sword jagged and his horn cracked, nor any fatally wounded, aging Beowulf...

You can't summon legions under the banner of happiness...

Indeed, no country wanted to part with its unhappiness, this wine that had been aging nicely in the cellar, where it was always on hand if needed. The strategic national stockpile of unhappiness. But now (for the first time) the moment had come to choose happiness.

3.

It was almost certain that **France** would choose its own happy and renowned *Les trente glorieses*, when the economy and prosperity were growing, everyone was in love with French cinema, Resnais, Truffaut, Trintignant, Delon, Belmondo, Anouk Aimée, Girardot, everyone was humming Joe Dassin's *"Et si tu n'existais pas"* and talking about Sartre, Camus, Perec... And behind all of that stood a well-oiled economic machine. The glorious and happy thirty, between 1945 and 1975. Clearly everything in France after the Sun

King had to last a long time, their happy periods were thirty years long, as were their wars . . .

Some wagered heavily on the '60s. Of course, there was a specific favorite year—1968—invented, filmed, and made into legend. To be young during 1968, who wouldn't choose that?

It turns out that the French themselves would not choose it. The '60s were a troublesome time, the colonies were leaving, Algeria was lost in 1962, clashes with those who considered you an oppressor rather than a patron. To whom you thought you were a patron. Paris in the '60s was nice for magazine articles, cinema, and a two-week vacation, but in the end a person always chooses to live in more nondescript times. Nondescript times are the most convenient for life. In fact, the '60s had no real chance at all.

I presume that 1968 did not exist in 1968. Nobody back then said, Hey, man, that stuff we're living through now, it's the great '68, which'll go down in history. Everything happens years after it has happened . . . You need time and a story for that which has supposedly already taken place to happen . . . with a delay, just as photos were developed and images appeared slowly in the dark . . . Most likely 1939 did not exist in 1939, there were just mornings when you woke up with a headache, uncertain and afraid.

One of the most curious movements to crop up alongside the referendum would be called "A Moveable Feast"—after Hemingway's memoir of the 1920s, set in the capital of the world. The Paris of cafés in the Latin Quarter, of Saint-Germain-des-Prés, of La Closerie des Lilas, La Coupole, La Rotonde, Saint-Michel . . . the home of Miss Stein, Sylvia Beach's Shakespeare and Company, which Joyce himself liked to stop into, the Paris of Fitzgerald, Pound . . . I've always loved that book, and if I could, I surely would have voted for that decade. The movement itself had been founded by a group of young writers. But when it came down to it, not everyone wanted to live in a moveable feast. A feast is good for feasting but inconvenient for life. It raises a racket, you can't sleep, as one woman, an elderly landlady in the central quarters, said in the news reports. Besides that, the problem was that the movement mainly staked its bets on just one city, never mind that it had been the capital of the world. But France was large and provincial—the fishermen of Breton, the farmers and apple-pickers of Normandy, the quiet towns in the south of France didn't care a fig about the orgies of some scribblers who meandered from café to café, trading women and rolling around without a penny to their names in cheap hotels. The lost cause of a lost generation. The movement would end up getting around four percent of the vote, which was not at all negligible, perhaps it equaled the exact number of writers at that moment in France.

Supporters of Marine Le Pen chose a strategy that turned out to be misguided. In the beginning they decided to boycott the referendum, which actually lost them quite a bit of time, without bringing them any particular ratings. They only joined in at the very end of the campaign and to everyone's surprise they supported the Gaullist wing that chose the late '50s as the decade to return to. De Gaulle was nevertheless the strongest defender of a great and autonomous France, the man was legendary for standing up to the big dogs and championing a "Europe of Nations." Their man, *par excellence*.

So many things influenced the choice, irrational and personal things above all, that when the results showed the victory for those who voted for the early '80s, that sweet timelessness of the outgoing Giscard d'Estaing and the incoming Mitterrand, analysts needed some time to explain why this was logical.

In the end, victory went to those who had been young and active then. The 1960s came in as a very close second, only about three percentage points behind, perhaps due above all to the current anarchist movements which were gaining strength and which wanted another chance to throw the cobblestones of 1968.

Only Le Pen's nationalists would announce that they refused to accept the election results. They declared their intention to block any decision on the case in the European Parliament.

4.

Spain, with its long experience of being *unhappy in its own way*, would have an easier time of it. When you've got a civil war that overflows into the Franco regime, you can bracket off half a century without a second thought, leaving far fewer years to choose from, which makes things much easier. And if at the beginning of the century you get rid of the first few decades due to the Spanish flu, the Rif War, and the dictatorship of General de Rivera, the situation becomes simple indeed. The '80s were brilliant years, wild years, one Madrileno said in a news report. After the Franco decades, as cold and gloomy as a ground floor, you suddenly step outside, the sun is shining, the world has opened up, waiting for you to experience everything you've missed out on, the sexual revolution and all those other revolutions, in one fell swoop.

Others claimed that they had never lived better than in the '90s. The post-Franco transition was already over, things had fallen into place, the economy was surging. *There was more money than work, there was a future ...*

I didn't have the right to open a bank account or to have a driver's license, I couldn't even get a passport without my husband's permission, one woman shouted during a discussion in which some elderly gentleman made so bold as to suggest that under Franco things had been calm, and hinted at the Spanish economic miracle of the '60s.

In the end, Spain chose the "release" of the '80s with La Movida Madrileña, Almodóvar, Malasaña ... The first bare tits in post-Franco cinema, sometimes justified, sometimes not. I remember how, when these films finally reached us (we must've been seventeen or eighteen), we would make bets that by the second minute there would be nude scenes, that's why we loved Spanish cinema.

In any case, there was not a civil war during the referendum, as some observers had predicted (the support for Franco was much lower than anticipated) and Spain happily returned to the fiestas of the 1980s.

Once I ended up in Madrid toward the end of a warm September, after midnight on a square filled with young people, beer drinkers, fire eaters, weed smokers, guitar players, laughing groups of friends ... A scene that would have fit well in at least several centuries. On my way home late that night, I caught glimpses of young men and women calmly pissing in the alleyways, right on the sidewalk between the cars. That's what Madrid smelled like, beer and urine, and there was joy in that smell.

Portugal, by analogy, after a long, cold regime that ended in the Carnation Revolution, would choose the mid-1970s as a new beginning, when the intoxication of 1974 was still alive. But also when the memory of Estado Novo, Salazar, and his heir Caetano was still fresh and could be counted as part of the unhappiness of being Portuguese. A myth, which had united people for several centuries after the Great Age of Discoveries, and which had only grown stronger after the Great Losses of the Newly Discovered Territories.

I remember how as kids we would play a game called "Nations." We would stand in a circle and everyone would pick a country according to a special rhyme (*round and round the globe does spin, now which country are you in?...*), then we'd all scream, "Let it be, let it be..." France, for example. We'd all run away, then France would shout, "Stop," and would have to say how many steps it would take to reach one of the other countries. If you guessed the right number of steps, you conquered the foreign territory. There were steps of different sizes—giant steps, human steps, mouse steps, ant steps, and I can't remember what else. A simple game, in which the most important thing seemed to be which country you chose. We all pushed and shoved to get to be Italy, Germany, France, the U.S., or even "Abroad." The girl I was secretly in love with always chose Portugal. Thus I duly chose Spain, so as to be near her. In any case, Portugal didn't have any other neighbors and that geographical location spared me inevitable jealousy. I recall now how well that country fit her.

What did we know about it? It was on the very edge of Europe, small, pressed up against the wall of the ocean. A country not really known for anything. Perhaps she chose it due to its mysterious name, which sounded like *portokal*, the Bulgarian word for "orange"? I was convinced that oranges lived mainly there, in Portugal. And since it was so far away, they rarely made it here. Someone ate them up during the long journey, most likely the truck drivers themselves, because who could resist the temptation? I didn't blame them, I wouldn't have been able to resist, either.

Portokalia Portugalova, that's what I called her. That name is all I can remember of her.

5.

Unlike Spain and Portugal, **Sweden**, for example, found it much more difficult to choose a happy time to return to due to very few unhappy decades, which left far too many choices available.

Okay, so the first fifteen years of the century could easily be excluded due to the unemployment caused by a sharp increase in population, which some historians attribute to vaccines and potatoes. Then, after two major wars and a cleverly cashed-in neutrality, everything fell into place. That which had decimated the Continent had been good for the country. There would always be a need for strong Swedish steel and machine parts, especially during wartime. This explained the fact that there, on the eve of the referendum, for the first time among all the other countries, a movement in favor of the 1940s arose and even gained popularity. Someone had obligingly excerpted passages from Astrid Lindgren's diary, which gave a short and sweet account of what could be found on a Swedish holiday table in those wartime years: *a leg of pork weighing 3.5 kilograms, homemade liver pate, roast beef, smoked eel, reindeer meat*, or a list of family gifts exchanged on Christmas 1944: *an anorak, ski boots, a sweater vest, a white woolen scarf, two sets of long underwear (I give him those every year), cuff links, slacks for everyday wear, a chain for his watch, books, a gray pleated skirt, a dark blue cardigan, socks, books, a puzzle, a very nice alarm clock, a bath brush, a little marzipan pig . . .*

I don't know why that little marzipan pig stuck in my head, but clearly it had the same effect on Swedish journalists. Sweden was not a marzipan pig during the war—protesters shouted this slogan against the movement. Such prosperity was a fact, but of course the problem of guilt remained. Could a person be happy and well fed amid the hell unleashed all around? In the end the polls showed the '40s with a rather modest percentage, which put them in fifth or sixth place in the rankings, without any practical chance of success. But the very fact that the specter of the war years had reared its head as a possibility was jarring enough.

According to analysts, the high percentage of supporters for returning to the 1950s, which all surveys showed to be leading in the campaign, was due precisely to the upswing in the previous decade along with the awkwardness of choosing war, after all. But the '50s were a strong decade in their own right. The media recalled how, amid a ruined Europe coming out of the war, Sweden stood strong, with unviolated resources and manufacturing. Life was growing ever cozier. *We had a nice semi-automatic washing machine, a television for the first time, and a refrigerator yea big* . . . a woman on TV was saying, spreading her arms as wide as she could. She was around seventy, well preserved for her years. And . . . here the camera panned to the man next to her, a tall, wiry old man with a red face, who added to the fridge his Volvo Amazon, the first model from 1957, *black with a light gray top, quite a piece of work* . . . And he thrust at the camera a black-and-white photo of the couple standing in front of the car, grinning from ear to ear. The Volvo resembled my father's Warszawa, which in turn was an exact copy of the Soviet Pobeda. Those sturdy, slightly hulking cars of the '50s, solid as tanks and almost as fuel-inefficient.

Another strong and undeniable ace up the sleeve of the movement for the '50s was, of course, IKEA. Yes, that was when IKEA published its first catalog, opened its first store, and, perhaps most importantly, introduced the idea of dismantling the legs from a coffee table so it would fit in your trunk and so you could put it together at home. That's how the '50s were—practical, sturdy, cheap, a bit raw, and simple.

Their big rival was the '70s, however. The 1950s, on the one hand, or the 1970s, on the other, despite the economic crises, those were the stakes in the Swedish referendum. There was something inherently scandalous in the '70s. During the 1970s and '80s, besides the Iron Curtain, the world was also split in two in an equally categorical manner by the question every man faced—the Blonde or the Brunette (sometimes also the Redhead) from ABBA. Posed just like that, not Agnetha vs. Anni-Frid (Frida). I, with all the wisdom of my ten years, was not among the target group, but secretly, like most men, I liked the Blonde. I also already knew, however, that that was banal and that it was cooler to prefer the Brunette. Or at least to say that you did. In any case, ABBA was everything northern, light, Swedish, dancing, glittering, white—in the '70s.

ABBA or the Poäng chair, for example, an IKEA creation from that same decade, such things turn eras upside down, not the gross domestic product and the export of wood and steel. In the end, despite the crises of the 1970s and the changes of government, despite the jump in gas prices and the subsequent new crisis, despite all of that, the *dancing queen* of the late '70s overtook the Volvo of 1957 with its huge refrigerator and semi-automatic washing machine. Romance no longer lay with the fridge, people felt like dancing, and a new sentimentality was hovering over the northern waters. So, after the referendum, Sweden woke up to a new 1977.

It was no surprise that **Denmark**, too, chose the 1970s in the end, although the '90s remained in the race until the very last. Yes, there was something Scandinavian about the '70s. They resembled those New Year's cards sprinkled with white sugar instead of snow, which we secretly licked.

Because in the 1970s we started taking pleasure in life, that's what a Danish friend of mine explained to me. But what about the sixties? I asked her, didn't the pleasure start there? She fell silent for a moment, then said: You're right, only we still didn't know what to do with it then. I got pregnant without meaning to, I had a child, the father disappeared, I left the child with my mother and father, went to Moscow, to a new life, I lasted a year, Yevtushenkos were screaming in the stadiums, Ahmadulinas, children of the sixties' thaw . . . While their real poets were underground, drunk, unpublished, exiled, and I had just discovered them and then they arrested me, I got sent back to Denmark via official channels. In short, that's how the sixties ended, like a college party where you've just gotten drunk, just gotten your buzz on, and suddenly the cops bust in. Only the hangover remains. In the 1970s I already knew how to handle pleasure, we all already knew, and we lived well. Rest assured that everyone will vote for them.

Well, not absolutely everyone, but still, she was right.

6.

. . . It rained the whole evening. I woke up to the sound and lay there with my eyes closed, listening to the droplets. There was no attic, only thick roof beams from way back when. I lay there and listened. The body and the rain have an old, ongoing conversation that I had forgotten. There is a simple life, a life in solitude, which I had grown unused to. Eating bread at a wooden table, gathering up the crumbs and tossing them to the sparrows. Slowly peeling an apple with a pocketknife and realizing that this gesture exactly re-creates your father's gesture, which re-creates the gesture of your grandfather's. The place is not the same, nor the time, nor the hand. But the gesture remembers. Opening up the local paper, *Zuger Woche*, to check the weather forecast, thinking of the newly sprouted onion and a blossoming cherry tree in the yard. Concerned about a world you do not belong to. At around five, the huge Franciscan clock beyond the wall sounded, no less booming than the bell. I got up, got dressed, sat down by the window as dawn was breaking. I opened a slim volume of Tranströmer's poetry, a pocket edition, and read slowly and with an enjoyment from another time. I closed the little book and thought, if nations go back to the '70s or '80s, what will happen to the poetry and books that are not yet written and which are forthcoming? Then I tried to recall what great things I had read from the past few years. I didn't think I would have regrets about any of it.

7.

What would happen with the referendum in the erstwhile East of Europe—that part which is always preceded by the modifier "former"? Of course, everyone had long since scattered, just like a former family that had been forced to live under one roof until the kids grew up, and then everyone went their own way. If they didn't hate one another, at best they did not harbor any curiosity toward one another, either. Each wanted to go to that (Western) mistress they had been dreaming about while sharing the common socialist nuptial bed.

My final hope for returning to a new 1968 after the French failure lay precisely in this (former) bloc. And naturally, the **Czech Republic** was the most likely place for this nation of '68. To be twenty-something and to be on the streets of Paris or Prague, what more could you want? After the vote in France in favor of the '80s, half of this dream died. Paris was lost, Prague remained.

But just as in France, that which looked good from the outside did not look quite the same from the inside. The legend of '68 sounded nice, time had smoothed out its rough edges, the Prague Spring was as seductive as the Garden of Eden, minus that episode where a wrathful God came storming in. But this storming in was nevertheless a fact, and God thundered like a Russian tank and was as vengeful as "brotherly troops," a true deus ex machina, and armored, at that.

After the Prague Spring, a summer of devastation followed, and as always when life breaks, everything changes places: those who had been in the street pass into the cold shadow of that summer and all summers thereafter, while the meek poke their noses outside and are called to take up the now-empty places. It's not the clashes, the broken windows, the exiled, the imprisoned, the beaten and raped, or even the murdered ones that crush you, but rather the subtle, chilling sense of meaninglessness in some subsequent afternoon, when you see people laughing on the street, getting together, making children within that same system that has already kicked you out of life for a good long while. History can afford to make a hash of fifty or sixty of its years, it's got thousands of them, to history, that's no more than a second, but what is that human-fly to do, for whom that historical second is his whole life? Because of the afternoons that followed '68, in Prague they had no desire to choose the '60s.

And yet in the Czech Republic a lengthy battle was waged between three possible past nations. Above all, the First Republic—the Golden '20s ... an economic miracle ... a cultural boom—ranked among the top ten economies in the world, the movement's media arm recalled. The enthusiasm of a young nation that was succeeding in everything. Then came the nation from the other end of the century, the Velvet Revolution of 1989. And bringing up the rear, the Prague Spring of 1968, which, albeit the third-ranking party, was also not to be taken lightly at first. Which nation to choose, their names alone were seductive—*golden, velvet,* or *spring*? A certain character with a certain mustache peeked out from behind the '20s, one who would welcome the Sudetenlanders and turn the blossoming nation into a protectorate. Behind Prague Spring stood a cold Russian summer, behind the Velvet Revolution—the subsequent disappointments of dreams not quite come true.

In the end, fear about that which followed the '20s turned out to be greater than the fear of what came after the '90s.

The great battle of fears. And so the Velvet Revolution was victorious for the second time and the Czech Republic returned to the 1990s.

Poland also had a movement pulling for the 1920s and betting on the Second Polish Republic, but without much success. In the end things were clearly leaning toward the 1980s, with two factions. Some wanted to return to the very beginning of the decade, to the resistance, the birth of Solidarity during 1980. Supporters insisted that the enthusiasm from back then had to be reinvigorated, to start things off on a high note. They recalled how in just a few months the membership of the first non-communist labor union allowed by the system reached ten million. 10,000,000. So many years later that figure continued to look impressive.

The other faction, however, brought out the scarecrow that was Jaruzelski from that same time period, the general in the dark glasses whom even my grandma in Bulgaria used to scare me with, *Go to bed before that fellow with the glasses comes.* After 1980 came martial law, repression, imprisonment . . . For that reason, they wanted to start over fresh at the very end of the decade, with the first semi-free elections, when Wałęsa won. In any case, the faction backing the early 1980s got the upper hand. Poland even went so far as to restart two years earlier, so as to also mark the selection of Pope John Paul II, a sign from God that had given rise to the glorious decade that followed.

In the end, almost all the countries from Eastern Bloc (with two exceptions, Bulgaria and Romania) chose the years around 1989 as the desired point for returning and restarting. Of course, in this there is both sound logic as well as a personal angle. Somewhere there, at the very end of the century, everyone was, we were, young for the last time. Including those from the 1950s, who believed that the end would come and who had waited for that end, as well as the young ones from the '68s that happened and didn't happen, who saw in '89 a happy inversion of those two numbers. And finally the youngest of the young, the twenty-somethings in 1989, for whom it was the first revolution, here I can speak in the first person. Finally, the unhappened seemed as if it would happen, everything was ahead of us, everything was beginning, and at the very end of the century, no less.

I will exercise my right to marginalia, to an eyewitness diversion, because I was there at the protests in the real 1989. I jumped, shouted, cried, and then suddenly got old in the bait-and-switch of the following years. Marginalia and sheepish mourning for the '90s. The system was changing before our very eyes, promising a wonderful life, open borders, new rules . . . And at warp speed, from one day to the next. I remember how on the squares of 1989 the following exchanges could be heard: So, dudes, I don't mean to be a downer, but surely it's gotta take a year or two before things get straightened out, a friend said, I wonder whether it wasn't K.? It might even take three or four, perhaps as long as five, another suggested cautiously. Good God, how we tore into him, we all but kicked his ass, booo, who's gonna wait your five years, huh, hello, our university exams start three months from now, enough of your five-year plans already . . . At that time there was still a strategic national stockpile of future and we boldly parceled it out. Absolutely naïvely, as would become clear.

A decade later, in the aughts, that reserve was already depleted, only its rock-bottom gleamed glassily before us. Sometime around then, at the end of one decade and the beginning of another, something happened with time, something went off the rails, something snapped, sputtered, spun its wheels, and stopped.

8.

If Scandinavia couldn't decide which one of its happy periods to choose, **Romania** was also wracked by doubt, but for the opposite reasons. The whole twentieth century—a time of historical staggering and terrible circumstances, bad choices about which horse to tie their wagon to—the German, English, or Russian one? Lost territories and battles, sieges, crises, internal coups. Even the revolution of 1989 was far from velvety. It was as if only in the late '60s and early '70s a window opened briefly (and it would be chosen for lack of any other option)—an attempt at independence in a divided world. Afterward the window would slam shut in the misery of the following decade of debt, empty stores, and Securitate.

All those happy, well-fed peoples, Frenchmen, Englishmen . . . Oh, I am not from here, I have centuries of constant misfortune behind me. I was born in a nation devoid of opportunities. Happiness ends in Vienna; beyond Vienna begins Damnation! The merciless Cioran.

This describes not only the Romanian case.

The vote in **Austria** seemed to be the most fragmented and unclear. Here we had the lowest rates of voter engagement, and among those who voted, several movements, which were themselves rather anemic, received equal percentages of the vote. The memory of that colorful and multilingual empire from the first decade of the twentieth century, served up above all in literature and Secession style, was slowly growing cold like a coffee forgotten out on the veranda with a dried-out slice of Sachertorte. And it didn't end well at all—the assassination of an archduke, the Great War, disintegration, and all the rest of it . . . Austria of the Anschluss received a worrisome—but similarly insufficient—percentage of votes. Some public shame, perhaps more a habit than a conviction, still hung in the air. Austria of the '70s and '80s, that guilty pleasure of the East and West, which had turned its permanent neutrality into a permanent source of income, was the other preferred slice of the electoral pie. And in the end came the '90s, when the secret from the preceding decades could finally be revealed—the briefcases were opened, the checks were cashed, double agents claimed what they were owed by the employers on both sides.

With these absolutely unclear and tied results, spread across several decades of the century, Austria risked annihilation, stuck between neighboring temporal empires, with Vienna left as nothing more than a museum-city, which is what it has always been. A border zone in the geography of happiness.

Nevertheless, in the end the '80s scraped out a win by only a few percentage points. This victory, which most suspected was backed by a hidden nationalist vote from the successors of Jörg Haider, whose star had risen in that very decade. Watching reports from Vienna and Salzburg, I imagined how the winners from the '80s would quickly pull together a new referendum, in which—now beyond the watchful eyes of Europe, in the privacy of their own home, as it were—the Anschluss of 1938 would come. Many buried things lay at the foot of 1939.

9.

Germany remained the major, decisive mystery. There, history danced the longest and Berlin was its stage, cabaret, place d'armes, shop window and wall, everything all at once. The first half of the century was amputated, despite attempts by the new ultra-right wing to place a prosthesis in that empty space. Germany would not go back there, not yet, despite the autobahns and Volkswagens that turned up on the black market during this race. But each of the following decades had a chance in its own way. *Sociologists are forecasting a win for the 1980s,* E. wrote to me from Berlin, horrified. *Can you imagine? Not the economic miracle of the '50s, not the '60s because of '68 and everything else, but the '80s, what a disgrace. You know that I am for the '90s, didn't we always say those were our '60s that never happened in Bulgaria: the Summer of Love, Prague Spring, all that. The '90s were our '68, okay, so maybe a little shabby, a little second-hand, but still ours. I feel like living in the early '90s and if we win, come and meet me there, in Berlin or Sofia ... Much love, E.*

Sweet E. She and I passed through the first years of the '90s together, it was a tumultuous relationship, as could only have happened then. All our waiting for the '60s has finally paid off, she would say with a laugh back then, handing me her cigarette in bed.

E. and I even managed to get married, a major mistake. In the 1990s no one got married, they only got divorced. Okay, well, we also managed to correct that mistake in the very same decade. We split up, then she left for Germany. All Bulgarian students with straight-A's in German left sooner or later. I had straight-A's in Bulgarian and so I stayed.

Still, she wasn't completely right about the '80s, at least not the German ones. Something was brewing there on both sides. *Wir sind das Volk!*˙—they screamed on Alexanderplatz and the squares of the East. *Atomcraft? Nein danke,*˙˙ they chanted in the West, human chains, peace marches, red balloons, Nena, HIV, and punk. In the end, it was interesting there on both sides. At the current time, however, few of those who wanted the '80s imagined that they would have to go back to a divided Germany. But there was a way around that as well, they voted specifically for 1989, the very eve of it. Hoping to drag it out for a year or two or three. If one could remain forever on the eve of the celebration and keep the herring of enthusiasm fresh for a long time (contrary to Bismarck) in a drawn-out delay of the future, what more could you want? I imagined a permanent tearing-down of the Wall and its secret rebuilding afterward, only to be torn down again. Spinning your wheels in happiness.

Frankly, 1968 didn't have much of a chance in Germany, either. With the exception of a hard-core yet negligible group of late Marxist and arthritic anarchists (anarchists age, too), the grand year of '68 was not overwhelmed by supporters. Mostly because after it came the 1970s. And they were not an easy choice—what with Baader-Meinhof and all those murders, bombings, kidnappings, bank robberies. Between Mao and Dao, "Bandiera Rossa," Che Guevara, Marcuse, Dutschke—the mess that was the '70s in Europe. And the Second World War had ended only twenty- or thirty-odd years earlier.

Sometimes we don't stop to think how some historical event only appears to be more distant than it actually is. When I was born, the

---

* "We are the people!"
** "Atomic energy? No, thanks!"

Second World War was a mere twenty-three years in the past, but it has always seemed like a completely different epoch to me.

As Gaustine would say: Warning, history in the rearview mirror is always closer than it appears . . .

In the end the '80s won out. No, it is more accurate to say that the West German '80s won out. Except that Berlin once again became a divided city. Interestingly enough, both sides insisted on this.

Elderly Germans voted for that decade thanks to the magnificent person of Helmut Kohl, who radiated stability and security. The young, or those who had been young then, i.e., the majority of voters, chose the remnants of disco of the '80s.

In the end, the banal always wins out, the trivial and its barbarians sooner or later invade and conquer the empires of weighty ideology. The big winners in the referendum were Falco, Nena, Alphaville, the whole West German soccer team from the '80s, Breitner's beard, the young Becker and Steffi Graf, the ponderous luxury of KaDeWe, *Dallas*, *Dirty Dancing*, Michael Jackson, whom everyone was wild about here, even that ennui-inducing New Year's celebration on *A Kettle of Color* on East German television.

You always say that the eighties are the decade that produced mostly boredom and disco in the East, E. wrote me after the elections, *but clearly that's what people want—disco and boredom.*

E. was right, but there was something else going on. People also likely chose the '80s because of their upcoming end. There was something strange about the voting and this gave us a clear sign. By choosing a decade or a year, you are actually also choosing what comes after it. I want to live in the '80s, so as to look forward to 1989.

(No one paid any attention to the fact that in most of Germany's eastern provinces, the sinister Party of the '30s came in second.)

10.

For several days (weeks?) I haven't spoken to anyone. I seem to be losing my sense of time. I get up, get dressed, go down into town for fish, it's market day. I try to call Gaustine again, no luck, just a strange signal on the other end of the line. I chat a bit with the olive seller. He speaks Italian, I reply in bad German. He ends up selling me as many olives as he had intended. I roll his last words around in my head like olive pits as I climb back up to the mon-astery on the hill—*prego, olive, grazie, prego, olive, grazie.* When I reach the top, I spit them out. I've bought cheese and fish as well. I clean the fish, cut a sour apple into thin slices, then olive oil, basil, lemon, a splash of wine, and a piece of white alpine cheese. In half an hour the fish is ready. I set it on the table on my nicest plate. I pour myself the rest of the wine. I sit down and realize that I have no appetite whatsoever.

11.

The Absentee Syndrome

So many places where I'm not. I'm not in Naples, in Tangier, Coimbra, Lisbon, New York, Yambol, and Istanbul. Not only am I not there, I am painfully absent. I am not there on a rainy after-noon in London, I am not there in the clamor of Madrid in the evening, I am not in Brooklyn in autumn, I am not there on the empty Sunday streets of Sofia or Turin, in the silence of a Bulgarian town in 1978 . . .

I am so very absent. The world is overcrowded with my absence. Life is where I am not. No matter where I am . . .

It's not just that I'm not there geographically; that is, I'm absent not just in space. Even though space and geography have never been merely space and geography.

I am not there in the fall of 1989, in that crazy May of 1968, in the cold summer of 1953. I am not there in December 1910, nor at the end of the 19th century, nor in the Eastern '80s, stuck in their disco groove, which I personally loathe.

A person is not built to live in the prison of one body and one time.

—Gaustine, New and Imminent Diagnoses

12.

Switzerland's turn comes around. The country's willingness to take part in the referendum without being a member-state is one of those flattering (if inexplicable) surprises.

Months earlier, Gaustine and I had been locked in the following argument.

Mark my words, I would say, these folks here will choose the 1940s without blinking an eye, to everyone else's horror.

Look here, he would say, amid a war-torn Europe, Switzerland may have looked like paradise, but believe me, that wasn't the case. They were expecting to be attacked at any moment, warplanes were circling the borders. Hitler didn't pussyfoot around. I assure you, he even had a detailed plan to conquer Switzerland, city by city.

I loved when Gaustine spoke as if he had been an eyewitness, although sometimes it got on my nerves. How can you argue with somebody who talks as if he had been there?

Still, preparing for war is not the same as being in the thick of it, right? I sniped back at him.

I'm not at all convinced of that, he replied, sometimes it's even worse. Hearing about all the horrors being visited upon your neighbors, sleeping with your rifle on your pillow, in full battle-readiness. Burrowing into the Alps to make yourself bunkers, we called them "redoubts," hiding in redoubts, always giving larger and larger loans and concessions to the Reich . . . Especially after they had trounced the French in no time. I recall that some cities were bombed by the Allies—Basel and Geneva, for example, if I'm not mistaken, and Zurich.

Navigational errors, I retorted, using the U.S. Air Force's official explanation. As they say, nobody bombs a bank that is holding his own money.

But just look at how much money those same Swiss poured into charitable funds right after the end of the war, the Marshall Plan, the Red Cross in Geneva, that can't be denied, Gaustine replied.

And yet, they will still choose the 1940s, mark my words. The influx of gold, money, and paintings was never greater. Banks and Old Masters.

That's true, but the money went to the banks, while the people were truly poor, especially outside of Zurich. They'll never choose the 1940s, Gaustine argued.

In the end, Gaustine was right. He always was right. Even though all polls indicated high levels of support for the war years, which put Brussels on tenterhooks. At the last minute, however, the old masters of the referendum made a decision that was so logical, yet at the same time absolutely unexpected. Switzerland, surprise,

surprise, chose neutrality. A peculiar, temporal neutrality, so to speak. It chose as its period the year, month, and exact date of the referendum.

But ... but that isn't the past, the European commissioners stuttered. On the contrary, it is already the past as we speak, the government responded calmly. And tomorrow it will surely be even more in the past. And so on with every passing day.

Remaining neutral has always been a game outside of time. I don't dance to your time—for a certain time, at least. But I can measure it out for you, if you're willing to pay, I'll time it with a stopwatch (Swiss-made, of course) and I'll sell you clocks, I'll guard your paintings, rings, diamonds, and all your baggage, while you're off playing or fighting.

No objection could be made to that.

After some debate, the Europeans admitted that, in fact, Switzerland's choice did offer certain advantages to everyone. It wasn't a bad idea in this historical overturning of time to have one country that everyone could set their clocks by. And what better clock to depend on than a Swiss one? It was good to have a preserved model, a gold standard of the time that the others had pushed off from. And also, if anyone experienced severe claustrophobia from the past, Switzerland could offer them temporary asylum. A shelter.

It was also decided that it was best for the independent European institutions that would oversee compliance with the new temporal borders to be situated in such a country. In the no-man's-land of time.

13.

P.S. Italy

I had given up all hope when, in the end, Italy, with typical southern dawdling, managed, albeit at the very last moment, to save the '60s. Especially when at first nothing hinted at this at all.

If we could go back to the time of Mussolini, but without Mussolini, so many things were built back then, one man was saying on RAI 1 before the vote, with a chubby belly and denim coveralls, leaning on his little fiat. Fortunately, over the course of the election campaign such statements became fewer and farther between, a different sort of nostalgia awoke, nearer and dearer than Mussolini's highways, which turned out not to be of such high quality. Il Duce was replaced by La Dolce.

Not Il Duce, but La dolce vita! supporters of the eponymous movement wrote on the walls. We had money and youth to spend, said an Italian woman from the Piazza di Spagna in Rome, while licking her gelato, and it was like a line from a film. The economic miracle of the '50s lasted into the '60s, there were enough TVs, washing machines, Vespas, little Fiats, Fellinis, Lollobrigidas, Mastroiannis, and Celentanos to go around.

In the referendum, Italy finally chose that decade which no one had dared choose in Prague, Paris or Berlin. "Italy Saves the '60s," shouted headlines in the *Corriere della Sera* and most of the major newspapers the following day. *"Vita Brevis, Dolce Vita longa!"*

The sixties were a film most likely created in the studios of Cinecittà, but who doesn't want to live in the movies? An Italy of sky-blue Vespas, an Italy of nights, raincoats, impossible divorces in Italiano, Fontana di Trevi. The Italy of Via Veneto, of terraces and legends of the private birthday party of the young Countess Olga di Robilant in early November of 1958, where the dancer Aïché Nana performed a sudden striptease and several leaked photos inflamed the imagination of the nation. The phrase was coined, and the '60s were ready, invented, and in high demand.

That sweet life, *La dolce vita*, was possible at least in one country.

I've always thought, and as I grow older I think it more and more often, that one day we'll all go live in the Italy of the '60s, perhaps not exactly in Palermo, but somewhere there in Tuscano, Lombardia, Veneto, Emilia-Romagna, Calabria . . . It's enough just to hold these names on your tongue, the melting gelato of the names, with their soft *l*, *gna*, and *m*, and with the occasional nut of the *r*.

Once, as a young man, I found myself in a little square in Pisa, and since then I've known what the thing I've always wanted looks like . . .

It was one of those nights that you realize is not meant for sleep. You sink down into the unfamiliar streets. After a few blocks the noise has died away completely. Then you discover a piazza, with a little fountain and a church in the corner. And with a little group of friends, a few guys and girls, who have come out to shoot the breeze in the coolness around midnight. You sit down on a bench at the other end of the square, you listen to their voices, and if anyone had asked you at that moment what happiness is, you would point silently toward them. Growing old with your friends on a square like this, chattering and sipping your beer on warm nights, in a quadrangle of old buildings. Unperturbed by the lulls in the chatter, followed by waves of laughter, you don't want anything more or less in the world, besides to preserve that rhythm of silence and laughter. In the inescapable nights of the coming years and old age.

That kind of Europe is what Gaustine and I were dreaming of, it seems to me, with small chatter-filled squares. Its mornings are Austro-Hungarian, its nights are Italian. The gravity and grief are Bulgarian.

14.

The new map of Europe would look like this.

In the end, in the referendum people chose the years when they were young. Today's seventy-year-olds were young in the 1970s and 1980s, in their twenties and thirties back then. The aging chose the years of their youth, yet the young, who were not even born then, would have to live in those years. There was a certain injustice in that—choosing the time the next generation would live in. As happens in all elections, actually.

Whether the young were entirely innocent is another question. Exit polls indicated that the majority of them voted, in even greater numbers than the old, for the decades of the previous century, which they had no memories of. Some kind of new conservatism, new sentimentality, imposed nostalgia passed down from generation to generation.

The empire of the 1980s took shape as the largest and most powerful bloc, like a spine running through the center of Europe, encompassing what had been Germany, France, Spain, Austria, and Poland. They would be joined by Greece as well, that poorer version of Italy.

The northern alliance of the 1970s was the other major grouping, with Sweden, Denmark, and Finland. Here the only southern exception was Portugal. But what could be better for the northerners from the '70s than having their very own southern colony and warm beaches on the other end of the Continent? Hungary also joined this alliance, as the "happiest barracks" in the socialist era.

The 1990s, which came in second in most countries, a second-place dream and in some sense the bright future of the empire of the '80s, were actually not to be discounted in the least. Here were the Czech Republic, Lithuania, Latvia, and Estonia, still intoxicated with their post-1989 independence. Slovenia and Croatia also ultimately chose the final decade of the twentieth century, with the special clause to be included in it only after the end of the Yugoslav Wars. This was a good choice for both liberally and the nationalistically minded voters, as they each saw horizons for development. Here, in that somewhat fragmented and agitated nation of the '90s, the Irish tiger lent a hand (or rather, a paw). More new immigrants were expected, coming from other countries. The empires of the '70s and '80s would end up dropping anchor here, sooner or later. In the end clearly everyone would come together at the point of 1989.

The concentration into only three or four main temporal alliances, all from the second half of the twentieth century, no less, was interpreted as a promising step toward future unification. For some time, however, all citizens had to remain within the borders of their country and the respective decade that had received the largest number of votes. The mixing of time periods was to be avoided, at least in the beginning, until things stabilized and got going.

After that the borders would be opened. Actually, there was sharp disagreement on this point. One group, known as the diachronists, supported the restarting of time and allowing for its natural progression after the first few chosen years. The other camp of synchronists, however, demanded that countries remain in their chosen decades for a longer period. The process of resetting the clocks was slow and unwieldy, and it was not at all clear how long it could be sustained . . .

Pandora's box with its evils of the past had already been opened . . .

15.

They searched for him everywhere, including in the '70s and '80s . . . They rummaged through the '60s, where he liked to linger, but there was no trace of him. Not in the clinics or the communities of the past. Doctors from Heliostrasse and Lord knows where else called me. I, in turn, tried calling him several days in a row and after he stubbornly refused to pick up, I finally took a train from the monastery to Zurich.

It was a nice day, invisible birds called from the crowns of the trees. One woman was sitting in the sun and had opened up a book. A woman reading on a balcony. The world was still the same.

Gaustine had disappeared, of course. This was not an unusual occurrence, as far as my experience with him was concerned, but still it struck me as quite strange and to some extent irresponsible in a moment like this. Perhaps he had sensed the ticking time bomb in this whole unleashing of the past? Perhaps he felt the atomic guilt of the physicists from the '30s? Perhaps the past had sucked him in again? Or perhaps his disappearance would be short-lived, a temporary tumble into another time, from whence he would resurface very soon. For a moment I thought that he had decided to put an end to himself.

But if I am alive, could Gaustine be dead?

I remembered the little room on the '40s floor where we had met for the last time. It was his latest secret office, so to speak. It would be equally frightening to find him there and to not find him there. I opened the door with trepidation. On the desk, next to the model airplanes, lay a big brown envelope with my name on it. Inside was a sheet of paper in his handwriting and with his signature, stating that everything connected to the clinic and the villages of the past was temporarily left under my direction, for an indefinite period of time. There was something else—a yellow notebook, one-sixteenth-inch format with soft covers, half filled. I would read it later. And a black-and-white postcard of the Main Rose Reading Room from the New York City Public Library, with two lines written on it in Gaustine's hand.

I need to go to 1939, I'll write when I get there.
Farewell, your G.

Typical Gaustine. Dropping everything with two sentences. (I must admit that I felt personally offended.) No instructions, no heart, no nothing. All his projects ever only made it this far. All his crazy schemes, I should say. And my own crazy schemes, since I had been part of them, I had bought into them, I had created them alongside him. He simply jumped from a moving time, from one century to another. He had known it when we saw each other that last time, it had already been decided. That's why he had fixed me with that piercing look when I had said that we'd meet at six before the war.

He had gone to defuse the bomb of '39. I would follow him sooner or later.

What should I do with these clinics and villages of the past, now that the past has crept out of them and officially settled into all the surrounding cities? What to do with Alzheimer's homes in an Alzheimer's world? I spent several nights thinking about that. How could he have dumped all of this on me? Of course, the clinics had to stay open, the patients had the right to a protected past. Especially given the temporal chaos outside. Even more so, given the temporal chaos outside.

V

DISCREET

MONSTERS

And when the demons came out of the past, they went into man . . .

—Gaustine, the yellow notebook

I do not know which of us has written this page.

—Jorge Luis Borges, "Borges and I"

1.

The box was open . . .

In the beginning, after countries had chosen their happy decades, things were relatively calm for several months. There was a noticeable boom in old movies, albums, vinyl records, and the production of record players. Magazines and newspapers from back in the day started publishing again, telegrams, typewriters, and ditto paper reappeared . . . People had forgotten how detailed the past is and they were gleefully rediscovering things, going down to the basement, digging out old stuff, cleaning it off, repainting it, getting it restored. Collections of stamps, matchboxes, napkins, and records were pulled out. Movie theaters were showing old films around the clock, directors were getting orders for remakes, retro dance clubs were springing up like mushrooms, ever more frequently on the streets you could spot old Ladas in the East or Opel Rekords in the West, light industry was switching tracks . . .

But there were also things that could eventually upset the applecart. Sometimes it is harder to forget than to remember. For example, giving up smartphones, the Internet, social media . . . Some people did it gladly, that was the whole point, after all—to forget, to toss things aside . . . but they were quite a small percentage. The heroin of the virtual had done its job. Most people, even those who had voted for the '50s or the '60s, didn't want to give these things up. The mobile operators and social media empires also were not happy about a possible reversal of fortune, and rumor had it that they were secretly pouring money into campaigns to boycott the new rules.

On the other hand, a rebellion was simmering among those who had "lost" the referendum. Those who had voted for the '90s, for example, refused to go along with the timelessness of the '70s. Everyone wanted the decade they had voted for and which had been awakened over the course of the campaign. Anarchism and centrifugal turmoil moved upon the face of the countries. Suddenly that which was supposed to be idyllic started breaking down... Discontents began breaking off into their own communities and enclaves, marking off small territories and populating them with different times. The local once again became important.

If an uninitiated person were to set out on a trip, they could unexpectedly find themselves in a different time, one not marked in any guidebook: an Eastern European village that had broken away into early socialism, with collective farms and old tractors, a town with late nineteenth century Bulgarian Revival–era houses where preparations for rebellion were in full swing, or a forest with wigwams, Trabants, and East German Indians straight out of 1960s Red Westerns. All sorts of past eras were rolling around the streets of the Continent, fusing together and taking place simultaneously.

The old road maps became time maps.

2.

The world had become a chaotic open-air clinic of the past, as if the walls had fallen away. I wondered whether Gaustine had foreseen all this—he, the one who always made me shut the doors tightly so as not to mix the times ...

The decades were flowing like streams feeding a river that had surged beyond its banks and was pouring over everything around it, churning through the narrow streets, flooding ground floors, climbing up walls, smashing windows and going into rooms, dragging branches, leaves, drowned cats, posters, street musicians' hats, accordions, photographs, newspapers, scenes from movies, a table leg, fragments of phrases, other people's afternoons, skipping records . . . A great tidal wave of the past.

It started to become clear that the time map of the new countries would last only a short while. The demons that the referendum had awakened could not be stuffed back into their bottles. Once they had crept out, they scurried around everywhere, exactly as Hesiod had described them—voiceless, yet seductive . . .

The world was returning to its original state of chaos, but not that primordial chaos, from whence everything arose, rather it was the chaos of the end, the cruel and chaotic abundance of the end, which would drown all available time along with all creation in it . . .

The demons had been set free . . .

3.

I chose two young and ambitious doctors to run the clinic. I equipped myself with an armload of books, empty notebooks, and pencils, and went back to the monastery on the hill, behind the walls of the seventeenth century, just beneath the bell tower. From the height of the monastery (and the seventeenth century) I could better observe where the flood of the past had reached, plus it would take some time before its waters would reach me here. I also took the yellow notebook that Gaustine had left me, filled with all sorts of observations, new and imminent diagnoses (that was what he had called them), personal notes, and blank spaces that seemed to have been left on purpose. I soon began filling them up. I first marked his notes with a "G.," and then my own with two ("G.G."), but then I stopped. Our handwriting was indistinguishable.

4.

Is it possible that God is rewinding the film? We are in the uncertain memory of a God who has started to forget. To lose all recollection of what he had said in the beginning. In a world made of names, forgetting them is its natural end.

God is not dead. God has forgotten. God has dementia.

—*the yellow notebook, G.*

That which I don't dare do (or say) turns into Gaustine.

But still, he is too radical with that "God has dementia." God has only just begun forgetting. Sometimes he mixes up times, gets his memories confused, the past does not flow in one direction.

What is going through the head of a God who holds all the stories in the world? Both the happened and the unhappened. All our stories in every second of this world.

—*the yellow notebook, G.G.*

5.

I don't recall when exactly he started to become more real than me. People were reading about Gaustine, they were intrigued, they were looking forward to his next appearance, they asked what was taking him so long. The magazine in which I published short stories about him from time to time doubled my honoraria. I could see Gaustine giving me that '60s wink: Dude, half of that's mine. You don't need anything, I would reply, after all, I thought you up, didn't I? Oh, did you, now? He would arch his eyebrow. Can't you think up something better than this turtleneck and these round glasses of mine? Why don't you write in a light blue Pontiac or at least a Mini Cooper for me?

Go on, get lost, I would snap, I can spare you a Vespa and nothing more.

Over the years it became ever more difficult to discern who was writing whom. Or perhaps some third person was writing us both, without much particular effort or consistency. Sometimes I am the happier and better man, that's how they write me and I soar, but just a paragraph later they clip my wings and I'm wobbling around like a pigeon in the dust. I tell myself: Don't forget that you're from the other side of the story, don't forget that you're from the other side of the story . . . You're writing it, it's not writing you. The second you start to get the feeling that someone else is writing you, your goose is cooked, the demons have captured you, that which you fear most is upon you, your brain is emptying out like a barn in winter. No, I'm still holding it together . . . I still shut the doors tightly, or so it seems to me.

I am the one who writes . . .

When I write, I know who I am, but once I stop, I am no longer so sure.

6.

All the radio stations play music and news from past decades. What's happening today doesn't matter anymore. It doesn't matter which decade was chosen in the referendum, everyone is living in their own. We thought that the past was organized like a family album with carefully ordered photos: Here we are as kids, here's graduation, here I am in the army, my first wedding, my daughter's birth ... Nothing of the sort.

I have found a small semi-legal radio station that tries to report today's news. But it, too, is forced to broadcast the past (in all of its anarchy).

7.

Today it occurred to me to cook something I haven't tried to make since I was a kid—egg on a newspaper. This is the simplest recipe I know. You set a piece of newspaper on the burner and crack an egg on top of it. Back in the day, the problem was that there were no eggs, now there are no newspapers. Thank God I found a newspaper. I turned the burner on low, and the room was filled with a scent I hadn't smelled since I was eight years old. The scent of egg and toasted paper, a dry scent. I recalled how some of the letters would be imprinted on the egg whites. I also recalled how back then newspaper was used for everything. My grandpa would wrap the cheese in it and when we sat down to lunch I could read the headlines on the hunk of feta.

In the summer people would put newspaper on the windows in place of blinds, and also so that flies wouldn't dirty up the glass. Speaking of flies, that brings to mind the bare light bulb sticky from flies that hung from the ceiling in the village; my grandma would make a lampshade of sorts for it out of newspaper, which would quickly get yellowed and scorched.

The egg in a newspaper turned out quite tasty.

8.

I slept badly, I dreamed of a flood and wild beasts, fires . . . in short, Old Testament dreams, a true nightmare. On top of everything, I was out of cigarettes, but I didn't feel like going out, I had enough of a supply of tobacco. I just needed to find rolling papers. I didn't have any newspaper left, and notebook paper was too thick . . . I had an old notebook made of thin sheets, almost rice paper, from back in the '90s, filled with old poems which were no good in any case . . .

9.

Blind Vaysha Syndrome

A case has been reported of a girl who sees only the past with her left eye and only what will happen in the future with her right. Sometimes the borders between the past and the future grow so thin that with her left eye she sees the moon setting while her right sees the sun rising. Other times the borders grow so distant that the face of the earth from the first days unfurls formless and empty before her left eye, while before her right—the planet in its final days, ravaged and once again formless.

Blind Vaysha Syndrome, as it would become known in science, is characterized by precisely this simultaneity of past and future, with the ability (and misfortune) to see the world in its before and after at one and the same time, but never in its present, here and now. It is different from the syndrome of those inhabiting the past or of those who live only in the future, and it is twice as severe.

Clinical picture: A painful sense of not belonging to any time, quick jumps between past and future, functional blindness despite having normally functioning pupils, attempts at self-harm and suicidal tendencies. Similar to so-called *Unbelongers Syndrome*.

Patients cannot go out unaccompanied, because the street they are walking down does not yet exist for one of their eyes, while for the other eye it is a highway with cars zooming past. Experts expect the frequency of cases to double in the next one to two years.

—*Gaustine*, New and Imminent Diagnoses

Sometimes G.—I'm not even going to write out his full name— truly infuriates me. He has infuriated me before as well, the funny thing is that now he is doing it even when he is not here. The very fact that he is not here, but instead is grinning between the lines, is outrageous. His whole unscrupulous monopolization of everything infuriates me. This fictitious fellow has run wild and forgotten himself, where does he get off? Hang on a second, I thought you up, I can write you off... A single sentence would be enough, for example, "Gaustine passed away on that first day of September," and it's all over.

My whole life someone has been taking advantage of my warm southeastern heart.

10.

Years ago, while I was still traveling, I stopped into a Sunday mass at the Dominican church in Kraków. It was February, cold and gloomy, snowflakes were flitting around me. I saw a girl in a short coat sitting on the steps, parents with a baby carriage and two sniveling kids pressed up against them fearfully, an old homeless man wagging his beard in rhythm like a metronome, the faces of anxious people. I had the feeling that I had seen these same faces and bodies, this same scene, at some point during the '40s, (I was born twenty years after that.) What will people's faces look like when the Last Days come? Will those faces be marked with a sign, or will they be the same as ours?

One afternoon, years later, after yet another terrorist attack somewhere in Europe, I spent hours in the museum at the Hague. As if in a shelter from another time. It was full of people who had run away from the news of the day. A girl in jeans and a sweater was standing in front of *Girl with a Pearl Earring*. I was standing a step away from them, not moving. Their faces one and the same. So time is merely a piece of clothing, an earring . . . The gallery guard resembled Vermeer.

11.

My notebooks are full of quickly sketched faces. Faces of people who don't exist . . . Here as well, in this notebook. Just as in all my notebooks over the years . . . I have no idea who they are, I don't look for resemblances.

Georgi Gospodinov

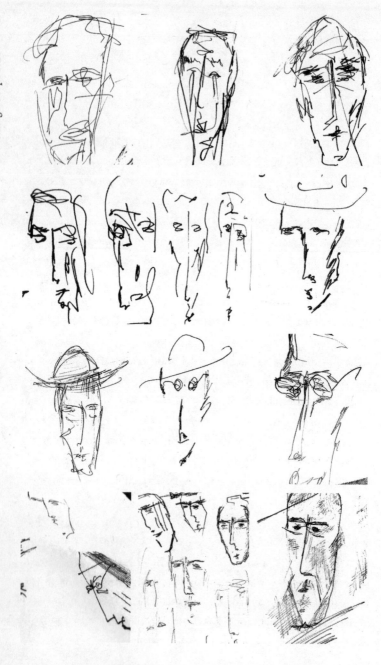

What are you doing?

    Drawing faces that don't exist.

    Have they not been born yet or they're already gone?

    They are not born yet and are already gone.

They've come up with software that combines facial features to design and produce unfamiliar faces, and they are absolutely realistic. Not a single one of them exists, as the article made sure to repeat under every photo. Yet I kept getting the feeling that I had seen them somewhere. There is something frightening in producing the faces of nonexistent people, but I can't even say exactly what.

12.

Hunger for faces. I'm nineteen years old, a guard on the Bulgarian-Greek border. I'll be there for a whole year, in that no-man's-land where if you see a human face, you should shoot it. No one has the right to cross. At the post there are twelve other soldiers and a commander—the only faces that are constantly before your eyes, morning, noon, and night. And this isn't even a prison. Every month you have the right to one day of leave. Most soldiers use that day to catch up on sleep. Sleep ranks among the most important things for a solider, right up there with food. Sex is an unattainable luxury. I use that day to go to a nearby provincial town, with a population of barely three thousand. I don't know anyone there. I get up before sunrise, walk a few kilometers, if I meet a horse cart on the way I hitch a ride, cars almost never pass by here. Two hours later I'm in town, exactly when they open the only café in the center. I sit down outside, place my order, either lemonade or Schweppes, and watch faces. I sit and watch—the faces of "civilians," as we called them back then. Non-military faces. My eyes follow them of their own accord. This is the only thing that brings me satisfaction and peace. That somewhere in this world, beyond that frontier post, there are people living normal lives. It seems so far away from me, and I'm afraid I'll never get back there "with all my faculties intact," as it says in a book, which I keep hidden in the bag with my gas mask.

The calming knowledge that there are different human faces, and the rising fear that yours is not among them. That perhaps it does not exist.

13.

I observe the world, shut up in a room from the seventeenth century, with Wi-Fi from the twenty-first century, writing on a wooden desk that is at least one hundred years old and sleeping in a bed with metal head- and footboards from the nineteenth century. I try to play out the past that lies ahead. My memory grows weak, my mind deserts me, that which I have thought up is chasing me hard on my heels, it catches up and passes me. Forgive me, O God of utopias, the times have mixed together and now you don't

know whether the story you are telling has already happened or is
yet to come.

14.

And so began the mass doubling of the happened and the
unhappened ...

In ever more detail, ever closer to the real events, sometimes even more
real than the originals. And no one could discern which was real and
which was the likeness anymore ... One will flow into the other and
when blood is spilled, real, warm, human blood, people will applaud
as if at the theater, while elsewhere red dye, extracted from poisonous
cinnabar, will be taken for blood and they shall fly into a blind rage ...

— *Gaustine,* On the Mixing of Times

15.

Burgtheater, 1925/2025

Peer Gynt, that northern Odysseus, comes home ... A furious
storm starts raging, lightning rends the sky, the sea has gone mad,
the ship shall be wrecked at any moment ...

   Suddenly, amid the thunderstorms on stage, revolver shots ring
out, coming from the audience. A woman screams in a box on the
first balcony. A bullet has passed through her right cheek, grazed
her tongue, and gone out the other side. Spectators on the ground
floor raise their heads. And, horror of horrors, a man's head is hanging over the railing. Drops of blood soak into the ash-rose dresses
of two terrified young ladies whose seats are directly below. The

266

Georgi Gospodinov

whole auditorium is on its feet. Several couples run out, there is crowding and jostling at the exits, others sit frozen . . .

At that moment a petite woman appears in the box holding a still-smoking Mauser, she offers a hand to the injured party, the murder victim lifts his bloodied face, and the three of them bow politely to the exulted audience . . .

End of the tragedy. The curtain silently comes down on the stage, even though no one is looking in that direction anymore.

One of the greatest attractions in Vienna—*Peer Gynt* at the Burgtheater. A full reenactment of the production from 1925, complete with the murder of the Macedonian revolutionary Todor Panitsa on May 8 of that same year, during the fifth act, the scene with the storm, right before the line "one dies not midmost of Act Five." The woman with the injured face is his wife. The petite woman who shot him is part of an enemy faction, her name is Mencha Karnicheva. (Her full name is Melpomena, the muse of theater, how ironic.)

The audience has come primarily for these few minutes—the shipwreck on stage and the blood in the auditorium. Who wouldn't want to get a taste of the 1920s with a murder at the theater? Tickets are sold out for a year in advance.

16.

Have we spent it yet, my dear friends, the paycheck of the future? The unbacked check of the future . . .

Even the past is now *no longer* and the future is now *not yet*—isn't that what St. Augustine says in Book XI of the Confessions?

In that *not yet* there is still some consolation, it is not here, but it will come. But what will we do when the future is *no longer*? How different is a future that is *not yet* from that which is *no longer*? How different that absence is. The first is full of promise, the second is an apocalypse . . .

— *Gaustine,* Notes on the End of Time

17.

Memory holds you, freezes you within the fixed outlines of a single, solitary person whom you cannot leave. Oblivion comes to liberate you. Features lose their sharpness and definitiveness, vagueness blurs the shape. If I don't clearly remember who exactly I am, I could be anyone, even myself, even myself as a child. Suddenly those games of Borges's, which you loved so much in your youth, those doubling games, become real, they happen to you yourself. What was once a metaphor has now become an illness, to turn Sontag on her head. There are no longer any metaphors here, as G. had said, when we met for the first time and discussed the death of mayflies at the end of the day. Here you really are no longer sure which side of history you're on. Here "I" becomes the most meaningless word, an empty shell that the waves roll along the shore.

The great leaving is upon you. They leave you one by one, all the bodies you have been. They dismiss themselves and take their leave.

The angel of those who leave and the angel of those who are left—sometimes one and the same . . .

18.

In the yellow notebook I came across the following note, which has not given me peace for a few days now.

> "While writing a novel about those who have lost their memories, he himself begins to lose his memory . . . He rushes to finish it before he forgets what he was writing."

Is he mocking me, threatening me, or offering me an idea?

19.

The embarrassment of forgetting names . . . Of course, everyone complains about this at a certain age. But I'm talking about the names of our nearest and dearest. For example, you can't forget the name of the woman you used to live with, whom you were married to for several years, and who now hands you a novel and smiles, expecting a very personal autograph. She had queued up in line at one of my rare public appearances a while ago. And . . . a total blank. I can remember her body in detail, where she has a mole, our first night together, those were five years of my life.

But her name . . . I run through a dozen or so names in my head and none of them is hers. This isn't the first time this has happened to me, but it has never been so frightening, never with someone so close. I look around helplessly, there is a line of people waiting. I know some tricks for such cases—if I see an acquaintance nearby, I'll introduce him to her so I can hear her name, but unfortunately there is nobody around right now. I go to plan B. I'll write an inscription that is sufficiently personal, but without a name. I write something like, *For the shared past we are made of.* I hand her the book. She opens it, then innocently hands it back to me: Come on, add my name, please . . .

In my anxiety I grip the transparent counter of the stand, something gives, and the glass comes crashing down at my feet. Blood gushes from my wrist, a woman in line faints, people crowd around me, the girl from the bookstore pours water on the cut and takes out bandages, the giving of autographs is suspended, the line disintegrates, two photographers are snapping away, tomorrow I'll see myself on some tabloid website . . . drowning in blood . . . but for me there is such relief in all this . . . Can I help with something? my wife asks anxiously, my ex-wife, that is, for whose sake I am bleeding like a stuck pig. Everything's fine, I say, noticing a bit of blood on her copy of the book, right by the inscription.

Would you like to exchange it? The girl from the bookstand asks.

Oh, no, thanks, it's more personal this way, Emma says, and leaves the scene of the crime.

Emma! Emma, of course, Emma . . . Like Emma Bovary.

20.

I went to see a neurologist friend of mine right away. In any case, he had long considered me a hypochondriac.

It's possible for this to be temporary coping mechanism, stress. You meet lots of people, and when we add all the ones you make up as well . . .

(He was right, I hadn't stopped to think that I also needed to keep in my head all the characters wandering around in my books; I am a softie and I don't kill them off easily like others do, which makes it ever harder to keep them in line.)

Of course, we're all growing a bit dimmer, the doctor said, neurons are burning out here and there, some connections have been deeply buried and seem lost, even though they can pop up unexpectedly one day. But not exactly at the moment we look for them. It's like with sleep—the more you tell yourself while lying in bed at night, *I must fall asleep, I must fall asleep,* the worse your chances of falling asleep become. Try to get more rest . . .

I left the office with a guilty feeling that they think I'm a faker, an inventor of my own paranoias. But what the hell was the doctor's name again? I wondered just a few yards down the hall, and went back to read the name on the sign on his door.

As is written, we drank from the waters of the Lethe before we were born, so as to completely forget our previous life. But why do we sometimes wake up in the middle of the night or why do we get a sudden flash of insight at three in the afternoon that we've already lived through this and we know what will happen from now on? Unexpected cracks have appeared. Cracks through which the light of the past streams in. And yet we are supposed to have forgotten everything.

The waters of the Lethe aren't what they used to be.

21.

I can't find in myths some great god of memory or at least a god of forgetting. Like those for love, fire, revenge . . . I can't even find demigods or nymphs. The whole of Greek mythology, which is otherwise swarming with deities, demigods, centaurs, heroes, and who knows what else, has forgotten the gods of memory and forgetting. Yes, there is Mnemosyne, but she's better known as the mother of the muses. There's also Lethe, but they are all always somehow in the shadows. Most likely when myths first appeared, the world was too young to start forgetting . . . Plus, people died young, before old age emptied their minds.

In the end, writing arises when man realizes that memory is not enough.

The early clay tablets with cuneiform from Mesopotamia do not hold any wisdom about the secrets of the world as we might expect, but rather completely practical information about the number of sheep in one herd or the different words for "pig." The first written artifacts were lists. In the beginning (and the end), there is always a list.

22.

Since nothing is happening in my life this year, I'm copying out my journal from last year day by day, a friend told me. Today, on November twenty-sixth, I'm copying down what happened to me last year on November twenty-sixth.

I've never heard of anything more depressing.

I kept a journal for a long time myself, without putting dates or years in it, noting only if it was day or night, at one point I even stopped doing that.

Now, when I find myself ever more estranged from my memory, I think it was a very stupid move. I've lost even the small reference points of the years and months. I recall some things as I read, but when they happened, a year ago or fifteen years back, it's already hard for me to reconstruct. Other things I have no recollection of at all, as if they had happened to a complete stranger and were written by someone else's hand.

My handwriting gets ever messier, smaller, and pointier. That's how I wrote as a child.

Some words are lost as soon as I write them, they simply turn to gibberish, their syllables become scrambled, the head goes to the tail, like some mythical creatures, like centaurs cobbled together quickly or metamorphized tadpoles.

Prayer—Yerpra.

Where was I starting from, what exactly did I want to say? . . . I'm trying to finish a book about memory receding and . . . I'm hurrying to finish it, before I forget what it is actually about. But if everything I write comes to pass, I need to escape into another person.

23.

First a few words disappeared. He turned it into a game, it was a long ago, they were still at the university. He told his wife and his friends those five or six disappearing words and when he needed one of them, they would prompt him—"cornice," "mercantile," "rosemary," "confrontation" . . .

One day, perhaps because he had split up with his wife and had quit seeing his friends, and because the words were multiplying, he decided to write them down. At first a single page was sufficient, then both sides of a sheet of paper. Then another, and another . . . Then he got himself a notebook. He called it *A Brief Dictionary of the Forgotten*. There was also a section for people's names. Gradually the number of sections increased—one for scents that reminded him of various things was added. Then one for sounds, he was going deaf on top of everything. (A doctor had told him that hearing loss and memory loss were related, they shared the same room in the brain.)

Finally yet another section appeared in the notebook, perhaps the most important of all—for that which had actually happened to him, so he could differentiate it from what he had read and from what he had invented.

Sooner or later everything would get mixed up—what had happened, what he had read, and what he had invented would jump up and switch places, until they gradually quieted down and faded away, but for now he was trying to hold the borders in place. Years later his ex-wife would line up for an autograph and he wouldn't be able to find her name in his head . . .

24.

It was the worst with names. And when he had to switch languages, it was a nightmare. He would forget even the right phrase to use to apologize and ask:

Sorry, your name escapes me . . . Sorry, your name . . .

Every morning he would take a blank sheet of paper and write these five words out by hand. It reminded him of punishment from back in school, when he was forced to write out words he had gotten wrong or some minor infraction like "I forgot my homework" a hundred times. From here arose his early discovery that repetition changes meaning, it removes the bones and the sense of what is written. Repeated one hundred times, everything (including guilt) disintegrates into meaningless syllables.

But no matter, he now enjoyed these memories. They were some of the few that had remained, and he cared for them as for a beloved pet; he called them over, stroked their ears, and spoke to them.

He knew that one day he would end up having to use this phrase as well:

Sorry, my name escapes me.

25.

He wondered how soon the moment would come when he forgot letters as well. They were the only thing he could not live without. He had learned to write quite young, at age four or five, which should mean that they would be the last thing to leave him. He could clearly imagine them filing out like little critters, ants or beetles, leaving this notebook, leaving the books in his library, crawling around, crossing the room and leaving en masse. The great migration of the letters. Now there's Щ, creeping out like a centipede, Б only waves and disappears with its stomach jutting out before it, О rolls around like a well-fed dung beetle, Й doffs its funny little hat in farewell, Ж leaps like a frog and vanishes through the door. I open a book at random, it's blank, only a little e drops out onto the ground and rolls behind the radiator.

A library with empty, abandoned books—with no titles, no authors, no texts. White pages, tabula rasa. A child's mind is a tabula rasa and we must write everything upon it. His teacher had said this at the ceremony to mark the start of first grade. He had remembered this strange phrase precisely because he didn't understand it. His mind was again a tabula rasa, except that now nothing more could be printed upon it. The film had been exposed.

26.

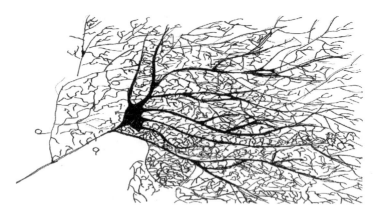

The neuron (from ancient Greek: νεῦρον—fiber, nerve) is an electrically excitable cell that processes and passes on information. Dendrites accept signals from other nerve cells, while the axon via thousands of branches transmits these signals to other neurons, which in turn ... (Anatomy for Seventh Grade)

That joyful (or alarming) communion of neurons, that constant buzzing. Flashes, the movement of ions, the vibration of membranes, axons, neurotransmitters, exchanges in the synapses, signals, impulses, *the happy buzz of work** ... And suddenly, or not so suddenly but rather gradually, they stop speaking to one another, they stop paying visits, stop making those neighborly exchanges of

---

* Line from the poem "Let's Work" by the patriarch of Bulgarian literature, Ivan Vazov (1850–1921).

flour, salt, gossip, the buzz dies down, everything in the workshop grinds to a halt, it corrodes, the lights go out . . .

27.

A friend of mine used to tell this story about his mother and his mother-in-law, women of around eighty, who almost simultaneously began losing their memories. There was no other choice, they had to take both of them into the family apartment in Sofia. And every morning, the following conversation would take place:

Who is this lady, where might she be from, exactly? one would ask.

Well, I'm from that place there, what's it called, on the seaside. (They no longer remembered their own names, let alone the names of their hometowns.)

Oh, is that so, I'm from the seaside as well, what a coincidence. And what are you doing here?

I've come to visit my son. He lives here with his wife. And to see my grandchild. What about yourself, madam?

Well, I've come to see my daughter. She lives here with her husband. I'm also here to see my granddaughter.

Ooh, well, what a coincidence! How old is your granddaughter, madam?

She must be seven or eight, and yours?

Good Lord, what a coincidence, mine is the same age. Here is her picture.

Are you serious, madam? the other would cry. That's my granddaughter.

Sometimes they got into arguments, sometimes they made peace, realizing that they were in the very same home visiting the very same family, and that one woman's daughter had married the other woman's son.

The next morning, my friend would say, everything would start over from the beginning.

Where might the lady be from, exactly...

28.

Salt

The old myths (and new ideologies) don't like looking back... Looking back, Orpheus loses Eurydice forever; looking back toward Sodom, Lot's wife turns into a pillar of salt; later those who look back are simply locked up. Everything must start out with a clean slate, with no memory. (New, so new is the star of communism, and there is nothing before it, the local party secretary used to recite back in the day.)

Remember Lot's wife. Remember Sodom and Gomorrah, the fire that rained from the sky. And don't you dare look back, that's what Luke reminds us. Everyone should remain where they are. No one on the rooftop should come down. Nor should anyone in the field leave when the apocalypse arrives. It sounds like orders from the police.

But what terrible crime has the past committed? Why not look back? Why is the past so dangerous, and why is looking back at it such a sin that you will be turned into a pillar of salt? The apocalypse comes precisely to destroy the past. It's not enough to leave Sodom and Gomorrah, that's the easy part, everyone flees from disaster. The real test is to forget it, to wipe it from your memory, to not miss it. Lot's wife left the city, but couldn't manage to forget it.

Time is not the last second that has just passed, but a whole series of failures going back (and up ahead), heaps of rubble, as Walter Benjamin puts it, before which the angel of history will stand aghast, his face turned away. Could the Angel of History (drawn by Klee as *Angelus Novus*) actually be Lot's wife?

Why does she stop and look back?

Because it is human to do so.

What did she leave there?

A past.

Why salt, exactly?

Because salt has no memory. Nothing grows on salt.

In the *Nuremberg Chronicle* by Hartmann Schedel from the end of the fifteenth century, there is an illustration of this scene: In the foreground are the father and his daughters, led by a cheerful angel who is chattering to him. They are striding forward, leaving behind the burning Sodom and its collapsing towers. In the middle between the departing group and the burning city stands a woman in white. She has turned her face back. In fact, she is looking slightly off to the side. The past, just like fire, cannot be looked directly in the eye. Her face is peaceful. There is no horror, no fear, no pain. Only salt. While her daughters and old Lot, led by the chattering angel, don't even notice her absence. They have already forgotten her.

29.

Do not store up for yourselves treasures in the present, where moth and rust destroy and where thieves break in and steal. But store up for yourselves treasures in the past, where neither moth nor rust destroy, and where thieves do not break in nor steal. For where your treasure is, there will your heart also be.

— *Gaustine,* Apocryphal Versions and New Testaments

30.

Nothing calms you like neat rows of identical sets of encyclopedias from different continents—old cherry-red, brown, and black.

This mantra of titles can be used against evil spirits and times:

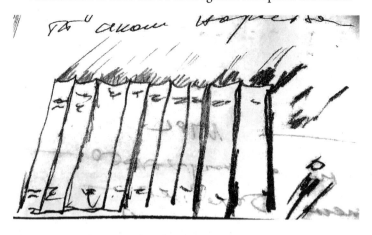

Enciclopedia general ilustrada del País Vasco
Enciclopedia de México
Nueva enciclopedia de Puerto Rico
Diccionario biográfico de Venezuela
Encyclopedia Britannica
The New York Public Library, Oriental Collection
The South in American Literature, 1607–1900
Poisonous and Venomous Marine Animals of the World
Nomenclator Zoologicus

Il grande libro della cucina italiana

The Cuisine of Hungary

Book-Prices Current (London), 1905/06

Subject Index of Books Published Before 1880

The Mother of All Booklists

*A Dictionary of Anonymous and Pseudonymous Literature of
    Great Britain*

Dicionário bibliográfico brasileiro

Catálogo de la bibliografía boliviana

*A Short-Title Catalogue of Books Printed in England,
    Scotland . . . , 1475–1640*

Catalogue of German Books, 1455–1600

Crime Fiction IV: A Comprehensive Bibliography, 1749–2000

Bibliografía de la literatura hispánica

31.

Somewhere in the Andes, they believe to this very day that the future is behind you. It comes up from behind your back, surprising and unforeseeable, while the past is always before your eyes, that which has already happened. When they talk about the past, the people of the Aymara tribe point in front of them. You walk forward facing the past and you turn back toward the future. What would the parable of Lot's wife sound like in this case?

We walk forward and enter the endless Elysian fields.

I walk forward and become past.

32.

I'm having that dream again. Somewhere, in the library of the world, in the main reading room with a high frescoed ceiling, wooden tables and lathe-turned lamps with the soft color of old gold, sits a man hidden behind an open newspaper. It's a large newspaper, hence an old one, as newspapers used to be way back when. I walk toward him amid people's faces (I see only the faces in the dream), which turn toward me. The faces of women and men, familiar from somewhere, but whose names have long been lost. I know (I don't know but I can sense) that everyone is watching us, it is an important scene. On the front page, the headline is written telegraph-style in large letters . . . what, I still can't read it.

It looks close, but in the dream the path lengthens on its own, my movements grow ever more difficult, as if I am wading through something sticky or I am simply afraid to reach him . . . My fear is twofold—first, I'm afraid of reading what is written there, even though somewhere inside myself I know what it says. (I know the whole newspaper by heart.)

My second fear is that when I reach him, the man will lower his newspaper and I will see my own face.

33.

There are days when everything seems to be okay, I can even write, I bring back the cities and rooms where I have been, my mind is clear like a bucket of rainwater, then everything gets muddled again, turns boggy... some people without faces show up, they stomp around the rooms, they speak, they threaten to make me happy, and afterward I don't remember anything, I stare at some point and don't have the strength to avert my gaze...

34.

A haircut in Brooklyn from Jani, a Tajik who hums Frank Sinatra, and when he flicks open his straight razor to shave my neck, I'm seized by that primordial fear of being slaughtered like a lamb. Then he pulls out an unbearably hot and moist towel, which he tosses over my face and presses down. And so, semi-slaughtered, semi-suffocated, doused in lavender-scented cologne as a finale, I open my eyes as if resurrected and give him a nice big tip, as if paying ransom for my survival. As soon as I'm back out on the sidewalk I add to my notebook the scent of barbershop cologne, which awakens memories of haircuts. Everyone has a memory and fear of that. Everyone has noted their own graying hair in the barber's chair.

That peculiar scent of the New York streets, coming from the rotting fruit of the ginkgo biloba. I write that scent down as well...

Ginkgo biloba in New York. What must its memory hold, that tree that remembers the end of the dinosaurs, those moving (and collapsing) skyscrapers from before the Ice Age. And alongside them, the collapsing of real skyscrapers as well—this is immeasurable, terrifying memory. Now do you understand why you have nightmares? I tell myself. Because you've been stuffing yourself with ginkgo biloba for years to fight forgetting, while it remembers terrible things.

I commute every day from Brooklyn to the New York Public Library on Fifth Avenue and Forty-Second Street. I gradually get used to all the details along the route. Coming up on the Manhattan Bridge, off in the distance the Statue of Liberty, the view of blind walls, chimneys, water towers, huge rooftop terraces with laundry hung out on them before the subway goes underground again. I get off at Times Square, I stand for a minute to read the billboards, as if glancing through the first few pages of the day's newspaper. Billboards are the new newspapers. What's written there—some monsters, going back to the future, blockbusters that scare us with the end of the world, clocks and loans . . . Clearly nothing good is on the horizon. I continue up Forty-Second, to the soundtrack of fire engines and police cars, like in a movie. I head into Bryant Park, past the green tables and chairs, passing beneath the tall plantains. I glance over at the Chrysler Building, that Secession in vertical, and sink into the cold cave of the library as if into another time, a time shelter.

35.

On the radio they're reporting that it is snowing in the desert in July, drifts are piling up on the pyramids, and I imagine the Sphinx with a snowy stocking cap. The snow disfigures public statues, as Auden wrote. I wonder what the camels in this snowy desert are doing. They feverishly search back through some deep memory for what to do in such cases, but there are no records, the time capsule of genes do not contain anything of the sort.

They say that when the end of time comes the seasons will get mixed up.

36.

I had a dream that I only managed to recall a single phrase from: the innocent monster of the past. I forgot the dream, the phrase remained.

37.

Sarajevo 1914/2024

The historical reenactments are becoming ever more brutal, ever more authentic. This ranks among the most popular ones in the Balkans—a spin around Sarajevo in a copy of Franz Ferdinand's car—a Gräf & Stift Phaeton, black, four cylinders. Plus the clothes, the crown prince's white shirt, the uniform, the saber, the route, the stops, the driver's fatal confusion—everything just as on that day.

"Don't stay outside, step inside history! Be Gavrilo Princip or Franz Ferdinand in Sarajevo 1914!"

The organizers, who by the way have connections to the city council, want to do something very special on the anniversary of the murder, June 28 (Gregorian style). Something heretofore unseen and hyper-realistic. It also happens to be a milestone anniversary of the outbreak of World War I. Thousands of locals engaged as extras and dressed in the clothing of the epoch have been strolling through the city for weeks. A detailed reenactment is unfolding in accordance with existing archival photographs and in consultation with historians from the university. But something is missing, there is no suspense, no threat. After all, this is not simply a jaunt about town by a royal personage on a fine June day . . . a war is commencing, after all, not a garden party. They have managed to track down a distant relative of the dynasty—from a rather collateral branch of the family, but still, royal blood is needed, isn't it?

For the role of Gavrilo Princip, they hold a casting call with young anarchist-leaning Serbian guys, unemployed and up for anything. It turns out that in the meantime the erstwhile Black Hand movement, which had given rise to the assassins back then, has also been reestablished. They choose a young man from its ranks. They suit him up with the proper pistol—a Browning FN M1910, small, flat, perfect for concealed carry. Loaded with blanks, of course, but at least the shots will still be heard.

June 28 rolls around, the whole city comes out to watch, some with tickets, others on the balconies of nearby buildings, kids hanging from the branches of trees. A striking resemblance to that June 28 in 1914, incidentally. Even the clouds are the same, as someone will later note, comparing the photos. A breeze is blowing, carrying the already fallen linden blossoms. The extras, some dressed in tails and top hats, others more eccentrically, are scurrying around impatiently. The women proudly wear their hats as large as storks' nests, dolled up in the style of an epoch coming to an end (due in large part to that very day).

The archduke putters up in his four-cylinder heavy black Gräf & Stift Phaeton. Everything happens as it did on that forenoon— the motorcade with the three cars sets out, the first unsuccessful attempt with the bomb, the stop at the town hall, where the archduke, visibly shaken, would say: I came here to see you, and you greet me with bombs. A stop by the hospital to visit the wounded, the cars taking the wrong route, the maneuver near the Latin Bridge before the eyes of the despairing Gavrilo Princip, who is guzzling a beer in front of the pub. At that moment the assassin raises his eyes and sees that the victim has come to him of his own accord. He takes out his pistol, leaps toward the car, which is turning in place like a heavy beetle, and shoots the archduke.

A red rose blossoms on the archduke's white shirt, blood gushes forth. Everything is so realistic that the people in the crowd are stunned, no one dares applaud. The wife Sophie crumples to Franz Ferdinand's feet, but no one pays any particular attention to this, just as is written in history as well. But something about the assassin's behavior is unexpected. It's as if he himself cannot believe what has happened, according to the script he needs to unsuccessfully try to shoot himself, to swallow cyanide, but instead he swallows his tongue.

A long, historically long second hangs over the center of Sarajevo, as if something clicks in time and we can see Gavrilo Princip standing there awkwardly with his still-smoking gun, the crowd is gaping in the frozen moment before they rush to tear him to pieces, the wind has died down, nothing can be heard, a child falls from the tree branches, but doesn't dare cry...

(For a moment I feel like I can see Demby's signature here, with his new open-air theater, tragicomedy dell'arte.)

And at that moment the archduke gasps, blood sprays out like a fountain. The man is truly breathing his last.

The guards hurl themselves upon Gavrilo Princip, or rather the one playing Gavrilo Princip, but it doesn't matter anymore, everything has been set into motion, just as before. The gun goes off one more time in the uproar and the supposed blank pierces the stomach of one of the guards. Then the crowd really does rush to tear the killer apart. Police sirens start howling, ambulances try to make their way through. Horses toss policemen from their backs and in the melee trample several ladies along with their hats. The chaos is uncontrollable and unscripted.

Afterward nobody will be able to explain how the supposedly blank bullets turned out to be live rounds. Once every hundred years even an empty rifle goes off, as the saying goes in this region, but who knows...?

The Austrian authorities immediately send a sharp note protesting the murder of their fellow countryman and descendant of the archduke. The European Prosecutor's Office brings charges against the organizers of the reenactment and calls for the immediate arrest of everyone involved and an investigation into the Black Hand anarchist movement. The local inhabitants of Sarajevo don't wait for invitations and the offices of several Serbian companies are trashed immediately.

Europe finds itself on the cusp of a second First World War.

38.

Something has changed, something is not the same.

I hear its dragging footsteps, heavy breathing. It wasn't like this before, there used to be rhythm, dancing, running.

For a moment, between the shadow of the leaves I catch a glimpse of the tired light of yesterday or of a forgotten afternoon years ago. Something seeps in, drop by drop, the sediment of other times.

On my palate I sense the taste of ash, with my nose I catch the scent of something burned. Like stubble or a forest that has set itself alight . . .

Something has changed, something is not the same.

With my fingers I touch another skin, cold and grainy. Before, it was warm and smooth, alive like a person's hand, now it is like the shed skin of a viper.

You stroll through the hot afternoon in August and suddenly out from behind some bush the stench of rot hits you. A corpse, of a rat most likely, but still a corpse.

Something has started to go rotten, go bitter, to stink, to go dark, and to grow cold, I feel it with my five senses.

Something has changed, something is not the same.

But what if time has already stopped? How will we know? Will the clocks stop? Will the calendars be stuck on one and the same day? Hardly, they actually don't feed on time, they do not live off it.

So what feeds on time, then?

Everything living, of course. The cats, cows, bees, and water snakes, the thistles, the lizard hawks and the lizards, the squirrels in the park, the earthworms and the fruit fly, the blue whale and redfish—everything that swims, crawls, silently creeps, climbs trees, grows, reproduces, grows old, and dies. Only these feed on time . . . Or time feeds on us. We are food for time.

For Christ's sake, we would notice if it died.

39.

And again back to the shelves of books, to convince myself that the world is bound and ordered. Here is WWI, wrapped up in twelve identical red volumes of some encyclopedia. Here is the Cold War, forever buried between the covers of these three big volumes, gray. Neither the Spanish Civil War (sleeping on the top shelf) nor the Second World War, with its two whole bookcases, is frightening anymore. Everything sooner or later ends up in a book, as Mallarmé put it in that quote so beloved by Borges. Which, when you think about it, is not such a bad result.

I stand in the Main Rose Reading Room beneath the Veronese-style suspended and frescoed heavens. I'm sitting close to the shelves of historical books. I've taken down, more as an alibi, the first volume in an *Encyclopedia of the Cold War*, published in 2008, letters A–D. I realize that I can tell stories from the front about this war, we fought in it even as children. I page through it, like a spy tossing secret glances at the people around me. Whatever you read is what you shall become. At the table in front of me there's a person whom I immediately recognize as homeless. I have always felt an inexplicable closeness to them. He's wearing a puffy winter jacket, quite large (I have a similar one) and a hat with earflaps sticking out on the sides. It's warm in the reading room, but it's better for him this way, all packed up, ready to leave immediately if they chase him out. I know that feeling of anticipatory guilt quite well.

He has placed a pile of books to his left. Actually, he is one of the few around me who is actually reading. The rest are staring at their phones, sending text messages, waiting for the rain outside to stop. The library is a shelter, a warm and dry place open to all. Years ago an attempt was made to prevent the homeless from coming in, but the management gave up on it. I am dying with curiosity to see what exactly he is reading, so I get up and pretend to be looking for something on the nearby shelves and turn around slightly. In front of him is a thick dog-eared *Chronicles of the Barbarians*. Beneath it I manage to make the title on the spine: *A Short History of India*. And on the very top of his pile . . . it can't be, Gaustine's *Selected Writings*. I involuntarily reach for it, the homeless man lifts his eyes, and only then do I read the cover correctly—Augustine, of course. (I could have sworn that the author was Gaustine just a short while ago.) I apologize, he stares at me, then hunches over the book he is holding again, an album with enormous Spanish houses from the nineteenth century.

40.

A few years ago I started slowly losing my hearing. A subtle hearing aid, prescribed to me with the promise that it would bring back the blackbirds in the morning and the crickets on summer nights, but it hardly helped at all. Through it I heard everything as if recorded on an old gramophone record, with a faint metallic echo and crackling here and there. A feeling of mechanical reproduction, as Walter Benjamin would put it. The soundtrack of yesterday's world, recorded and played back on an infinite loop.

Birds sang even during the war. I turn this phrase in my head while listening to Messiaen's *Quartet for the End of Time*, written and performed for the first time in January 1941 in a French prisoner-of-war camp. I've turned up the volume to the max. In the beginning of the quartet, Messiaen has put those words from the Apocalypse—about the angel who announces the end of time. A cold rain fell that afternoon, the concert was outside in the open, but none of the four hundred prisoners or guards left. An unexpected combination of piano, clarinet, violin, and cello—those were the musicians available among the prisoners . . . The first movement, "Crystal Liturgy," opens with the awakening of the birds, the clarinet imitates a blackbird in a marvelous solo, and the violin follows after it—a nightingale, endless, repetitious, oblivious, mellifluous, and alarmed, at one and the same time calm and anxious.

Birds sang even during the war. Therein lies the whole horror . . . and consolation.

41.

Even though Ecclesiastes teaches us that there is a time for everything, a time for this and a time for that, all of a sudden in the last book of the Book they announce to us the end of time. This is what the angel in Revelation proclaims, with one foot in the sea and the other on land, holding a scroll in his hands. The scroll John has to eat. When we say, "I absolutely devoured that book," somewhere an echo of that voice can also be heard.

Take it and eat it, says the angel, handing the book to John. It will be bitter in your stomach, but in your mouth it will be as sweet as honey. (As a young and devoted reader I once ate a page, I don't remember which book now, I think it was a poetry chapbook, they use the least ink. It was already bitter in my mouth.)

And right at that moment in Revelation the angel announces that there shall be no more time. That's it. He doesn't proclaim the end of the world, but the end of time.

The cages of the days shall be opened and all times will gather as one.

. . . And God will call back the past.

42.

. . . **M**y whole life is sewn together from other people's lives. Even the one I'm living is some other life, I can't know whose. I feel like a monster cobbled together from different times. I sit in an unfamiliar city constantly filled with fire-truck sirens, as if it is always engulfed in flames. I spend all my days at its library, in the cold hall under a painted sky, surrounded by the encyclopedias of the world, red covers and gold letters. I read old newspapers and look at people's faces. I am afraid that at any moment someone will turn up, will look around, and will head straight for me . . .

I sit in a library, the library of the world. Every morning I read papers from one and the same day in 1939. Everything is familiar to me, I have been there, I have had drinks in a dive on Fifty-Second, the rains of that autumn have fallen on me. The newspaper is merely a doorway. Into the petty and insignificant, isn't that how the saying goes, there hides the past with its clockwork that must be defused. Somewhere there amid the last sales of the season and the article about gas masks in German schools with a large photo on page three in the *New York Times* (all the students from a high school standing in front of the building, holding hands with their oтъзъ~ ~ coats, ~~se ещ~

⑧-СЧ~ bere a cele~ feen co~
Emerson
self-powered
Portable

~~w~~

gas masks on, with no faces). I'll peruse offers from the movie
theaters and nightclubs, I'll sit in the Cinzano bar on page thirty-
seven, I'll switch on my new Emerson wireless and antenna-free
radio set for only $19.95, I'll hear the latest news from abroad, I'll
spend the night in the little ads for rooms for rent in Lower Manhattan, and I'll look at the faces of the people who have come out
toward evening in the gossip columns. I can't miss anything, the
trigger is there somewhere, in one of the final August evenings . . .
Yours, G.

I stand at the window with a letter in my hand, both sender and
receiver, I read and think that the world is always a little before
September 1, at the end of summer, with ads in the paper and the
distant roar of a just-started war . . . The afternoon of the world, in
which our shadows grow long under the waning sun, before evening falls.

43.

The less memory, the more past.

As long as you remember, you hold at bay the times gone by. Like lighting a fire in the middle of a forest at night. Demons and wolves are crouching all around, the beasts of the past are tightening the circle, but they still don't dare step into it. The allegory is simple. As long as the flame of memory burns, you are the master. If it starts to die out, the howling grows louder and the beasts draw closer. The pack of the past.

Shortly before the end, times get mixed up. Because the cages have been opened, and everyone will creep out ... If it weren't for the days, where will we live, a poet asked, what was his name again. But the days are done ... The calendar has dismissed itself, there is only one day and one night and they repeat eternally ...

I remember, so as to keep the past in the past ...

—the yellow notebook

44.

I'm seven ... We're visiting friends in another town, some celebration is going on. There are swarms of people, I reach their waists, they're jostling, stepping on me, somebody spits the shells of sunflower seeds on me, I cling to my father's pants, then I let go, I stop in front of a shooting booth, but my head barely reaches the counter, I don't recall how long I stood there, I turn around ... my father and mother have disappeared. Now what? Hansel and Gretel's father took them for a walk in a strange forest and ... when they turned around, he was gone.

I run through the crowd, I shout, I break out of the swarm, it's late afternoon, the streets of the town are full, people are coming home from work. I stop a woman my mother's age, Auntie, I'm lost, I sob. I can't remember the name of the street or the number of the house where we're staying. All I know is that it has a green door ... Ah well, they're all green, little boy, I'm on my way home from work, ask somebody else. I ask another woman, I don't dare stop the men, I'm in a hurry, son, I'm in a hurry, there must be a nice police officer somewhere around here, don't worry ... It's getting completely dark, cars are whizzing past, the streets are emptying out, it's getting cold, no one notices me, blood starts dripping from my nose ... And suddenly a hand grabs me, two whistling slaps, Do you have any idea how worried we've been? ... I'm saved.

45.

I'm six, my brother is four, we're wearing shorts and sandals, but with long hair like the Beatles (I'm John, he's Paul) at the village square, in front of a monument to a partisan. The photo was taken by my father a minute before he took us (accompanied by the village policeman) to Grandpa Petre, who was under orders from the mayor to shave our heads. He would also do the same to my father, who, in addition to having long hair, had also grown a mustache. There is no barbershop in the village. Grandpa Petre sits us down on a stump, his donkey is snorting nearby. I watch my hair fall in light blond locks, and I don't even dare to start bawling, I'm afraid of the policeman. Maybe you're not allowed to cry, since you're not allowed to have long hair . . .

In the end, the three of us—my father, my brother, and I—with our heads shaved like prisoners and spritzed with Grandpa Petre's cheap cologne, hurry home. Don't you dare cry, my father says through clenched teeth, he can tell we are on the verge of bawling our heads off.

Strawberry fields forever . . .

46.

I'm getting old. Exiled ever further from the Rome of childhood in the distant empty provinces of old age, from which there is no return. And Rome no longer answers my letters.

Somewhere the past exists as a house or a street that you've left for a short while, for five minutes, and you've found yourself in a strange city. It's been written that the past is a foreign country. Nonsense. The past is my home country. The future is a foreign country, full of strange faces, I won't set foot there.

Let me go back home . . . my mother told me not to be late . . .

47.

I must be three years old. Just as tall as the roses in the garden, I'm standing barefoot on the warm soil, holding my mother's hand and staring at a rose point-blank for a long time. That's the only thing I remember. The first and the last.

48.

Unbelongers Syndrome

No time belongs to you, no place is your own. What you are look-ing for is not looking for you, that which you are dreaming about is not dreaming about you. You know that something was yours in a different place and in a different time, that's why you're always crisscrossing past rooms and days. But if you are in the right place, the time is different. And if you are in the right time, the place is different.

Incurable.

— *Gaustine*, New and Imminent Diagnoses

Epilogue

Novels and stories offer deceptive consolation about order and form. Someone is supposedly holding all the threads of the action, knowing the order and the outcome, which scene comes after which. A truly brave book, a brave and inconsolable book, would be one in which all stories, the happened and the unhappened, float around us in the primordial chaos, shouting and whispering, begging and sniggering, meeting and passing one another by in the darkness.

The end of a novel is like the end of the world, it's good to put it off.

Death has been preoccupied in reading and has forgotten, its scythe is rusting by its side. It could be a Dürer engraving or a detail from Bosch.

I have never liked endings, I don't remember the ending of a single book or a single film. I wonder if there's such a diagnosis—an inability to remember endings. And what is there really to remember about an (always already known) ending?

I only remember beginnings.

I remember how, for a long time, I used to go to bed early...I remember when they brought ice to the village for the first time and my dad brought me to see the Gypsy ... I've forgotten his name. I remember a terrible winter storm and the candle that was burning at home, the candle was burning ... I remember a rose that I am staring at face-to-face, I'm just as tall as it is. I remember sitting around in a wet greatcoat in the trenches of some war, smoking short, harsh cigarettes. I sit in one of the dives on Fifty-Second, uncertain and afraid ... Or I tie my sandals and raise my shield, which gleams in the sun.

They say that my life was entirely different.

I agree, so as not to irritate them. But I myself do not have any other life.

I don't remember anymore whether I thought up Gaustine or he thought me up. Was there really such a clinic of the past, or was it just an idea, a note in a notebook, a scrap of newspaper I randomly came across? And whether this whole business about the coming of the past has already happened or whether it will start from tomorrow ...

o.

1939/2029

The troops are assembled and waiting. The first shots will be fired by the ship *Schleswig-Holstein* at the military depots on the West-erplatte Peninsula near Danzig. It has long been in the works, they have been waiting for the right moment, some anniversary. Everything will be precisely re-created hour by hour. There is a minor preliminary debate over the exact minute, some claim the beginning was at 4:44 a.m., others at 4:48 a.m. The war will claim its first casualty, the Polish sergeant Wojciech Najsarek. The Luftwaffe will support the attack by air . . . Several submarines will be waiting in the Baltic Sea.

I know what will happen. With a million and a half troops at the ready, it only takes a single shot, and . . . the tanks will roll through the trees, the old ship will start showering rounds, the hidden machine gun nests will be revealed and will start cutting everything down with a rat-a-tat-tat—the first body will be torn apart, *aaah*, someone has switched the blanks with live ammunition, the other side will return fire . . . the howling of crazed foxes, frightened crows, signal flares that slice the sky, everything has been waiting, everything has been building up, only to open the floodgates now . . . I know from somewhere that on the first day about twenty will be killed, four from the Polish and sixteen from the German side, and in the end—millions . . .

The largest-ever military reenactment, life-sized, with a million and a half extras as soldiers from the Wehrmacht, positioned along the whole sixteen-hundred-kilometer border with Poland, sixty-two divisions, fifty-four of them in full combat readiness, twenty-eight hundred tanks, two thousand warplanes (old Junkerses or Stukas have been tuned up), artillery installations wait hidden in the forest, submarines, battleships, a flotilla of destroyers, a flotilla of torpedo boats.

We are re-creating this war so as to end all wars, someone will say on the radio, and this absurd tautology will unleash everything.

Tomorrow was September 1.

—1.

Жгмццрт №№№№кктррпх ггфпр111111111. . . .
внтгвтгвнтгггг777ррр . . .

ACKNOWLEDGMENTS

For a person who loves the world of yesterday, this book was not easy. To a certain extent it was a farewell to a dream of the past, or rather to that which some are trying to turn the past into. To a certain extent it was also a farewell to the future.

Various places and shelters were part of the journey of this novel.

My thanks to the Cullman Center, New York Public Library, where I spent ten months in 2017–18 happily reading and taking notes.

Thanks also to the Literaturhaus Zurich for their kind invitation in 2019, which gave me time and fresh air to write.

One thinks that writing is done in isolation, but it constantly leads to conversations in one's head with other people and books. Thanks to all of them, you will most likely discover echoes of these in absentia exchanges in the novel. Thanks also to Gaustine, who was always somewhere nearby.

Thank you to the people with whom I shared ideas while writing or who were my first readers—Boyko Penchev, Ivan Krastev, Nadezhda Radulova, Dimiter Kenarov, Bozhana Apostolova, Angela Rodel, Galin Tihanov . . .

For the research, especially for the chapter about the referendum on the past, I would like to thank Helle Dalgaard, Marie

Vrinat-Nikolov, Maria Vutova, Henrike Schmidt, Magda Pytlak, Jaroslaw Godun, Hellen Kooijman, Borislava Chakrinova, Giusppe Dell'Agata, Vesselin Vačkov, Marinela Lipcheva, and Martin Weiss.

Thanks also to the Wissenschaftskolleg Berlin, where I finished the book in the leap month of February 2020. I had pleasant and encouraging conversations with friends and colleagues there, such as Efraín Kristal (Borges was with us the whole time), Wolf Lepenies, Thorsten Wilhelmy, Barbara Stollberg-Rilinger, Katharina Biegger, Daniel Schönpflug, Stoyan Popkirov, Luca Giuliani, David Motadel, Felix Körner ...

Thank you to Bozhana Apostolova, who unflinchingly supported this manuscript, just as she has all my previous books published by Zhanet-45.

Thanks to Nedko Solakov, Lora Sultanova, Hristo Gochev, Nevena Dishlieva-Krysteva, and Iva Koleva, who worked on the book during a pandemic.

Thank you to my parents for the patience and love with which they waited for this book and tolerated my absences.

And finally, as is always the case, thanks to those who were by my side and put up with me while I wrote this novel—to Biliana, who read and edited, and to Raya, who is critical and forgiving. (As she put it, Your characters don't have names so that you don't forget them. And she was right.)

Thank you to everyone who will sit down some afternoon in the time shelter of this book.

G.G.
February 29, 2020,
Berlin